Carpenter
and
Quincannon

PROFESSIONAL DETECTIVE SERVICES

Carpenter and Quincannon

PROFESSIONAL DETECTIVE SERVICES

BILL PRONZINI

Crippen & Landru Publishers
Norfolk, Virginia
1998

Cover painting by Carol Heyer; cover design by Deborah Miller

Crippen & Landru logo by Eric D. Greene

ISBN (limited edition) 1-885941-24-2

ISBN (trade edition) 1-885941-25-0

FIRST EDITION

10 9 8 7 6 5 4 3 2 1

Crippen & Landru, Publishers
P. O. Box 9315
Norfolk, VA 23505

E-Mail: CrippenL@Pilot.Infi.Net
Web: www.crippenlandru.com

For Doug and Sandi,

with thanks

CONTENTS

PREFACE: ANATOMY OF A SERIES

Sabina Carpenter and John Quincannon, unlike the majority of series characters these days, were an unplanned detective duo. Conception and birth both came about in spite of the fact that I had no real desire to father another series. In their infancy I would cheerfully have given them up for adoption to anyone interested in raising the little dears. And more than once, I'm ashamed to say, I abandoned them for lengthy periods of time.

The pair, as created for a 1985 novel entitled *Quincannon*, were wholly different individuals from the ones depicted in these pages. Quincannon at that time was an operative of the San Francisco branch of the U.S. Secret Service, and a somewhat bleak and hard-edged alcoholic who blames himself for an accidental shooting in which a pregnant woman was killed. When he meets Sabina, during the course of a counterfeiting investigation in Idaho, she is masquerading as a dressmaker; in fact she is an undercover operative for the Pinkerton agency in Denver, a widow whose Pinkerton husband was killed in the line of duty. (Yes, indeed there were women private investigators in the 1800s. Sabina is loosely based on Kate Warne, the first female P.I., who worked for Allan Pinkerton in his Baltimore agency during and after the Civil War.) By the end of the novel the two have become friends detecting in concert. Quincannon is in the process of overcoming his drinking problem, and there is a suggestion that they may become partners in a San Francisco detective agency. The suggestion was my way of providing an upbeat ending; there was no serious intent to do anything further with either character.

Nevertheless I had established an effective scenario for a series—a fact I was reminded of about a year later when my wife, Marcia Muller, and I decided to write a second collaborative novel. Our first collaboration, *Double* (1984), which featured Sharon McCone and the "Nameless Detective" working in tandem, had been such an enjoyable experience that we were eager to repeat it. Another McCone/"Nameless" wasn't feasible because by then we had different publishers for our respective series. Marcia was then writing a second series featuring Elena Oliverez, a Chicana museum curator in Santa Barbara, and we wondered if it would be possible to concoct a mystery in which a contemporary sleuth such as Elena could team with an 1890s detective such as

Quincannon to solve a common case. Writers love that sort of challenge.

After considerable brain-cudgeling, we developed a story that begins during the 1846 Bear Flag Rebellion in California and involves a hidden cache of valuable religious artifacts. Quincannon is hired in 1894 to locate these artifacts by an heir of the original owner; he solves part of the mystery surrounding them, but is frustrated in his efforts to locate the artifacts themselves. Elena comes into the case in the present day when she discovers a folder containing Quincannon's investigator's reports. Using the reports as a basis, and by correctly interpreting clues hidden in them, she solves the rest of the puzzle and recovers the treasure. The story was told in alternating sections, beginning in an 1846 prologue and then shifting back and forth between Quincannon and Elena as they conduct their respective investigations. In this novel, Carpenter and Quincannon, Professional Detective Services was a well-established agency; Quincannon had become a teetotaler, and his determined but constantly repelled efforts to seduce his partner was an established subplot; and the tone was much lighter, with more tongue-in-cheek humor. The book was published late in 1986, under the title *Beyond the Grave*.

Despite fairly enthusiastic critical and reader response, the careers of Carpenter and Quincannon seemed destined to end with that novel. I sent out a few feelers to publishers for a solo book featuring the characters; there were no takers. So I moved on to other projects.

Another year passed. Then came a letter from Jack Adrian, a British writer and anthologist who was compiling a volume of Yuletide mystery shorts to be called *Crime at Christmas*. Would I write an original story for the book? I would. But Jack didn't want a "Nameless" or a story with a contemporary setting. He wanted a period mystery, and because he'd read and liked *Beyond the Grave*, his preference was a period mystery with Quincannon as the protagonist. A somewhat different version of "No Room at the Inn," the first entry in these pages, was what he got. His excellent editorial suggestions led to a much better story.

After *Crime at Christmas* was published, I sent out a few more feelers. Still no takers. Frustrated, I consigned C&Q to fictional limbo. And there they remained for five years, and would have continued to remain if it weren't for a good and supportive editor named Elana Lore.

Early in 1993 Dell Magazines announced the launching of a new bi-monthly, *Louis L'Amour Western Magazine*. This would be something of a test case, a bedsheet-sized, slick-formatted periodical featuring high-quality art-work, interviews with major players in the fields of Western fiction and nonfiction, and original articles and short stories. Elana, who had been given the editorial reins, formerly worked as an assistant editor on both *Alfred Hitchcock's Mystery Magazine* and *Ellery Queen's Mystery Magazine*; she knew my work, knew that I wrote Westerns now and then, and asked if I would contribute a story to *LLWM*'s premier issue. I delivered an offbeat, if traditional nonseries piece called "Doc Christmas, Painless Dentist," thinking that that was the sort of thing Elana had in mind.

Yes and no. She bought "Doc Christmas," but for the first issue of *LLWM*, she said, she would prefer a Quincannon story. Both she and Louis L'Amour's son, Beau, were aware of the two novels containing the C&Q characters and thought they would make a good series for the new magazine. Flattered, I sent her "Burgade's Crossing." Both the first issue and the story were well received, firmly establishing the magazine and my commitment to the series.

Over the next year and a half I produced five more C&Q Western/mystery hybrids, four of which were published in *LLWM*. The fifth, "The Horseshoe Nail," was purchased and in inventory when the conglomerate owner of Dell Magazines, in spite of strong subscription and newsstand sales, summarily decided to end *LLWM*'s short life with the January 1996 issue. The official line was that it was too expensive to produce and there wasn't enough ad revenue to support it, i.e. that it was no longer "cost effective"; but in fact the conglomerate was getting ready to divest itself of *EQMM*, *AHMM*, and Dell's science fiction and large line of crossword puzzle magazines, and the new buyers weren't interested in *LLWM*. The manuscript of "The Horseshoe Nail" was returned to me, and I immediately resubmitted it to *EQMM*; editor Janet Hutchings bought it while *EQMM* was still part of the old regime, and thus I was paid twice for the novelette by the conglomerate—a nice bit of "cost effective" irony.

By this time, I was enjoying the research and writing of the C&Q stories too much not to want to continue the series. *EQMM* has proven to be a receptive market, and I hope will remain so. I would very much like to write a C&Q novel, but given the current state of publishing and my own tenuous position in it, I suspect that wish will be unfulfilled. More's the pity. I like to think Carpenter and Quincannon and their 1890s milieu would fare even better in a new novel than they did in *Quincannon* and *Beyond the Grave*.

A few words about the stories. While some liberties have been taken, the California and Nevada locales are for the most part historically and geographically accurate; the same is true of such 1890s pursuits as Delta ferryboating, pluviculture, gambling (the character of Lady One-Eye is based on a real person, one "Madame Moustache"), counterfeiting, train travel, logging, spiritualism and mediumistic trickery, and Chinese tong rivalry. Six of the nine tales employ some variation on the impossible crime theme, a longstanding favorite of mine that seems well suited to the time period, and all are stories of detection complete with clues and (sometimes quirky) ratiocination. Not for nothing am I an admirer of John Dickson Carr and other proponents of the classic detective yarn. And finally, even though Quincannon is the primary and viewpoint character and does the lion's share of the sleuthing, Sabina is by no means a minor member of the team. She figures prominently in most cases, helps to solve or provides the solution to some, and is clearly the more level-headed and probably the smarter of the duo (Quincannon's bellows of protest notwithstanding). Despite the prevailing attitudes of the time, I've taken pains to keep sexism in limbo where it belongs.

You may now proceed to the adventures of my two unplanned offspring, Sabina Carpenter and John Quincannon. I may have been a mediocre, if not downright poor, parent to them in their early years, but Jack Adrian, Elana Lore, Janet Hutchings, and Douglas and Sandi Greene of Crippen & Landru, among others, have taught me to properly appreciate the pair. And made me fond and proud of them, too.

Bill Pronzini
Petaluma, California
February 1998

NO ROOM AT THE INN

W hen the snowstorm started, Quincannon was high up in a sparsely populated section of the Sierra Nevada—alone except for his rented horse, with not much idea of where he was and no idea at all of where Slick Henry Garber was.

And as if all of that wasn't enough, it was almost nightfall on Christmas Eve.

The storm had caught him by surprise. The winter sky had been clear when he'd set out from Big Creek in mid-morning, and it had stayed clear until two hours ago; then the clouds had commenced piling up rapidly, the way they sometimes did in this high-mountain country, getting thicker and darker-veined until the whole sky was the color of moiling coal smoke. The wind had sharpened to an icy breath that buffeted both him and the ewe-necked strawberry roan. And now, at dusk, the snow flurries had begun—thick flakes driven and agitated by the wind so that the pine and spruce forests through which the trail climbed were a misty blur and he could see no more than forty or fifty rods ahead.

He rode huddled inside his fleece-lined long coat and rabbit-fur mittens and cap, feeling sorry for himself and at the same time cursing himself for a rattlepate. If he had paid more mind to that buildup of clouds, he would have realized the need to find shelter much sooner than he had. As it was, he had begun looking too late. So far no cabin or mine shaft or cave or suitable geographical configuration had presented itself—not one place in all this vast wooded emptiness where he and the roan could escape the snapping teeth of the storm.

A man had no sense wandering around an unfamiliar mountain wilderness on the night before Christmas, even if he was a manhunter by trade and a greedy gloryhound by inclination. He ought to be home in front of a blazing fire, roasting chestnuts in the company of a good woman. Sabina, for instance. Dear, sweet Sabina, waiting for him back in San Francisco. Not by his hearth or in his bed, curse the luck, but at least in the Market Street offices of Carpenter and Quincannon, Professional Detective Services.

Well, it was his own fault that he was alone up here, freezing to death in a snowstorm. In the first place he could have refused the job of tracking down Slick Henry Garber when it was offered to him by the West Coast Banking Association two weeks ago. In the second place he could have decided not to come to Big Creek to investigate a report that Slick Henry and his satchel full of counterfeit mining stock were in the vicinity. And in the third place he could have remained in Big Creek this morning when Slick Henry managed to elude his clutches and flee even higher into these blasted mountains.

But no, Rattlepate John Quincannon had done none of those sensible things. Instead he had accepted the Banking Association's fat fee, thinking of that *and* of the $5000 reward for Slick Henry's apprehension being offered by a mining coalition in Colorado *and* of the glory of nabbing the most notorious —and the most dangerous—confidence trickster operating west of the Rockies in this year of 1894. Then, after tracing his quarry to Big Creek, he had not only bungled the arrest but made a second mistake in setting out on Slick Henry's trail with the sublime confidence of an unrepentant sinner looking for the Promised Land. Only to lose that trail two hours ago, at a road fork, just before he made his third mistake of the day by underestimating the weather.

Christmas, he thought. 'Tis the season to be jolly. Bah. Humbug.

Ice particles now clung to his beard, his eyebrows; kept trying to freeze his eyelids shut. He had to continually rub his eyes clear in order to see where he was going. Which, now, in full darkness, was along the rim of a snow- skinned meadow that had opened up on his left. The wind was even fiercer here, without one wall of trees to deflect some of its force. Quincannon shivered and huddled and cursed and felt sorrier for himself by the minute.

He should never have decided to join forces with Sabina and open a detective agency. She had been happy with her position as a female operative with the Pinkerton Agency's Denver office; he had been more or less content working in the San Francisco office of the United States Secret Service. What had possessed him to suggest, not long after their first professional meeting, that they pool their talents? Well, he knew the answer to that well enough. *Sabina* had possessed him. Dear, sweet, unseducible, infuriating Sabina—

Was that light ahead?

He scrubbed at his eyes and leaned forward in the saddle, squinting. Yes, light—lamplight. He had just come around a jog in the trail, away from the open meadow, and there it was, ahead on his right: a faint glowing rectangle in the night's churning white-and-black. He could just make out the shapes of buildings, too, in what appeared to be a clearing before a sheer rock face.

The lamplight and the buildings changed Quincannon's bleak remonstrations into murmurs of thanksgiving. He urged the stiff-legged and balky roan into a quicker pace. The buildings took on shape and definition as he approached. There were three of them, grouped in a loose triangle; two appeared to be cabins, fashioned of rough-hewn logs and planks, each with a sloping roof, while the bulkiest structure had the look of a barn. The larger cabin, the one with the lighted window, was set between the other two and farther back near the base of the rock wall.

A lane led off the trail to the buildings. Quincannon couldn't see it under its covering of snow, but he knew it was there by a painted board sign nailed to one of the trees at the intersection. *TRAVELER'S REST,* the sign said, and below that, in smaller letters, *Meals and Lodging.* One of the tiny roadhouses, then, that dotted the Sierras and catered to prospectors, hunters, and foolish wilderness wayfarers such as himself.

It was possible, he thought as he turned past the sign, that Slick Henry Garber had come this way and likewise been drawn to the Traveler's Rest. Which would allow Quincannon to make amends today, after all, for his earlier bungling, and perhaps even permit him to spend Christmas Day in the relative comfort of the Big Creek Hotel. Given his recent run of foul luck, however, such a serendipitous turnabout was as likely to happen as Sabina presenting him, on his return to San Francisco, with the holiday gift he most desired.

Nevertheless, caution here was indicated. So despite the warmth promised by the lamplit window, he rode at an off-angle toward the barn. There was also the roan's welfare to consider. He would have to pay for the animal if it froze to death while in his charge.

If he was being observed from within the lighted cabin, it was covertly: no one came out and no one showed himself in the window. At the barn he dismounted, took himself and the roan inside, struggled to reshut the doors against the howling thrust of the wind. Blackness surrounded him, heavy with the smells of animals and hay and oiled leather. He stripped off both mittens, found a lucifer in one of his pockets and scraped it alight. The barn lantern hung from a hook near the doors; he reached up to light the wick. Now he could see that there were eight stalls, half of which were occupied: three saddle horses and one work horse, each nibbling a pile of hay. He didn't bother to examine the saddle horses because he had no idea what type of animal Slick Henry had been riding. He hadn't got close enough to his quarry all day to get a look at him or his transportation.

He led the roan into an empty stall, unsaddled it, left it there munching a hay supper of its own. Later, he would ask the owner of Traveler's Rest to come out and give the beast a proper rubdown. With his hands mittened again he braved the storm on foot, slogging through calf-deep snow to the lighted cabin.

Still no one came out or appeared at the window. He moved along the front wall, stopped to peer through the rimed window glass. What he could see of the big parlor inside was uninhabited. He plowed ahead to the door.

It was against his nature to walk unannounced into the home of a stranger, mainly because it was a fine way to get shot, but in this case he had no choice. He could have shouted himself hoarse in competition with the storm before anyone heard him. Thumping on the door would be just as futile; the wind was already doing that. Again he stripped off his right mitten, opened his coat for easy access to the Navy Colt revolver he carried at his waist, unlatched the door with his left hand, and cautiously let the wind push him inside.

The entire parlor was deserted. He leaned back hard against the door to get it closed again and then called out, "Hello the house! Company!" No one answered.

He stood scraping snowcake off his face, slapping it off his clothing. The room was warm: a log fire crackled merrily on the hearth, banking somewhat because it hadn't been fed in a while. Two lamps were lit in here, another in what looked to be a dining room adjacent. Near the hearth, a cut spruce reached almost to the raftered ceiling; it was festooned with Christmas decorations—strung popcorn and bright-colored beads, stubs of tallow candles in bent can tops, snippets of fleece from some old garment sprinkled on the branches to resemble snow, a five-pointed star atop the uppermost branch.

All very cozy and inviting, but where were the occupants? He called out again, and again received no response. He cocked his head to listen. Heard only the plaint of the storm and the snicking of flung snow against the window-pane.

He crossed the parlor, entered the dining room. The puncheon table was set for two, and in fact two people had been eating there not so long ago. A clay pot of venison stew sat in the center of the table; when he touched it he found it and its contents still slightly warm. Ladlings of stew and slices of bread were on each of the two plates.

The hair began to pull along the nape of his neck, as it always did when he sensed a wrongness to things. Slick Henry? Or something else? With his hand now gripping the butt of his Navy, he eased his way through a doorway at the rear of the dining room.

Kitchen and larder. Stove still warm, a kettle atop it blackening smokily because all the water it had contained had boiled away. Quincannon transferred the kettle to the sink drainboard. Moved then to another closed door that must lead to a bedroom, the last of the cabin's rooms. He depressed the latch and pushed the door wide.

Bedroom, indeed. And as empty as the other three rooms. But there were two odd things here: The sash of a window in the far wall was raised a few inches; and on the floor was the base of a lamp that had been dropped or knocked off the bedside table. Snow coated the window sill and there was a sifting of it on the floor and on the lamp base.

Quincannon stood puzzled and scowling in the icy draft. No room at the inn? he thought ironically. On the contrary, there was plenty of room at this inn on Christmas Eve. It didn't seem to have any people in it.

On a table near the bed he spied a well-worn family Bible. Impulse took him to it; he opened it at the front, where such vital statistics as marriages, births, and deaths were customarily recorded. Two names were written there in a fine woman's hand: Martha and Adam Keene. And a wedding date: July 17, 1893. That was all.

Well, now he knew the identity of the missing occupants. But what had happened to them? He hadn't seen them in the barn. And the other, smaller cabin—guest accommodations, he judged—had also been in darkness upon his arrival. It made no sense that a man and his wife would suddenly quit the warmth of their home in the middle of a Christmas Eve supper, to lurk about in a darkened outbuilding. It also made no sense that they would voluntarily decide to rush off into a snowstorm on foot or on horseback. Forced out of here, then? By Slick Henry Garber or someone else? If so, *why?*

Quincannon returned to the parlor. He had no desire to go out again into the wind and swirling snow, but he was not the sort of man who could allow a confounding mystery to go uninvestigated—particularly a mystery that might involve a criminal with a handsome price on his head. So, grumbling a little, his unmittened hands deep in the pockets of his coat, he bent his body into what was swiftly becoming a full-scale blizzard.

He fought his way to the barn first, because it was closer and to satisfy himself that it really was occupied only by horses. The wind had blown out the lantern when he'd left earlier; he relighted it, but not until he had first drawn his revolver. One of the animals—not the rented roan—moved restlessly in its stall as he walked toward the far end. There were good-sized piles of hay in each of the empty stalls as well, he noticed. He leaned into those stalls with the lantern. If anyone were hiding in a haypile it would have to be close to the surface to avoid the risk of suffocation; he poked at each pile in turn with the Navy's barrel. Hay and nothing but hay.

In one corner of the back wall was an enclosure that he took to be a harness room. Carefully he opened the door with his gun hand. Buckles and bit chains gleamed in the narrow space within; he saw the shapes of saddles, bridles, hackamores. Something made a scurrying noise among the floor shadows and he lowered the lantern in time to see the tail end of a packrat disappear behind a loose board. Dust was the only other thing on the floor.

He went back toward the front, stopped again when he was abreast of the loft ladder. He climbed it with the lantern lifted above his head. But the loft contained nothing more than several tightly stacked bales of hay and a thin scattering of straw that wouldn't have concealed the packrat, much less a man or a woman.

No one in the main cabin, no one in the barn. That left only the guest cabin. And if that, too, was deserted? Well, then, he thought irascibly, he would sit down in the main cabin and gorge himself on venison stew while he waited for somebody—the Keenes, Slick Henry, the Ghost of Christmas Past —to put in an appearance. He was cold and tired and hungry, and mystery or no mystery he was not about to wander around in a blizzard hunting for clues.

Out once more into the white fury. By the time he worked his way through what were now thigh-deep drifts to the door of the guest cabin, his legs and arms were stiff and his beard was caked with frozen snow. He wasted no time getting the door open, but he didn't enter right away. Instead he let the wind hurl the door inward, so that it cracked audibly against the wall, while he hung back and to one side with his revolver drawn.

Nothing happened inside.

He waited another few seconds, but already the icebound night was beginning to numb his bare hand; another minute or two of exposure and the skin would freeze to the gunmetal. He entered the cabin in a sideways crouch, caught hold of the door and crowded it shut until it latched. Chill, clotted black encased him now, so thick that he was virtually blind. Should he risk lighting a match? Well, he would have to. Floundering around in the dark would mean a broken limb, his luck being what it was these days.

He fumbled in his pocket for another lucifer, struck it on his left thumbnail, ducked down and away from the flare of light. Still nothing happened. But the light revealed that this cabin was divided into two sparsely furnished bedrooms with an open door in the dividing wall; and it also revealed some sort of huddled mass on the floor of the rear bedroom.

In slow strides, holding the match up and away from his body, he moved toward the doorway. The flame died just as he reached it—just as he recognized the huddled mass as the motionless body of a man. He thumbed another match alight, went through the doorway, leaned down for a closer look. The man lay drawn up on his back, and on one temple blood from a bullet furrow glistened blackly in the wavering flame. Young man, sandy-haired, wearing an old vicuna cloth suit and a clean white shirt now spotted with blood. A man Quincannon had never seen before—

Something moved behind him.

Something else slashed the air, grazed the side of Quincannon's head as he started to turn and dodge, and drove him sideways to the floor.

The lucifer went out as he was struck; he lost his grip on the Navy and it went clattering away into blackness as thick as the inside of Old Scratch's fundament. The blow had been sharp enough to set up a ringing in his ears, but the thick rabbit-fur cap had cushioned it enough so that he wasn't stunned. He pulled around onto his knees, lunged back toward the doorway with both hands reaching. Above him he heard again that slashing of the air, only this time the swung object missed him entirely. Which threw the man who had swung off balance, at the same instant Quincannon's right hand found a grip on sheepskin material not unlike that of his own coat. He yanked hard, heard a grunt, and then the heavy weight of his assailant came squirming and cursing down on top of him.

The floor of an unfamiliar, black-dark room was the last place Quincannon would have chosen for hand-to-hand combat. But he was a veteran of any number of skirmishes, and had learned ways to do grievous damage to an opponent that would have shocked the Marquis of Queensbury. (Sabina, too, no doubt). Besides which, this particular opponent, whoever he was, was laboring under the same disadvantages as he was.

There were a few seconds of scrambling and bumping about, some close-quarters pummeling on both sides, a blow that split Quincannon's lip and made his Scot's blood boil even more furiously, a brief and violent struggle for possession of what felt like a long-barreled revolver, and then, finally, an opportunity for Quincannon to use a mean and scurrilous trick he had learned in a free-for-all on the Baltimore docks. His assailant screamed, quit fighting, began to twitch instead; and to groan and wail and curse feebly. This vocal combination made Quincannon's head hurt all the more. Since he now had possession of the long-barreled revolver, he thumped the man on top of the head with the weapon. The groaning and wailing and cursing ceased abruptly. So did the twitching.

Quincannon got to his feet, stood shakily wiping blood from his torn lip. He made the mistake then of taking a blind step and almost fell over one or the other of the two men now lying motionless on the floor. He produced another lucifer from his dwindling supply. In its flare he spied a lamp, and managed to get to it in time to light the wick before the flame died. He located his Navy, holstered it, then carried the lamp to where the men lay and peered at the face of the one who had tried to brain him.

"Well, well," he said aloud, with considerable relish. "A serendipitous turnabout after all. Just what I wanted for Christmas—Slick Henry Garber."

Slick Henry Garber said nothing, nor would he be able to for a good while.

The young, sandy-haired lad—Adam Keene, no doubt—was also unconscious. The bullet wound on his head didn't seem to be serious, but he would need attention. *He* wouldn't be saying anything, either, for a good while. Quincannon would just have to wait for the full story of what had happened here before his arrival. Unless, of course, he got it from Adam Keene's wife . . .

Where was Adam Keene's wife?

Carrying the lamp, he searched the two bedrooms. No sign of Martha Keene. He did find Slick Henry's leather satchel, in a corner of the rear room; it contained several thousand shares of bogus mining stock and nine thousand dollars in greenbacks. He also found evidence of a struggle, and not one but two bullet holes in the back wall.

These things, plus a few others, allowed him to make a reasonably accurate guess as to tonight's sequence of events. Slick Henry had arrived just before the snowstorm and just as the Keenes were sitting down to supper. He had either put his horse in the barn himself or Adam Keene had done it; that explained why there had been *three* saddle horses present when only *two* people lived at Traveler's Rest. Most likely Slick Henry had then thrown down on the Keenes: he must have been aware that Quincannon was still close behind him, even if Quincannon hadn't known it, and realized that with the impending storm it was a good bet his pursuer would also stop at Traveler's Rest. And what better place for an ambush than one of these three buildings? Perhaps he'd chosen the guest cabin on the theory that Quincannon would be less on his guard there than at the other two. To ensure that, Slick Henry had taken Adam Keene with him at gunpoint, leaving Mrs. Keene in the main cabin with instructions to send Quincannon to the guest cabin on a pretext.

But while the two men were in this cabin Adam Keene had heroically attempted to disarm Slick Henry, there had been a struggle, and Keene had unheroically received a bullet wound for his efforts. Martha Keene must have somehow heard at least one of the shots, and fearing the worst she had left the main cabin through the bedroom window and hidden herself somewhere. Had Slick Henry found her? Not likely. But it seemed reasonable to suppose he had been out hunting for her when Quincannon came. The violence of the storm had kept him from springing his trap at that point; he had decided instead to return to the guest cabin as per his original plan. And this was where he had been ever since, waiting in the dark for his nemesis to walk in like the damned fool he often was.

This day's business, Quincannon thought ruefully, had been one long, grim comedy of errors on all sides. Slick Henry's actions were at least half doltish and so were his own. Especially his own—blundering in half a dozen different ways, including not even once considering the possibility of a planned ambush. Relentless manhunter, intrepid detective. Bah. It was a wonder he hadn't been shot dead. Sabina would chide him mercilessly if he told her the entire story of his capture of Slick Henry Garber. Which, of course, he had no intention of doing.

Well, he could redeem himself somewhat by finding Martha Keene. Almost certainly she had to be in one of the three buildings. She wouldn't have remained in the open, exposed, in a raging mountain storm. She would not have come anywhere near the guest cabin because of Slick Henry. And she hadn't stayed in the main cabin; the open bedroom window proved that. So, she was in the barn. But he had searched the barn, even gone up into the hayloft. No place to hide up there, or in the harness enclosure, or in one of the stalls, or—

The lamp base on the bedroom floor, he thought.

No room at the inn, he thought.

"Well, of course, you blasted rattlepate," he said aloud. "It's the only place she can be."

Out once more into the whipping snow and freezing wind (after first taking the precaution of binding Slick Henry's hands with the man's own belt). Slog, slog, slog, and finally into the darkened barn. He lighted the lantern, took it to the approximate middle of the building, and then called out, "Mrs. Keene! My name is John Quincannon, I am a detective from San Francisco, and I have just cracked the skull of the man who terrorized you and your husband tonight. You have nothing more to fear."

No response.

"I know you're here, and approximately where. Won't you save both of us the embarrassment of my poking around with a pitchfork?"

Silence.

"Mrs. Keene, your husband is unconscious with a head wound and he needs you. Please believe me."

More silence. Then, just as he was about to issue another plea, there was a rustling and stirring in one of the empty stalls to his left. He moved over that way in time to see Martha Keene rise up slowly from her hiding place deep under the pile of hay.

She was young, attractive, as fair-haired as her husband, and wrapped warmly in a heavy fleece-lined coat. She was also, Quincannon noted with surprise, quite obviously with child.

What didn't surprise him was the length of round, hollow glass she held in one hand—the chimney that belonged to the lamp base on the bedroom floor. She had had the presence of mind to snatch it up before climbing out of the window, in her haste dislodging the base from the bedside table. The chimney was the reason neither he nor Slick Henry had found her; by using it as a breathing tube, she had been able to burrow deep enough into the haypile to escape a superficial search.

For a space she stared at Quincannon out of wide, anxious eyes. What she saw seemed to reassure her. She released a thin, sighing breath and said tremulously, "My husband . . . you're sure he's not—?"

"No, no. Wounded I said and wounded I meant. He'll soon be good as new."

"Thank God!"

"And you, my dear? Are you all right?"

"Yes, I . . . yes. Just frightened. I've been lying here imagining all sorts of dreadful things." Mrs. Keene sighed again, plucked clinging straw from her face and hair. "I didn't want to run and hide, but I thought Adam must be dead and I was afraid for my baby . . . oh!" She winced as if with a sudden sharp pain, dropped the lamp chimney and placed both hands over the swell of her abdomen. "All the excitement . . . I believe the baby will arrive sooner than expected."

Quincannon gave her a horrified look. "Right here? Now?"

"No, not that soon." A wan smile. "Tomorrow . . ."

It was his turn to put forth a relieved sigh as he moved into the stall to help her up. Tomorrow. Christmas Day. Appropriate that she should have her baby then. But it wasn't the only thing about this situation that was appropriate to the season. This was a stable, and what was the stall where she had lain with her unborn child but a manger? There were animals in attendance, too. And at least one wise man (wise in *some* things, surely) who had come bearing a gift without even knowing it, a gift of a third—no, a half—of the $5000 reward for the capture of Slick Henry Garber.

Peace on earth, good will to men.

Quincannon smiled; of a sudden he felt very jolly and very much in a holiday spirit. This was, he thought, going to be a fine Christmas after all.

BURGADE'S CROSSING

Quincannon heard the calliope ten minutes before the Walnut Grove stage reached Dead Man's Slough. The off-key notes of "The Girl I Left Behind Me" woke him out of a thin doze; he sat up to listen and then peer through the coach's isinglass window. He saw nothing but swamp growth crowding in close to the levee road. Sounds carried far here in the river delta, particularly on cold, early-winter afternoons such as this one. And the rusty-piped sound of the calliope was familiar even at a distance: the *Island Star* had drifted downriver and tied up at Burgade's Crossing, just as he'd expected.

The stage's only other passenger, a mild little whiskey drummer named Whittle, lowered the dime novel he'd been reading and said tentatively, "Sounds festive, doesn't it?"

"No," Quincannon growled, "it doesn't."

Whittle hid his face again behind the book. It was plain that he was intimidated by a man twice his size who wore a bushy, gray-flecked freebooter's beard and was given to ferocious glowers when in a dark mood. He was pretending to be a drummer himself, of patent medicines, and Whittle had tried to engage him in brotherly conversation by telling a brace of smutty stories. Quincannon had glowered him into silence. Ordinarily he was friendly and enjoyed a good joke, but today he had too much on his mind for frivolous pursuits. Besides, Whittle's stories were graybeards that hadn't been worth a chuckle even when they were new.

The *Island Star*'s calliope stopped playing for a time, started up again with the same tune just before they reached the north-bank ferry landing at Dead Man's Slough. The coach's driver clattered them off the levee road, down an embankment steep enough to cause the rear wheels to skid and the brake blocks to give off dry squeals. Quincannon had the door open and was already swinging out when the stage came to a halt.

A chill wind assailed him. Overhead, dark-edged clouds moved furtively; the smell of rain was heavy in the air. The coming storm would break before the passenger packet *Yosemite*, bound upriver from San Francisco, reached

Burgade's Crossing at midnight. There were possible benefits in a stormy night, Quincannon thought bleakly, but the potential dangers far outweighed them.

He took a pipe from the pocket of his corduroy jacket, packed and lit it as he surveyed his surroundings. He had seen Burgade's Crossing from a distance several times, from the deck of one or another of the Sacramento River steamers, but he had never been here before. It was a sorry little backwater, with no attractions for anyone except the misguided souls who chose to live in or near it.

There was nothing on this side but the road and ferry landing; the town's buildings were all on the south bank. The ferry ran across Dead Man's a few hundred yards from where the slough merged with the much wider expanse of the Sacramento. West of the ferry, on the river, was a steamboat landing; east of the ferry, on the slough next to a continuation of the levee road, stood Burgade's Inn—a long, weathered structure built partly on solid ground and partly on thick pilings over the water. The rest of Burgade's Crossing ran east in a ragged line to where the slough narrowed and vanished among tangles of cattails and swamp oaks choked with wild grapevine. Its sum was a dozen or so buildings, a dozen or so shantyboats and houseboats tied to the bank, and a single sagging wharf.

The *Island Star*, Gus Kennett's store boat, was moored at the wharf. The calliope on her foredeck was again giving forth, monotonously, with "The Girl I Left Behind Me." The music had drawn a small crowd; Quincannon could see men, women, a few children clustered on the gangplank at the battered little steamer's waist.

He shifted his attention to the broad, flat-bottomed ferry barge. It had been tied on the south side, and at the stage driver's hail the ferryman had come out of his shack and was now winching it across. The scow was held by grease-blackened cables made fast to pilings on a spit of north-side land a hundred yards upslough. The current pushed the ferry across from shore to shore, guided by a centerboard attached to its bottom and by the ferryman's windlass.

When the barge nudged the bank, the ferryman quickly put hitches in the mooring ropes, collected the toll, then lowered the approach apron. The stage driver took his team of four aboard, their hooves and the coach's wheels clattering hollowly on the timbers. Quincannon, scowling and puffing on his pipe as if it were a bellows, followed on foot. A minute later the cable whined thinly on the windlass drum and the scow began moving again, back across.

The wind was stronger on open water, sharp with the smells of salt and swamp and impending rain. It made the slough choppy, which in turn caused the ferry to buck and squirm even with its heavy load. Again, Quincannon felt worry at what lay ahead tonight. Why the devil couldn't Noah Rideout have been sensible and spent another night—or better yet, another week—in San Francisco?

He touched the pocket where he'd stowed the telegram that had arrived for him in Walnut Grove this morning. Its contents were what had thrust him into his bleak mood.

```
EFFORTS   HERE   STILL   FRUITLESS   STOP   NJR
RETURNING TONIGHT ON YOSEMITE STOP COULD NOT
DISSUADE  HIM  COMMA  STATES  BUSINESS  HERE
FINISHED  AND  IS  NEEDED  AT  HOME  STOP  LS
ACCOMPANYING  HIM  BUT  NO  ONE  ELSE  COMMA
REFUSED BODYGUARDS STOP URGENT YOU MEET HIM
AT BURGADES CROSSING AT MIDNIGHT

                                        SC
```

NJR was Noah J. Rideout, of course. LS was Leland Stannard, the foreman of Rideout's huge Tyler Island farm. And SC was Sabina Carpenter, the other member of Carpenter and Quincannon, Professional Detective Services.

There were still some narrow-minded dolts who questioned the wisdom of a former U. S. Secret Service operative entering into private partnership with a woman, even though Sabina had, like Kate Warne before her, worked for several years for Allan Pinkerton. The truth of the matter was, she was the equal of any man at detective work. In fact, Quincannon admitted grudgingly to himself, if never to Sabina or anyone else, she was not only his equal but in many ways his better. If her efforts in San Francisco were continuing to prove fruitless, then there was nothing to be found there.

The weight of the case was now all on his shoulders. And it was a dual burden: to find out, if he could, who wanted Noah Rideout dead; and to prevent, if he could, the act of murder from taking place. There had been one bungled attempt in San Francisco—that was what had led Rideout to hire

Carpenter and Quincannon, Professional Detective Services—and he was certain there would be another tonight. The one lead he and Sabina had uncovered had led him to Walnut Grove, and that lead had preceded him here to Burgade's Crossing: Gus Kennett, owner of the *Island Star*, who was rumored to be the man hired as Rideout's assassin.

The ferry trip took less than ten minutes. And five minutes after the barge landed on the south bank, the stage was on its way along the levee road to Isleton—empty now, for Whittle as well as Quincannon was stopping here. The two men, Quincannon carrying his old warbag, the drummer lugging a heavy carpetbag, trudged uphill to the inn without speaking. Inside, a bearded giant who identified himself as Adam Burgade took three dollars from each of them. The fee entitled the weary traveler to a meal and a room.

Burgade had at least two other guests at present. They were in the common room, and an odd pair they were: a young nun, dressed in a black habit, sitting before the glowing pot-bellied stove; and an old man with a glass eye and a fierce expression, standing with hands on hips before Burgade's liquor buffet.

Whittle stood blinking at the nun. Then, jerkily, he tipped his hat and said, "Good afternoon, Sister. Will you take offense if I say I am surprised to find you here?"

"Not at all, sir. I'm surprised myself to be here."

The old man glared with his good eye. "An outrage, that's what I call it. A damned outrage."

Burgade said, "Watch your language, Mr. Dana. I won't tell you again."

"This is no place for a nun," Dana said. "Besides, I'm a veteran, I served with McClellan's Army of the Potomac in the War between the States. I'm entitled to a drink of whiskey when I have the money to pay for it."

"The buffet is temporarily closed," Burgade explained to Whittle and Quincannon.

"You hear that?" Dana said. "Temporarily closed. Not a drop of good spirits sold while that woman is in the house. And me with a parched throat. It ain't right, I tell you, Burgade. I ain't Catholic. I ain't even religious."

"Well, I am."

The nun seemed embarrassed. "Really, Mr. Burgade, as I said before you needn't close your buffet on my account. I don't mind others using alcohol in moderation."

"Mr. Dana don't use it in moderation," Burgade said. "It's best this way,

Sister Mary."

"Bah," Dana said.

"Mr. Whittle here is a whiskey drummer," Burgade told him. "Maybe he has a bottle in his grip that he'll sell you."

"I would, and gladly," Whittle said, "but I've no samples left. This is my last stop, you see, Mr. Dana—"

"Bah."

Burgade said, "Gus Kennett's store boat is in, tied up at the wharf. He'll have a jug of forty-rod for sale, if you don't mind paying his price."

"I'll pay any price. But can I bring it back here to drink?"

"No. Burgade's Inn is a temporary temperance house."

"Temporary temperance house. Bah." Dana started for the door, stopped abruptly when he passed Quincannon, and turned back to face him, scowling. "Well, looky here. A Johnny Reb."

"Johnny Reb?"

"That's right. Southerner, ain't you?"

"I was born in Baltimore," Quincannon admitted, "but I've lived in California for fifteen years."

"Once a Johnny Reb, always a Johnny Reb. Spot one of you a mile away. Only good Reb's a dead one, you ask me."

"The Civil War has been over for thirty years, Mr. Dana."

"Tell that to my right eye. It's been pining for the left one for more'n thirty years. Damned Reb shot it out at Antietam."

He clumped out and banged the door behind him.

"Don't mind him, gents," Burgade said. "Nor you either, Sister. He's only like that when he's sober and on his way upriver to the doctor. His bark's worse than his bite."

Whittle said, lowering his voice, "We can do business, can't we, Mr. Burgade? Even though the inn is a temporary temperance house? I've some fine buys on Kentucky sour mash—"

"In the kitchen, Whittle, in the kitchen."

The two men went through a door next to the buffet. Rich aromas wafted out, reminding Quincannon that he hadn't eaten since a sparse breakfast. No time now, though; he could have supper later. As for the closing of the buffet, it was of no consequence to him. He had given up the use of spirits when he entered into partnership with Sabina two years ago.

He found his way down a central corridor at the rear, to the room he'd been given. It was not much larger than a cell, windowless, furnished with a narrow bed and a washstand. He stayed there just long enough to deposit his warbag on the mattress and to double-check the loads in the Navy revolver he carried under his coat.

Outside, the wind pushed him along a muddy branch of the levee road toward the wharf. The *Island Star*'s calliope was mercifully silent and the number of customers had dwindled to a handful as dusk approached. The little steamer was old and weatherbeaten, her brasswork greening from lack of polish, her short foredeck cluttered with crates and barrels. She was one of a handful of store boats that prowled the fifteen hundred square miles of sloughs and islands between Sacramento and Stockton, peddling everything from candy to kerosene to shantyboaters, small farmers, field hands, and other delta denizens.

Gus Kennett had more profitable sidelines, however. He bought and sold stolen goods, a crime for which he had been arrested twice and convicted once, and was rumored to be involved in a variety of other felonious activities, including robbery and assault. Murder, too, if what Quincannon had heard rumored was true.

As he drew abreast of the gangplank, the old man, Dana, came hurrying out of the lamplit cargo hold, clutching a bottle of forty-rod whiskey. Dana glared at him in passing, muttered something, and scooted off to find a place to do his solitary drinking. He was evidently the last of Kennett's customers. No one was visible in the hold and the decks were deserted except for a deckhand who lounged near the rusty calliope.

Quincannon sauntered across the plank, entered the hold. It had been outfitted as a store, with cabinets fastened around the bulkheads, a long counter at one end, and every inch of deck space crammed with a welter of sacks, bins, barrels, boxes, tools and other loose goods. Gus Kennett was perched on a stool behind the counter, a short-six cigar clamped between yellow horse teeth. He was a barrel of a man, Kennett—no, a powder keg of a man—with short stubby arms and legs, a small head, and a huge powerful torso.

"Afternoon," Kennett said around the stump of his cigar. "Help you with something, friend?"

"A plug of cable twist, if you have it."

"Don't. Never had a call for it."

"What kind of pipe tobacco do you sell?"

"Virginia plug cut and Durham loose."

"The plug cut, then."

Kennett produced a sack of cheap tobacco and named a price that was half again what it would cost even in Walnut Grove. Quincannon paid without protest or comment.

"Don't believe I've seen you in Burgade's Crossing before," Kennett said. "Big gent like you, nice dressed, I wouldn't forget."

"I've never been here before.

"Passing through?"

"On business."

"What kind of business?"

"Patent medicines," Quincannon said. "Dr. Wallmann's Nerve and Brain Salts, guaranteed to cure more afflictions and derangements than any other product made. I don't suppose I might interest you in a bottle?"

Kennett laughed. "Do I look like I need nerve and brain salts?"

"No, sir, you don't. But some of your customers might."

"Got my own supplier for patent medicines."

Quincannon feigned a sigh. "Little enough business for me here, it seems. Or anywhere in these backwaters. I believe I'll catch the next steamer for Sacramento. There is one due tonight, isn't there?"

"I couldn't say, friend. Ask Adam Burgade."

"I'll do that. Doesn't appear to be much business for you here either, if I may say so.

"Never is in Burgade's Crossing."

"So you'll be moving on soon yourself?"

"That I will," Kennett said. "Was there anything else, friend?"

Quincannon had taken the conversation to its limit; if he tried to prolong it, he would succeed only in making the store boat owner suspicious. He said, "No, friend, nothing," and took his leave.

He was uneasy again as he left the *Island Star*. How was Kennett planning to commit murder tonight? There had been nothing aboard the store boat and nothing in Kennett's manner to provide a clue. A distant rifle shot through rain-soaked darkness was pure folly. A pistol shot or knife thrust at close quarters were more certain methods, but Noah Rideout would not be alone when he left the *Yosemite* and the odds were short that an assassin would be identified or killed himself before he could escape. No, Gus Kennett would not risk his own neck, no matter how much he was being paid. He was sly and slippery, not bold.

Would he enlist the help of others? His deckhand, perhaps? That was another troubling thought.

As was the question of who had hired him and why.

Noah Rideout was a man of many enemies. A hard man, uncompromising in his business dealings and personal life. In his fifty-seven years he had had two wives, several mistresses, and three sons, all of whom, by his own free admission, hated him enough to want him dead. He owned much of the rich Tyler Island croplands; he had forced several small farmers to sell their land to him at low prices, and earned the hatred of others by his tireless and expensive campaign to build more levee roads as a means of flood control. And he had been a leader in the legal battle against hydraulic gold mining in the Mother Lode, the dumping of billions of cubic yards of yellow slickens that had clogged rivers and sloughs and destroyed farmland. The California Debris Commission Act, passed two years before in 1893, had made the discharge of debris into the rivers illegal and virtually put the hydraulickers known as the Little Giants out of business.

Rideout himself had been unable to narrow down the field, although it was his opinion that "one of the damned hydraulickers" was behind the murder plot. His battle with them had been long and bitter, involving bribery and intimidation of witnesses on the part of the miners, and he felt that some were not above mayhem as a means of revenge. But neither Quincannon nor Sabina had been able to find a link between Gus Kennett and one of the Little Giants, or any other evidence to support Rideout's contention.

Restlessly Quincannon prowled through the meager town, but there was nothing there to enlighten him. Full dark had closed down when he started back to the inn. The wind had sharpened and the first drops of rain iced his skin. The clouds were low-hanging now, so low that the tops of some of the taller trees in the swamp were obscured by their drift.

Diagonally across the road from the inn was a barnlike building that he took to be the livery. One of the doors was open and a buttery lampglow shone within. The light drew him. Inside he discovered four horses in stalls, an expensive Concord buggy, and the hostler asleep in the harness room.

He had a look at the buggy. He thought it might belong to Noah Rideout, and gold monogrammed letters on its body—NJR—confirmed it. Could

Kennett's plan have something to do with the rig? Or with the livery barn? Not the rig; Quincannon checked the wheels and hubs, the axletrees, the transverse springs, even the calash folding top and under the wide leather seat, and found nothing out of order. The barn, though, was an excellent place for an ambush. He would have to keep that in mind.

The rain was gathering momentum as he came out of the livery. Thunder rumbled faintly; so did his empty stomach. He hurried across to the inn.

Sister Mary had the common room to herself. She was still sitting before the stove, working now with cloth and thread on a sampler. He nodded to her and sat down at the long puncheon table.

She asked, "Has it begun to storm?"

"It has."

"I thought I heard thunder. Will it rain heavily tonight, do you think?"

"From all indications. Are you waiting for the midnight packet, Sister?"

"No, I'm going downriver. I'll be leaving in the morning."

"It's unusual for a nun to travel alone, isn't it?"

"Yes. My brother in Isleton is ill."

"I'm sorry to hear that. Seriously ill?"

She nodded gravely. "I am afraid so."

A Chinese waitress entered and Quincannon asked for supper. It turned out to be a plate of fried catfish, potatoes, and corn, and a cup of bitter coffee. He wolfed it all down and requested another helping, after which he found room for a slab of peach pie. His appetite had always been prodigious. He had inherited all of his father's lusty appetites, in fact, along with his genteel Southern mother's love for cultural pursuits.

Sabina had once remarked that he was a curious mixture of the gentle and the stone-hard, the sensitive and the unyielding. He supposed that was an accurate assessment. And the reason, perhaps, that he was a better detective than Thomas L. Quincannon, the rival of Pinkerton in the nation's capital during the Civil War. He knew his limitations, his weaknesses. His father had never once admitted to being wrong, considered himself invincible—and had been shot to death while on a fool's errand on the Baltimore docks. John Frederick Quincannon intended to die in bed at the age of ninety. And not alone, either.

In his room, he lit his pipe and tried to read one of the books of poetry he habitually took along for relaxation on field investigations. But he was too keyed up to relax tonight. And the verses by Whitman and Wordsworth made him yearn for Sabina. It was a sad but true fact that she had become more than a business partner to him. He had made numerous advances to her that were only partly of a lustful nature; she had rejected each gently but firmly. "We work splendidly together, John," she'd said. "If we were to become lovers, or more, it might damage our professional relationship."

He didn't agree with this, and he was ever willing to put the matter to the test. There were times when he felt that she cared deeply for him and that she was weakening; at other times he was convinced she would never weaken. It made his life difficult, and at the same time highly stimulating . . .

After a while the restlessness drove him back to the common room. Sister Mary had retired and there was still no sign of old man Dana. He watched Whittle and Burgade play chess. Burgade was surprisingly good at the game; the whiskey drummer made a poor opponent. Eventually Whittle wearied of losing and went to his room, and Quincannon took his place at the board.

He played an excellent game himself in normal circumstances, but his mind kept slipping away to Gus Kennett and Noah Rideout's imminent arrival. Burgade won three matches and they played a fourth to a draw. Outside, rain hammered on the inn's roof and the wind moaned and chattered ceaselessly. A foul night. And a foul deed no doubt planned for it.

But a deed that would not be done. No, by Godfrey, not with a fee balance of one thousand dollars yet to be collected from Mr. Rideout.

♦ ♦ ♦

It was just eleven-thirty by his stemwinder when he left the inn. Burgade registered surprise at his departure, and to forestall questions Quincannon explained that he was meeting an acquaintance on the *Yosemite* and felt the need of some fresh air before the packet arrived. A bit lame, but Burgade accepted it without comment.

In the wet darkness he pulled the brim of his hat down and the collar of his slicker up to keep water out of his eyes and off his neck. Visibility was no more than a few yards. He could barely make out the daubs of lanternlight that marked the ferryman's shack and steamboat landing. Wind-gusts constantly changed the slant of the rain so that it was like a jiggling curtain against the night's black wall.

Shoulders hunched and body bowed, he set off along the muddy road toward town. The surface was still solid along the edges, but if the rain continued to whack down with such intensity, by morning this track and the levee road would be quagmires.

Faint scattered lights materialized as he neared the town buildings, but none shone at the wharf. At first he thought the *Island Star* had slipped out of Dead Man's Slough under cover of the storm. But no, she was still moored there, the bumpers roped to her strakes thumping against the pilings as the rough waters rolled her from side to side. All dark as she was, she looked like a ghost boat. There was no sign of Gus Kennett or his deckhand. No sign of anyone in the vicinity.

Quincannon heeled around, started back toward the inn. He had gone only a few yards when a lull between gusts brought a sound to his ears. It was faint and far-off, an odd hollow chunking. He paused, straining to hear over the storm's wailings and moanings. There it was again . . . and again. It seemed to be coming from on or across the slough, but he couldn't be certain. He waited to hear it another time—and heard only the wind, the harsh slap-and-gurgle of the water as it punished the bank below.

He plowed ahead, bypassing the inn and then the ferryman's shack. The steamer landing, he saw as he approached it, was deserted. He veered off to check behind the landing's rickety lean-to shelter, to peer among the willows and cottonwoods that leaned over the river nearby. He startled a bird of some sort, a snipe or a plover, and sent it whickering off through the swamp growth. Nothing else moved there except the storm.

He stood shivering under the lean-to, his hand still resting on the butt of his revolver, alternately watching the river and the road down from the inn. It wasn't long before he heard the first shrill blast of the *Yosemite*'s whistle: she was on schedule despite the foul weather. Less than a minute later her three tiers of blurred lights appeared; and at almost the same instant lampglow spilled out through the front door of the inn and a slicker-clad figure emerged. Quincannon tensed, drawing back against the shelter wall.

The figure came down to the landing, not hurrying, tacking unsteadily through the mud and rain. Whittle? No, it was the old man with the glass eye, Dana. He didn't see Quincannon until he was almost upon him. And when he did, he started so violently that he came close to losing his balance and toppling into the river.

"Hellfire!" he shouted when he recovered. He leaned close to peer at Quincannon's face, breathing whiskey fumes at him. "Is that you, you damn

Johnny Reb? What're you lurking here for?"

"I'm not lurking, I am waiting for the *Yosemite*."

"Sacramento bound, eh?"

"No. Meeting someone."

"Another Copperhead, no doubt. Say, you got relatives fought at Antietam?"

"No."

"Reb that shot my eye out looked just like you."

Dana belched, moved off to stand at the far side of the shelter. He watched the *Yosemite*'s approach with his good eye and Quincannon watched him.

The packet's captain was experienced at landing in the midst of a squall. He brought the *Yosemite* in straight to the landing, her whistle shrieking fitfully, and held her there with her stern buckets lashing the river while a team of deckhands slung out a gangplank. As soon as the plank was down, two men wearing slickers and toting carpetbags hurried off. After which Dana, with a one-eyed glare at Quincannon and a muttered, "Damn all Johnny Rebs," staggered on board. The deckhands hauled in the plank and the steamboat swung out toward mid-channel again. The entire operation had taken no more than minute.

When Quincannon recognized Noah Rideout as one of the disembarkees, he stepped forward and identified himself. Rideout peered up at him; he was half a head shorter and had a habit of standing with his feet spread wide, a pose that was both belligerent and challenging. He reminded Quincannon of a fighting cock.

"What are you doing here?" Rideout demanded.

Quincannon told him in brief, clipped sentences. Rideout was neither concerned nor impressed.

"Well, let this man Kennett come ahead with his dirty work. I am armed and so is Leland. So are you, I trust. That makes three guns against one."

"Kennett may not be planning to use guns. And he may have help, for all we know."

"What sort of ambush could he be planning, then?"

"I haven't a clear idea. The man is shrewd and unpredictable. I suggest we get inside as quickly—"

"Inside? Inside where?"

"The inn, of course."

"That rathole," Rideout said contemptuously. "I wouldn't spend five minutes in Adam Burgade's house."

"It's the only place here to stay the night."

"I am not staying in Burgade's Crossing. I'll sleep in my own bed."

Quincannon stared at him. "You mean you're thinking of traveling home in this weather?"

"Not thinking of it," Rideout said, "about to do it."

"Sir, I strongly advise—"

"I don't care what you advise. Why should I stay here, if this is where some blackguard plans to assassinate me?"

"He could just as easily make the attempt on the road, with the rain and dark to conceal him. It would be safer at the inn."

"Damn the inn. If this rain keeps up, the levee road will be impassable tomorrow. I refuse to stay in Burgade's Crossing one night, let alone two, when I can be home in three hours." He turned to Leland Stannard, a dark, heavyset man who sported mutton-chop whiskers. "Enough of this shilly-shallying. Leland, go up to the livery barn and fetch the buggy and team."

"Right away, Mr. Rideout." Stannard started off.

"Quincannon, you go with him, give him a hand."

"No, sir, I'm staying with you."

"I don't need a bodyguard."

"You hired my firm to prevent your death and that is exactly what I intend to do. If it means accompanying you to your home tonight, then there will be three in your buggy, not two."

"Stubborn, aren't you?"

"No more than you, sir."

Rideout seemed to want further argument, changed his mind when the wind gusted sharply, pelted him with stinging rain. He shouted, "Have it your way," and stomped off toward the ferryman's shack.

Quincannon followed, grumbling to himself. He would have to leave his warbag at the inn; Rideout wouldn't go with him to pick it up, and he wouldn't let the farmer out of his sight for a minute until they reached his Tyler Island farm. A charge for the inconvenience would be added to Rideout's bill.

The burly ferryman did not take kindly to being wakened from a sound sleep, and even less kindly to a crossing on such a night as this. It was dangerous, he said; the wind was a she-devil, the current was flood-fast—

Rideout cut him off with a curt word and a gold coin that flashed in the light from the ferryman's bug-eye lantern. There were no more protestations. The ferryman had the landing apron down and was making ready with the windlass when Stannard drove the Concord buggy down the embankment.

The two horses were skittish; it took all four men to coax them onto the rocking barge. Stannard set the brake and then swung down to help Rideout hold the animals while the ferryman hooked the guard chain, cast off the mooring ropes, and bent to his windlass. Quincannon braced himself against the buggy's off rear wheel, scanning as much of the shore and slough as he could make out through the downpour. He thought he saw someone up on the road near the inn, a shape like a huge winged vulture, but he couldn't be sure. If they *were* being watched, whoever it was stood still as a statue.

Progress was slow, the barge rolling and pitching on the turbulent water. They were less than halfway across when Quincannon heard a moaning in the storm's racket—a split of wind on the ferry cable, he thought, or the strain on the scow produced by the load and the strong current. Then all of a sudden the barge lurched, made a dancing little sideslip that almost tore loose Quincannon's grip on the buggy wheel.

The ferryman shouted a warning that the wind shredded away. In the next instant there was a loud snapping noise and something came hurtling through the wet blackness, cracking like a whip. One of the cables, broken free of its anchor on the north bank.

Swirling water bit into the scow, drenched Quincannon to the knees as it sluiced up across the deck. The ferryman was thrown backward from the windlass; the drum spun free, ratcheting. He shouted again. So did Rideout, who was clinging to the horse on Quincannon's side. The barge, floating loose now and caught by the current, heaved and bucked toward the dark sweep of the river.

The terror-stricken horses reared, and a hoof must have struck Stannard; he screamed in pain and was gone into the roiling slough. Quincannon felt the deck canting over, the buggy beginning to tip and slide away from him. He lunged toward Rideout, caught hold of his arm. In another few seconds the buggy would roll, and the weight of it and the horses tumbling would capsize the scow. There was nothing to be done but to go into the water themselves, try to swim clear while they were still in the slough.

The ferryman knew it too. He yelled a third time—"Jump, jump!"—and dove over the guard chain. But Rideout fought against going overboard. He clawed desperately to free himself, to cling to the side rail, all the while shouting, "I can't swim! I can't swim!"

Quincannon was bigger and stronger, and there was no time left for such concerns. He wrenched the little farmer around, locked an arm about his waist, and jumped both of them off the tilting deck.

Rideout's struggles grew frenzied as the chill water closed over them. Quincannon nearly lost his grip on the man's slicker, managed to hold on and to kick them both up to the surface. Rideout continued to flail and sputter in panic, which left Quincannon no choice in this matter either. He rapped the farmer smartly on the chin with a closed fist, a blow that put an abrupt end to the scuffling.

The current had them by then, but it was not half as powerful here as it would be in the river. Quincannon shucked one arm out of his slicker, shifted his grasp on Rideout, and then worked the other arm free; without the dragging oilskins, he could move more easily in the water. It took him a few seconds to get his bearings, to pick out the faint light on the ferryman's shack. Then, towing the unconscious man, he struck out toward the bank.

The wind and the current battled him at every stroke, bobbing the pair of them like corks. Once an eddy almost took Rideout away from him. His right leg threatened to cramp; the cold and exertion numbed his mind as well as his body. The bank, the light, seemed far away . . . then a little closer . . . and closer still. . .

It might have been five minutes or fifteen before his outstretched arm finally touched the shore mud. He got his feet down, managed to drag himself and his burden up through the silt. Lay there in the pounding rain waiting for his breath and his strength to return.

Shouts penetrated the storm, roused him. He sat up weakly. At his side Rideout lay unmoving. Three men were sloshing toward them along the edge of the embankment, Adam Burgade in the lead. Behind him were the burly ferryman and the drummer, Whittle.

When Burgade helped him to his feet, Quincannon said, "Look after Rideout. I'm all right."

Burgade squatted to examine the farmer. "He's alive but he's swallowed a quart or two. I'll get it out of him." He rolled Rideout onto his stomach, straddled him and began forcing the water out of his lungs.

Quincannon turned to the ferryman, who was sodden but appeared none the worse for his own hard swim. "The other man on the barge—Stannard?"

"Drowned, looks like. There's no sign of him."

So Gus Kennett would stand trial for murder after all.

Whittle asked, "What happened out there?"

"Cable snapped," the ferryman said. "Don't know how—'twas new enough, and strong the last I checked it."

Quincannon knew how. Even the strongest cable could not withstand the blade of an ax. The odd hollow chunking he'd heard earlier had been ax blows. Kennett must have known of Rideout's stubborn refusal to spend a night at Burgade's Inn, that he would put his buggy on the ferry barge even in a squall; and he must have rowed a skiff over to the spit anchor and cut most of the way through the cable, leaving just enough for the ferry to be winched out into midstream before it snapped. A diabolical plan. Kennett might have killed four men for the price of one, and evidently without qualms.

He said nothing of this now; there would be time enough later for explanations. He watched the innkeeper finish emptying Rideout, stand and hoist the limp form into his giant's arms.

"He'll live," Burgade said, "if pneumonia don't set in."

"Same might be said for all of us."

Quincannon was still shaky-legged; the ferryman had to lend an arm as they trudged back along the bank, up the steep incline to the road. He was able to walk then under his own power. The ferryman veered away to his shack for dry clothing; the rest of them slogged to the inn.

Sister Mary was waiting anxiously inside. She clasped her hands at the damp front of her habit when she saw Rideout cradled in Burgade's arms. "Is he dead?"

"No, Sister. But he come pretty close."

"Do you think he'll live?"

"Chances are. Say a prayer for him."

Burgade carried the farmer into one of the rear rooms. Quincannon followed, helped strip off Rideout's soggy clothing and get him into bed.

"Hot coffee," he said then, "and plenty of it."

"Whiskey's better for taking off a chill. This is no longer a temperance house, nun or no nun."

"Just coffee for me," Quincannon said, and went out and down the hall to the room he'd occupied earlier. His warbag was still on the bed. A good thing, after all, that he hadn't been able to come back for it before boarding the ferry. He shucked out of his own soggy clothing, noticed then, for the first time, that he'd lost his Navy Colt in the slough. Rideout would pay for a replacement, he thought darkly, and no argument. New clothing and a new slicker, too.

He rubbed himself dry, dressed, and returned to the common room. Burgade and Whittle were alone there, sitting at the puncheon table with steaming mugs of coffee in front of them. A third cup waited for Quincannon.

"You sure you don't want a shot of Whittle's rotgut to go with it?" Burgade asked him.

"Rotgut?" Whittle was offended. "Mr. Burgade, you know very well—"

Quincannon cut him off. "Where's Sister Mary?"

"Gone to minister to Rideout," Burgade said. "She said she . . . hey! What's got into you?"

Quincannon had turned and was running back along the corridor. He yanked open the door to Rideout's room—and just in the nick of time. The woman in the black habit was bending over the bed, a pillow clasped tightly in both hands and pressed down over Rideout's face. The farmer was conscious enough to grapple with her, but too feebly to save himself.

Quincannon rushed in, tore the pillow from her grasp and flung it aside. She clawed at him, cursing, then tried to ruin him with her knee. He put an end to this lethal behavior by swinging her around and bear-hugging her from behind, pinning her against his body.

"Here, what do you think you're doing?" Whittle said from the doorway. His tone was outraged. "How dare you treat a nun that way!"

"She isn't a nun. Listen to what she's saying, drummer. No nun ever used such language as that."

The woman continued to curse and struggle, trying now to back-kick Quincannon's shins; he sidestepped nimbly. Her hood had come askew and strands of bright hennaed hair poked free.

Rideout pushed up onto one elbow, staring at her in dull-witted confusion. "Melissa?" he said.

"You know her, eh? I thought so. Who is she?"

"Melissa Pelletier. She . . . I knew her in Sacramento last year . . ."

"Knew me?" the woman shouted. "You promised to marry me, damn you. Instead you left me to die with scarlet fever."

"Scarlet fever? I never knew you were ill . . ."

"Nearly a year before I recovered. A year! I swore I'd make you pay dearly and I would have if Gus Kennett wasn't a blundering fool. And if this"—she called Quincannon a colorful name—"hadn't stopped me just now."

Quincannon was remembering the tune the *Island Star*'s calliope had played over and over today: "The Girl I Left Behind Me." Coincidence? Perhaps, but he didn't think so. Melissa Pelletier had likely paid Kennett for that bit of satisfaction, too.·

Burgade had pushed past Whittle. "What in blazes is this all about?" he demanded of Quincannon. "And what does Gus Kennett have to do with it?"

"Help me put this, ah, lady where she can't do any more harm and I'll explain."

Together they locked Melissa Pelletier in one of the other rooms.

Then they returned to Rideout's room, where the farmer was now sitting up in bed with a mug of coffee in one hand. With the other he gingerly rubbed a large bruise on his chin.

"I'll thank you for saving my life," he said to Quincannon, "not once but twice tonight. But dammit, man, was it necessary to crack my jaw?"

Not only necessary, Quincannon thought, but a pleasure.

He proceeded to tell his tale to Burgade and Whittle. The innkeeper took an angry view of such goings-on in his town; he was all for rushing down to the *Island Star* with rifle and pistol and either shooting Gus Kennett or placing him under citizen's arrest. Quincannon dissuaded him. He had neither the desire nor the stamina for any more heroics tonight. Even if Kennett realized he had been found out and managed to slip away in his boat, he would not get far. The sheriff of Walnut Grove and the law elsewhere in the delta would see to that.

"You seemed to know Sister Mary wasn't Sister Mary," Whittle said. "What made you suspect her?"

It had been more than one thing. She had told him her brother was seriously ill in Isleton and she was bound there to visit him; yet she had remained in Burgade's Crossing to wait for passage on tomorrow morning's downriver packet, rather than taking the stage from Walnut Grove that had brought him and Whittle here this afternoon. Then there was the figure he'd seen watching the ferry as he and Rideout boarded it. It had resembled a huge winged vulture, the very shape a woman dressed in black robes with a slicker held fanned out over her head would make. He had known she'd been outside, too, because of the dampness of her habit. And there was no reason for her to have stood watching in the rain unless she knew what was about to happen and wanted to see it done.

Quincannon did not articulate any of this. Nor would he to anyone but Sabina, who would properly appreciate such clever deductions—and, he very much hoped, properly reward him as well. Instead he smiled an enigmatic smile.

"Detective work, gentlemen," he said. "That is all I can say. A man in my profession must never reveal his secrets."

THE CLOUD CRACKER

The old watchman's shack was at the south end of the Delford railroad yards, a short walk from the station. Quincannon spied it as soon as he stepped down from the Stockton train. It was a ramshackle affair, listing a few degrees farther south on one side, its dusty windows blinded by squares of monk's cloth. Half a dozen citizens lounged in the shade of a row of locust trees nearby—far fewer, no doubt, than had been in attendance when the man calling himself Leonide Zacks began his rain-conjuring experiments five days ago.

The length of brand-new stovepipe that poked up more than a dozen feet through the shack's roof, and the streams of yellowish gas pouring from the pipe, gave the structure the look of a weirdly distorted steam boiler. An actual steam boiler was hidden from curious eyes inside—one of the items that made up Zacks' "miracle cloud-cracking machine." Among the others were a variety of chemicals, coils of copper tubing, a galvanic battery, and two large earthenware crocks. The crocks, Quincannon thought wryly, ought to have been given names: lightning mug for one, thunder mug for the other.

Alongside the shack stood a newly constructed platform, on top of which sat another odd contraption—a cross between a small-caliber cannon and a gigantic slingshot. It was in fact a kind of mortar whose alleged purpose was to assault the heavens with rockets containing a "secret chemical gas." Stretched between the platform and the building was a silken banner festooned with ribbons that hung limp in the hot dry air. Even from a distance Quincannon could read the crimson words emblazoned on the banner.

LEONIDE ZACKS
"THE CLOUD CRACKER"
Peerless Drought Breaking
by the King of Pluviculturists
Results Guaranteed

Not a trace of a cloud, cracked or otherwise, marred the smoky blue of the sky overhead. Quincannon would have been amazed if there had been. He would have been even more amazed to have smelled rain among the sharp odors of summer dust, river water, and the noxious perfume of the chemical gas. The heat here in the Central Valley was intense. Sweat slicked his forehead, trickled through the hairs in his gray-flecked freebooter's beard as he turned to peer in the opposite direction.

The town of Delford stretched out there, some five square blocks of it, its main street defined by orderly rows of gaslight standards—electricity hadn't yet come into general use here—and zinc-sheathed telegraph poles. There was not much activity, owing to the heat and the fact that this was a farm community still caught in the vise of a lengthy drought. Wheat fields surrounded it, broken only by the Southern Pacific tracks on one side and the San Joaquin River on the other.

"Mr. Quincannon."

He swung toward the open doors to the station. One of his clients, Aram Kasabian, had appeared there and was hurrying toward him. Fiftyish, portly, wearing muttonchop whiskers and a black cheviot suit, Kasabian looked exactly like the prosperous small-town banker he was. He had been on edge in San Francisco last week; today he appeared worried to the point of twitchiness.

"Well, Mr. Kasabian. Good of you to meet me."

"I wanted to see you right away. I must say I'm relieved that you're here."

"Difficulties with Zacks and the Coalition?"

"Zacks and O.H. Goodland."

O.H. Goodland was Quincannon's other Delford client. He was one of the larger wheat farmers in the area, and based on their meeting in San Francisco, something of a narrow-minded hothead. Upon learning that the other half of Carpenter and Quincannon, Professional Detective Services, was a former female operative of the Pinkerton Agency's Denver office, Goodland had made disparaging remarks that earned him Quincannon's dislike. Men who saw no purpose to a woman other than cook and bed partner were horses' hindquarters.

"What's happened?" he asked the banker.

"O.H. threatened to kill Zacks last evening."

"Did he now. For what reason?"

"Evidently Zacks made improper advances to his daughter. Perhaps even seduced her. Molly denied the seduction, but O.H. isn't convinced."

Quincannon felt no surprise at this turn of events. The rainmaker had a reputation as a womanizer. "When were the advances made?"

"While O.H. and I were in San Francisco. He found out yesterday afternoon, when he came upon Molly crying in her room."

"The girl is smitten with Zacks?"

"It seems she was, before the advances."

"Does Mrs. Zacks know about this?"

"She wasn't present when O.H. accosted her husband, but I don't see how she could fail to have heard. Zacks' assistant, Collard, was there and it was in public, outside the Valley House."

"Accosted? Were blows struck?"

"Worse than that." Kasabian mopped his forehead with a silk handkerchief. "O.H. was carrying his revolver and he drew the weapon when Zacks gave him no satisfaction. Tom McCool disarmed him—he's our town marshal, if you remember—and warned against any further violence. But O.H. is stubborn and a grudge-holder; there's no telling what he might do."

"Is he back in town today?"

"He never left town," Kasabian said. "Took a room last night at the hotel, down the hall from Zacks' room. He's in the hotel saloon this very minute."

"Building his courage with whiskey?"

"Yes. O.H. is temperamental enough when he's sober, but under the influence he is twice as unpredictable."

This information made Quincannon scowl. He had no use for men who sought to solve their troubles with the aid of strong drink, having been such a man himself not so long ago. Toward the end of his fourteen-year stint as a U.S. Treasury operative he had accidentally shot and killed an innocent by-stander during a gunfight, and this had led him into a prolonged period of drunkenness. Now, thanks in no small part to Sabina Carpenter, he was an ex-drunkard and a better flycop than he'd been a government agent.

He said, "Leave Mr. Goodland to me. Has there been any other trouble?"

"No, thank heaven."

"How is the Coalition taking Zacks' failure to bring rain?"

"There has been some grumbling, but he's a slick-tongued devil. Most of the people still have faith in him. He and Collard fired those chemical bomb-shells of theirs the last two nights and plan to do the same twice more. That's all it will take, he says. He promises at least one-half inch of rain by Monday morning or he'll return the advance payment."

"Which means," Quincannon said, "that unless a natural storm appears, he intends to vanish with the money by Sunday night. He won't, however. He'll be behind bars long before then."

Kasabian brightened. "He will? Mrs. Carpenter's wire said you were bringing good news . . ."

"I'll share it after we've collected Mr. Goodland."

Quincannon allowed the banker to pick up his carpetbag, lead the way through the station and north along Main. The heat lay heavy on his neck; that and O.H. Goodland's activities had tempered his good humor somewhat. He preferred San Francisco, with its cool fogs, and clients who acted in a reasonable fashion, thus permitting him to finish the task he had been hired to do and to take proper credit for it.

He and Sabina had accomplished this job swiftly. And he intended to be back in the city no later than Friday, two days from now, with the balance of their fee and a full compliment of satisfaction and good will. Leonide Zacks was a ruthless confidence man; bringing him to justice would be a feather in the caps of Carpenter and Quincannon, as well as save the Delford Coalition, a group of wheat farmers and merchants who had suffered hardest under the long drought, the three thousand dollars they had already paid to have rain clouds collected and cracked. But the feather wouldn't be half as tall if Zacks were shot dead by an irate father.

The collecting and cracking of Leonide Zacks would be done tomorrow, legally and according to Quincannon's arrangements—a fact he meant to impress on O.H. Goodland. With the barrel of his Navy Colt, if necessary.

♦ ♦ ♦

The Valley House was a plain, two-story building opposite the bank. It had two entrances, one marked *Hotel* and the other *Gentlemen's Saloon*. When he followed Kasabian through the latter, Quincannon found himself in a dim, stuffy room ripe with the smell of beer and spirits. He wrinkled his nose, scanning the handful of patrons. O.H. Goodland was not among them.

Kasabian was asking the barman where Goodland had gone when loud, angry voices rose from the adjacent hotel lobby. One, a tolerable bellow, Quincannon recognized as the farmer's. He hurried through the archway separating the saloon from the lobby.

At the foot of the staircase to the upper floor, Goodland stood nose to nose with a slender young man in a cutaway coat and brocade vest. A fair-haired woman dressed in shirtwaist and Balmoral skirt was making an effort to push Goodland away. He took no notice; she might have been pushing at a rooted tree.

". . . all of you out of town before noon tomorrow," the burly farmer was shouting, "or you'll suffer the consequences." The words carried a faint whiskey slur. Veins stood out on his thick neck; his face was the color of eggplant. "Hear me, Collard? By noon tomorrow!"

Ben Collard, Leonide Zacks' alleged assistant, was four inches shorter and fifty pounds lighter, but he too stood his ground. Flashing eyes and the hard set of his mouth belied the dandified appearance given him by a curled mustache and sleekly pomaded hair. He was neither afraid of Goodland nor intimidated by him.

"Your threats are worthless," he said. "We'll stay until we've fulfilled our contract to bring rain—"

"Rain! Not a cloud much less a cloudburst in five days."

"We are scientists, not wizards."

Goodland uttered a rude word that brought a gasp from the woman. Quincannon thought the gasp was theatrical; Nora Zacks had likely heard— and spoken—far worse in her twenty-eight years. She was small and soft-looking, but there was sand and steel at the core of her.

She said with spirit, "You are vulgar, sir, as well as a drunkard and a fool."

"Better a vulgar fool than a charlatan and a debaucher."

"My husband did not seduce your daughter."

"You can't deny he made advances to her."

"I can and I do. Now will you kindly allow us to proceed to our rooms?"

"Proceed to the devil, the lot of you. You'll be welcomed with open arms."

At this insult Collard's control deserted him. He launched a blow without warning, one that had a good deal of force when it landed on the farmer's chin. Goodland reeled backward and went down, but only for the time it took him to shake his head and roar out an oath; then he scrambled to his feet with fists cocked. He would have charged the smaller man if Quincannon hadn't caught both his arms from behind, pinned them at his sides.

Goodland struggled, and when he couldn't break loose he swivelled his head to see who had him in such an iron grip. "Who in the name of . . . oh, it's you, Quincannon. Let me go."

"Not until you agree to behave."

"That damned fop hit me—"

"You gave him good reason."

Goodland repeated the rude word, tried again to pull free

"You've had too much to drink and it's an infernally hot day. A bad combination, Mr. Goodland." Quincannon applied pressure on the man's right arm, until Goodland grunted with pain and subsided. "Will you behave now?"

". . . All right, blast you. You needn't break my arm."

Quincannon shoved him to a nearby wing chair and bent him into it, none too gently. The farmer stayed put, massaging his arm and muttering to himself.

Nora Zacks said, "You have our gratitude, Mr. . . . Quincannon, is it?"

He bowed. "John Quincannon, at your service."

She introduced herself and Collard. "I don't believe I've seen you in Delford before today."

"Mr. Quincannon is from San Francisco," Kasabian said.

"A reporter with the *Call-Bulletin*," Quincannon lied glibly, "come to witness the marvels of pluviculture first-hand. I had hoped to arrive earlier in the week, but another matter kept me in the city. I seem not to have missed either a deluge or a sprinkle, so far."

"You may well see the latter by morning," Collard said.

"Indeed? And the former?"

"By the first of next week. Given enough time, the Cloud Cracker's miracle formula always produces the desired results."

"I look forward to meeting the great man."

"He'll want to meet you too," Nora Zacks said. "Come to the rail yards before seven this evening and Mr. Collard or I will introduce you."

"He'll be bruising the sky again with his rockets?"

"Yes. Promptly at seven."

When she and Collard had gone upstairs, Quincannon wasted no time in hoisting O.H. Goodland out of the wing chair, then marching him past a wide-eyed desk clerk and out through the hotel's rear door. The farmer's protests were mild; heat, exertion, and alcohol had combined to make him sluggish. Kasabian tagged along behind.

In the shade of the hotel livery barn Quincannon sat him down again on a bale of hay. A water pump and trough beckoned nearby. He pumped half a dipperful and then unceremoniously doused the farmer's head with it. This roused Goodland, brought him sputtering to his feet.

"How dare you! You . . . you . . ."

"Are you sober enough now to listen to reason?"

"Mr. Quincannon has news for us, O.H.," Kasabian told him hastily. "Good news about Zacks."

"That rascal's death is the only news that would cheer me." Goodland dried his face with the sleeve of his shirt. His spurt of anger seemed to dry with it. He regarded Quincannon through eyes that were bleary but focused. "Well? What's this news of yours?"

"Andrew Beadle."

"Beadle? You mean the county sheriff?"

"I do. He'll be arriving on the noon train from Fresno tomorrow. With two deputies and a warrant for the arrest of Cora and Leo Saxe and Harry Pollard."

"Saxe? Pollard?"

"The real names of the Cloud Cracker and his cohorts."

"They're wanted criminals, then?" Kasabian asked.

"In four midwestern states."

"For what crimes?"

"The two men for confidence swindles dating back ten years, to their days as theatrical performers in Chicago.

"Theatrical performers?"

"Low comedy and specialty acts in variety beerhalls. More confidence men than you might think have such backgrounds. Since becoming professional swindlers they've left a trail of victims in Illinois, Ohio, Kansas, and Nebraska. Rainmaking is their most recent dodge, begun when Zacks married Cora Johnson in Omaha two years ago. Before that they posed as mining stock speculators, purveyors of a fountain-of-youth elixir, and inventors of an electric cancer-cure."

"Frauds and highbinders," Goodland said. "By God, I knew it all along."

Kasabian asked, "How on earth did you find out so much so quickly, Mr. Quincannon?"

The truthful answer was that he and Sabina had sent wires to other detective agencies across the country, providing specific information on the three rain-makers and their methods. The Pinkerton Agency's Chicago branch had been the most helpful. One of their operatives had developed a fascination with fraudulent pluviculturists after the debunking of the "Australian Rain Wizard," Frank Melbourne, who had achieved widespread publicity by allegedly "squeezing rain from cloudless skies as one would squeeze water from a sponge" in Ohio and Wyoming in 1891.

Melbourne had so thrived at first that other opportunists began claiming to have fantastic chemical or electrical machines and formulas of their own. Some, such as Clayton B. Jewell and the Kansas-based Inter State Artificial Rain Company, were quasi-legitimate exploiters who utilized Melbourne's trick of consulting long-range almanac forecasts and then gambling on natural storms to follow their cloud-milking folderol. These men operated on a "no rain, no pay" basis. The out-and-out fleecers such as the Cloud Cracker worked only in communities where they were able to inveigle drought-weary citizens to pay half their exorbitant fees up front. If no natural storms arrived, allowing them to collect the balance, they were content to disappear with the half already paid.

Miffed as he was at O.H. Goodland, Quincannon was not inclined to tell the simple truth. He answered Kasabian's question by saying, "Detective work of the most advanced and perspicacious sort. Did you think you'd hired a commonplace agency when you came to us?"

"No, no, not at all . . ."

Quincannon turned to the farmer. "Do you still consider me a fool for having a woman as my partner?"

"I never said you were a fool. I merely said it seemed a misguided choice."

"Misguided. Bah." Quincannon fixed him with a steely eye. "I trust *you* won't make a misguided choice, Mr. Goodland."

"What do you mean by that?"

"Taking the law into your own hands."

"Put your mind at rest, Quincannon. Now that I know Zacks or Saxe or whatever the scoundrel's name is headed for prison, I'll not try to avenge my daughter's honor."

"You'll return to your farm, then?"

"No, that I won't do. Not until I see him arrested with my own eyes." Goodland paused, frowning, as a thought struck him belatedly. "Why aren't Beadle and his deputies already here to do their duty? Why are they waiting until tomorrow?"

"They have more urgent business in Fresno."

Goodland said, "More urgent business," in disgusted tones. He added his favorite rude word and stalked away to the hotel.

♦ ♦ ♦

Town marshal Tom McCool was a middle-aged, lantern-jawed man whose peacekeeping duties were mostly limited to the arrest of drunks and rowdies on Saturday night. Stolid and unimaginative, he had staunchly supported the Delford Coalition—the reason Kasabian and Goodland had bypassed him in their determination to expose the Cloud Cracker and gone to Carpenter and Quincannon instead.

Now, however, with matters coming to a head, it was necessary to enlist McCool's aid. Quincannon took Kasabian with him to the marshal's office, where he showed McCool wires from the Chicago Pinkertons and Sheriff Beadle as proof of the rainmakers' criminal backgrounds and imminent arrest. McCool offered no argument. He'd "grown some leery" of Zacks, he said, and also been worried over O.H. Goodland's lack of good sense. He promised to keep a sharp eye on the farmer and the three swindlers.

When Quincannon returned alone to the Valley House, to claim the room Kasabian had arranged for him, the desk clerk handed him a Western Union telegram that had just been delivered. It was from Fresno and it read:

```
ARRIVAL  DELAYED  UNTIL  SIX  PM  TOMORROW
EARLIEST  STOP  REGRET  ADDITIONAL  DELAY
POSSIBLE WILL NOTIFY ASAP IN THAT EVENT

                        A BEADLE
```

"Hell and damn!" Quincannon said explosively, startling the clerk.

He read the wire again. "Regret additional delay possible" might mean Friday or even Saturday before Beadle and his deputies finally showed up in Delford. The prospect scratched at his temper like a thorn. The longer the delay, the shorter the odds that Goodland would lose his head or that Zacks would attempt to abscond with the Coalition's three thousand dollars. The only sure way to avoid either of those occurrences was for him and McCool to make a citizens' arrest of the four individuals, and he was hesitant to do that except as a last resort. The legalities were tricky without the proper warrants.

There was another reason the delay rankled him. If he wasn't back in San Francisco by early Saturday morning, his and Sabina's plans for the weekend

would have to be canceled. And important plans they were, confound it . . .
He went from the hotel to the telegraph office and sent a wire to Sabina.

```
BEADLE  DELAYED  STOP  RETURN  SF  BY  SATURDAY
MORNING  IN  JEOPARDY  STOP  IF  MUST  CANCEL
EXCURSION WILL SUFFER GRAVE PAIN AND HEART-
BREAK
```

JQ

Grave pain and heartbreak indeed, he thought as he handed message and coins to the telegraph agent. Sabina's adamant refusal to permit their relationship to go beyond the professional had been a source of misery and frustration to him for nearly two years now. She was a handsome, desirable widow, and while simple seduction had been his motive at first, this had rapidly changed to deeper and more poignant feelings. Now . . . well, he was smitten and no denying it. John Quincannon, confirmed bachelor, man of the world, hard-headed survivor of numerous misadventures, mooning and pining like a lovesick boy. Sad but true. This and the fact that his affections were un-requited made him desperate to break down Sabina's defenses.

It had taken him months to convince her to join him on an overnight pleasure trip, and her reluctant agreement to spend the coming weekend at Muir Woods seemed a sure sign that her defenses were crumbling at last. They would have separate rooms at their lodging-house, to be sure; but if all went well, such sleeping arrangements *could* be modified. At the very least they would be together in intimate surroundings. If the excursion had to be canceled, Sabina might balk at rescheduling—and in that event his frustrations would become intolerable.

"Hell and damn!" he exclaimed again, startling the telegrapher this time. Scowling and grumbling, he stomped out into the heat-drugged afternoon.

♦ ♦ ♦

Quincannon was sitting in a wing chair in a corner of the hotel lobby, pretending to read a two-day old copy of the Stockton *Record*, when Nora Zacks came downstairs. She was alone; her husband was still at the watchman's shack, and Collard had left twenty minutes earlier. He watched her walk across the lobby and outside. On her way to supper, he judged, before joining the men for the rocket assault. He consulted his Hampden pocket watch; the time was a quarter of six.

He laid the paper aside, climbed the stairs to the second floor. He had learned from the desk clerk which rooms were occupied by the Zacks and by Ben Collard; he went to the Zacks' suite first. The door was locked, of course, but this presented little difficulty for a man of Quincannon's talents. The handy little tool he carried in his pocket gave him access in less than a minute.

A thorough search of luggage and furnishings turned up no hint of the Coalition's three thousand dollars. Finding and confiscating the cash was one way of ensuring that the three humbuggers remained in Delford until Sheriff Beadle's arrival. But it was a small hope at best. Chances were the greenbacks rested in a money belt worn around the Cloud Cracker's waist.

Quincannon relocked the door and then picked the latch on the one adjacent. The money was not in Collard's room, either. But he did find one item of interest, in plain sight on the stand next to the bed: a timetable for Southern Pacific's Central Valley passenger trains, with notations written in ink at the top. The notations read: *Stockton Limited, Thursday, six p.m.*

The day and time puzzled him. This Thursday, tomorrow? It would seem so; it was highly unlikely that the trio intended to remain here another eight days. And yet, it also seemed unlikely that they would be planning to leave so soon, by train and in broad daylight.

Their usual pattern was to dismantle the mortar under cover of darkness, load it and the rest of their rainmaking apparatus into their converted dougherty wagon abandoning only the steam boiler, which had been obtained locally— and then vanish in the middle of the night.

Did they propose to abandon everything this time? If so, why? And how did they expect to be able to slip away by coach with the Coalition's money?

On the other hand, if the Cloud Cracker *wasn't* fixing to leave by train tomorrow evening, why had Collard marked the timetable?

♦ ♦ ♦

Quincannon took his supper at a sidestreet establishment called the Elite Café, which advertised "the best meal in Delford" (if this was true, the worst was probably lethal), and then walked down to the railyards. At a quarter of seven some of the day's heat had eased, but the sky was still summer-hazed and cloudless. A small crowd had begun to gather under the locust trees near the watchman's shack. The mood was not festive; facial expressions ranged from wary optimism to half-weary, half-sullen pessimism. It would not be long—three more days at the outside—before the more militant among the disillusioned took to cooking tar and gathering feathers.

As he approached the shack he could hear a rumbling, fluttering noise coming from within, not unlike the activity in a hive of hornets. It had an impressive sound, as befitted a miracle cloud-cracking machine, but it was in fact nothing more than the workings of the steam boiler and galvanic battery. Noxious yellow gas still issued from the stovepipe jutting above the roof: a combination of hydrogen and oxygen produced by mingling muriatic acid, zinc, and a little hydrogen, which was then pumped skyward through the boiler. The mortar rockets contained a similar and equally worthless chemical mixture.

Quincannon was about to take up a position near the mortar platform when the shack's door opened and two men emerged. One was Ben Collard; the other, heavyset, bearded, with a flowing silver-black mane, would be the infamous Leonide Zacks. Both were in shirt sleeves, sweating profusely from the heat inside, and each carried a pair of long, slender mortar shells. Nora Zacks, dressed in a fancy green and blue outfit, a squash-blossom necklace at her throat, followed after them, smiling and waving at the crowd. Even though she, too, had been in the shack, she looked cool and dry and unruffled.

Zacks and Collard brought their burdens to the platform, laid them at the foot of the slingshot mortar. Quincannon joined them at that point; he said, "Good evening, gentlemen, Mrs. Zacks," and doffed his derby to the woman. "Preparations for tonight's entertainment are nearly complete, I see."

Zacks bristled at this. He was an imposing gent up close, as most successful confidence men were; his black eyes were piercing and his manner imperious. "Entertainment? Hardly that, sir. Hardly that. Drought-breaking is serious business. And who might you be, may I ask?"

"This is Mr. Quincannon, Leonide," Nora Zacks said, "the San Francisco newspaperman I told you about."

"Ah, yes." Zacks' irritation vanished behind a mask of good fellowship. He pumped Quincannon's hand vigorously. "A pleasure, sir. I am in your debt for saving my wife and assistant from harm this afternoon."

"Not at all. Mr. Goodland was too far under the influence to have inflicted much harm on anyone."

"A ticklish situation, nevertheless," Zacks said. Then he frowned and said to Collard, "Here, Ben, what're you doing?"

The smaller man had climbed onto the platform, was picking up one of the rockets. Before he answered he began inserting the missile into the cannon's muzzle. "Loading the mortar, as you can plainly see."

"There's time enough for that."

"I'd rather have done with it now."

Zacks said to Quincannon, sounding irritated again, "Insolent fellow. I may have to hire a new assistant. Now if you'll excuse me, sir, there is more work to be done inside. We'll talk again, I'm sure."

"Oh, yes. We'll have much to say to each other later on."

Zacks turned away. Collard, who had finished loading the mortar, leaned over to take Nora Zacks' hand and help her onto the platform. Then he dropped down beside Quincannon, nodded curtly, and followed the larger man into the shack. The door shut firmly behind him.

Quincannon retraced his steps past the platform, where Nora Zacks was now soaking the tip of a long firebrand in kerosene. Under a locust tree, while he fed shag-cut tobacco into his pipe, he saw Aram Kasabian and Tom McCool approaching. O.H. Goodland was not with them, nor anywhere else among the gathered.

"We saw you talking to Zacks and Collard," the banker said when he and McCool reached him, "and wondered why."

"A testing of the waters, you might say."

"I'm not sure I—"

"There isn't a speck of worry in Zacks, though I detect some in Collard. He is the dominant partner and he doesn't seem ready to skip yet."

"That's good." Kasabian looked more closely at Quincannon's face and added, "Isn't it?"

"Perhaps."

"You're still concerned about O.H.?"

"Should I be?"

"Well, he was in his room a few minutes ago. I stopped by to have a word with him."

"Sober?"

"Yes, but he was pacing like a cat. It won't surprise me if he takes it in his head to come out here tonight—"

McCool said thinly, "Already has. Look."

Quincannon and the banker both turned. O.H. Goodland was striding purposefully toward the shack from the opposite direction.

At a distance he appeared grim-faced and hard-eyed. His hands were empty, but he wore his cowhide coat buttoned at the waist; it was impossible to tell if he was armed or not.

Quincannon said, "Hell and damn!" and called out Goodland's name. The wheat farmer took no notice. He was at the shack's door now, and he beat on it once with a closed fist. It opened immediately. And immediately he pushed his way inside.

"Oh, Lord," Kasabian moaned, "if he's come to do harm to Zacks—"

"Good citizens of Delford! Cover your ears and cast your eyes to the heavens! Your parched land will soon be drenched in a life-giving downpour —the time is close at hand!"

These words came from Nora Zacks atop the platform. They brought all eyes her way, momentarily froze Quincannon and the other two men in place. She had put a lucifer to the firebrand, he saw, and now stood with it poised over the mortar's fuse vent.

McCool said in a tone of awe, "By Godfrey, the woman's fixin' to fire that thing all by herself—"

He broke off as Nora Zacks lit the fuse, then dropped the firebrand, raised her skirts, and scurried down off the platform in unladylike haste.

In the next instant there was a tremendous concussive *whump!* The slingshot cannon bucked, the platform shuddered, and the chemical rocket Collard had inserted hurtled skyward with an earsplitting whistle. After several hundred feet the missile arced, then burst with a flash that unleashed streams of colored smoke.

Quincannon saw this at the edge of his vision; he was moving by then, his attention on the shack's closed door. It remained closed until he had gained the far end of the platform and then it popped open to reveal Ben Collard. Collard stepped out, yanked the door shut behind him; when he spied Quincannon he began gesticulating wildly. His handsome face was a sweat-sheened mask of distress.

"Mr. Quincannon!" he shouted. "Marshal McCool! Come quickly!" On the last word he spun on his heel, lunged back to the door. By the time Quincannon rushed up behind him he had the knob in both hands and was rattling it frantically. "Locked—Goodland's locked it!"

"What the devil's happened?"

"He made threats, drew his pistol and ordered me to leave . . ." Collard punished the door again. "Leonide! Are you all right?"

From inside a voice cried in muffled terror, "No, Goodland, no, don't shoot! Don't kill me!"

Quincannon tried to force Collard out of the way, so he could get his own hands on the knob, but the small man couldn't be budged.

McCool and Kasabian were there now, too, pushing in behind Quincannon with several other men at their heels.

Another cry came from within: "Please, spare my life!"

Seconds later there was the report of a gun.

Quincannon's reaction was immediate. He hurled his weight against Collard, with sufficient force to send the door crashing inward. Both men were off balance as they burst inside; Quincannon staggered, righted himself just in time to avoid tripping over O.H. Goodland, who was huddled on one knee on the rough plank floor. Between Goodland and the rainmaking apparatus at the far wall, Leonide Zacks lay supine in a twisted, motionless sprawl. The front of his shirt was splotched with blood.

Goodland appeared to be hurt; his face was twisted with pain and his left hand cradled the back of his head. In his right hand, held limply, was a Colt's New Pocket Revolver. Quincannon yanked the weapon free of his grasp, without resistance from the farmer.

Kneeling beside Zacks, Collard said heavily, "He's dead. Shot through the heart."

The door under the boiler stood open to reveal the pulsing flames within. With all the windows closed and sealed, the heat in the room was stifling. Quincannon breathed shallowly through his mouth as he scanned the dim confines. The only light came from the fire and from a single coal-oil lamp, but his sharp eyes picked out the glint of something on the floor near one of the earthenware crocks. He sidestepped Goodland and the dead man, bent to scoop up the small object—and almost dropped it because it was hot to the touch.

A wailing voice rose from outside: "Let me through, oh please let me through!" The knot of men clogging the doorway parted to permit the entrance of Nora Zacks. When she saw her husband she flung herself down beside him, caught up one of his hands and hugged it to her bosom, sobbing.

Quincannon glanced at the object he'd found. It was a spent cartridge shell.

He drew out his handkerchief, wrapped the casing in it.

O.H. Goodland still clutched his scalp, grimacing, blinking now as if his eyes refused to focus properly. Dizziness overcame him when he tried to stand; he sank down again to one knee. "My head . . . feels cracked like an eggshell . . ."

Collard said, "He must have fallen somehow when he shot poor Leonide."

"Shot? I didn't shoot anyone . . ."

McCool stepped forward, relieved Quincannon of the Colt's revolver and peered at it. "This here's your gun, Mr. Goodland."

"Tell you, I didn't shoot anyone."

"He's guilty as sin," Collard said. There was no one else here, no one else could have done it. You see that, don't you, marshal?"

"I see it," McCool agreed grimly. "Mr. Goodland, I got no choice but to arrest you for the crime of murder."

♦ ♦ ♦

Quincannon did not accompany the marshal and his prisoner to the jailhouse. Nor did he follow Collard and a still-sobbing Nora Zacks to the hotel. Instead he remained at the shack, waiting outside until everyone else had gone, then shutting himself inside.

The first thing he did was to examine the door and its sliding bolt. Then he searched among the jars of chemicals, spare rockets, and other items that littered the floor around the boiler and crocks; searched every nook and cranny until he satisfied himself that there was nothing else to be found, least of all the Coalition's three thousand dollars. The money hadn't been on Zacks' person, either; he had given the body a quick frisk before the town's undertaker arrived to claim it.

From the rail yards he went to the Western Union office, where he sent a night wire to the Pinkerton agency in Chicago. The wire asked specific questions and ended with the words URGENT REPLY NEEDED. If the Pinks heeded this, as he was certain they would, he would have an answering wire early in the morning.

Warm, dusty darkness was settling when he left the telegraph office. Word of the shooting had spread quickly; gaslit Main Street was packed with citizens discussing the Cloud Cracker's violent demise. They would have a great deal more to discuss within the next twenty-four hours, Quincannon thought as he made his way to the jailhouse to question O.H. Goodland. And they weren't the only ones with surprises in store for them.

By sundown tomorrow the name most often spoken in Delford would not be Leonide Zacks or O.H. Goodland. It would be John Quincannon.

♦ ♦ ♦

The reply to his Chicago wire was waiting when he stopped at the telegraph office at ten o'clock Thursday morning, on his way back from a brief visit with the railroad station agent. The answers to his questions were all just as he had expected. They brought a smile to his mouth and led him to send another wire, this one to Sabina in San Francisco.

CLOUD CRACKER MURDERED LAST NIGHT IN BIZARRE CIRCUMSTANCES STOP YOUR TRUSTED PARTNER HAS ALREADY SOLVED CRIME STOP BEADLE ARRIVAL UNIMPORTANT NOW EXPECT TO REACH SF TOMORROW AS PLANNED STOP GLORIOUS WEEKEND CELEBRATION INDICATED WILL PROVIDE DETAILS OF BRILLIANT DETECTIVE WORK EN ROUTE MUIR WOODS

Whistling, his step jaunty, he crossed the street to the bank to collect Aram Kasabian. The two men then went to the jailhouse to collect Tom McCool. And the three men then proceeded to the Valley House to collect Ben Collard and Nora Zacks.

The time for unveiling his brilliant deductions had arrived.

The place of the unveiling was the marshal's tiny office, where the five of them crowded together with an unfettered and head-bandaged O.H. Goodland. Mrs. Zacks wore mourning black and a stoic expression, which remained unchanged even after Quincannon revealed his true profession, his purpose in Delford, and the upcoming arrival of Sheriff Beadle and the arrest warrants. Collard, too, seemed determined to play the innocent. He said indignantly, "This is all an intolerable misunderstanding. We are legitimate pluviculturists—obviously the victims of mistaken identity. We've committed no crime in the midwest or in Delford."

"None here except willful homicide," Quincannon said.

"Faugh! You can't mean the murder of poor Leonide. The man who shot him has already been arrested—and why isn't Goodland locked in a cell where he belongs?"

"Mr. Goodland did no shooting last night."

"How can you make such a statement? You were at the shack, you know what happened as well as I do. He and Leonide were locked together inside. No one else could have done it."

"But someone else did. You, Collard."

Collard drew himself up in feigned outrage. "Have you taken leave of your senses, Quincannon? I was outside with you when the shot was fired. How could I possibly be guilty?"

"By means of clever planning, careful timing, and the help of your accomplice. Or rather, your paramour."

Nora Zacks said flatly, "That's a ridiculous accusation."

"Not at all. Your husband was a womanizer. Before the three of you left Omaha for California, his illicit affairs drove you to take his partner as your lover. His advances to Mr. Goodland's daughter, successful or not, were the final straw: they drove you to conspire in his murder."

"Preposterous!" Collard shouted. "Nefarious!"

"Fact," Quincannon said. "As for your motives, you'd grown to hate Zacks for a different reason. He'd taken over the handling of your swindles, reduced you to a subservient role by the force of his will. With him dead, you could have his wife and his money, and be your own master again."

"Utter rot, I say."

"Mr. Goodland's rash behavior two days ago gave you the impetus and the perfect foil for your plan. And the plan itself worked smoothly enough. If I hadn't come to Delford, you might well have gotten away with it—and with the Coalition's three thousand dollars. Before anyone thought to ask you for the money, you and Mrs. Zacks would have been gone on the six o'clock train for Stockton tonight. The station agent confirmed that you purchased the tickets this morning."

"What of it? I am escorting Mrs. Zacks to Stockton, yes—but I intended to return the money before departing. Leonide's murderer is in custody, or so we thought. There is no good reason for us to stay here—"

"You may have purchased the tickets today," Quincannon interrupted him, "but the date and time were settled much earlier."

"How could you possibly know that?"

"The railroad timetable in your room, the written notations in your hand. I saw them yesterday afternoon, in the course of my investigation, two hours *before* the murder."

The woman said, "That proves nothing and you know it."

"By itself, no. Tell me, Mrs. Zacks, why did you fire the mortar last night?"

The question caught her off guard. "Why . . . I was the only person on the platform. My husband and Ben were inside the shack with Goodland."

"Why didn't you wait for them to come out?"

"The launching was scheduled for seven. Rather than delay, I went ahead on my own."

"But you'd never fired the mortar before."

"Not in Delford, but elsewhere—"

"No. Your frightened actions after lighting the fuse prove otherwise. Last night was the first time and it was done by prearranged plan. That's the reason Collard loaded the mortar while I was talking to your husband—so it would be ready for you. Properly loading such a launcher is more difficult and dangerous than firing it."

Quincannon shifted his attention to O.H. Goodland. "Mr. Goodland, why did you go to the shack after I warned you to stay away?"

"A message was slipped under the door of my room. Signed with Zacks' name and asking me to come promptly at seven to settle our differences. The word promptly was underlined."

"My husband did write such a note," Nora Zacks lied. "He told me he had, which is the reason I was unconcerned when I saw Goodland arrive."

"No, Mrs. Zacks. The note was written by you, I suspect—a careful forgery."

She started to deny it, changed her mind, and said nothing.

Quincannon produced the Colt's New Pocket Revolver, which McCool had let him have earlier. He showed it to Goodland and asked him, "Is this your weapon?"

"It is."

"Did you take it with you last night?"

"I did not. I had no weapon when I went to the shack and Zacks had no damned idea what I was doing there. He was telling me that when Collard clubbed me from behind."

"When did you last have the gun in your possession?"

"Tuesday afternoon, after I made the mistake of threatening Zacks with it.

McCool took it away from me."

The marshal said, "I emptied it and put it in his saddlebag at the hotel livery. Collard was there; he saw me do it. He could've come back later and swiped it."

"I won't stand for any more of this." Collard's voice had risen. He was sweating now. "How dare you accuse me when you know damned well it's impossible for me to be guilty. I was outside when Leonide was killed. You saw me, marshal. And you, Quincannon, you heard him beg for his life and you heard the fatal shot. You can't deny the truth of that."

"I can't and won't deny what I seemed to hear."

"Seemed? What do you mean, seemed?"

Quincannon displayed another object from his pocket. "I found this on the floor, shortly after we broke into the shack. When I picked it up it was hot to the touch."

"Couldn't have come from Mr. Goodland's gun," McCool said. "Revolvers don't eject spent shells. Only one bullet was fired from that Colt's, and the empty was in the cylinder.

Kasabian asked, "Then where did that one come from?"

"The fire inside the boiler," Quincannon said, "where Collard placed it after he clubbed Mr. Goodland, shot Zacks, and put the revolver in Mr. Goodland's hand. A blank cartridge. The heat exploded the powder, simulating a gunshot, and the explosion kicked the casing out through the open fire door. Collard had used the trick before—I'll explain where and how shortly—and so he was able to gauge within a minute or so when it would go off."

"Amazing. And the shot that actually killed Zacks—?"

"Fired when Mrs. Zacks launched the rocket promptly at seven. The boom of the mortar drowned the report. Timing, you see?"

"What about the locked door?"

"It wasn't locked. Collard pretended it was by holding onto the knob and rattling it, while he blocked the doorway with his body. The bolt wasn't damaged, a fact that was overlooked in the excitement—by everyone except me."

Collard knew he was caught, but in desperation he played out his last card. "Leonide was still alive when we were all outside. You know he was, you heard him beg for his life—you heard him!"

"No," Quincannon said, "I didn't."

He paused dramatically and then asked the banker, "Mr. Kasabian, do you recall my telling you Zacks and Collard were once variety performers in Chicago?"

"Yes. Low comedy and specialty acts, you said."

"I didn't know for certain what the specialty acts were until this morning, when I received a wire from the Chicago Pinkerton office. One act was a magic show in which a supposedly invisible pistol was fired on command. Zacks was the magician, Collard the one who invented and staged the trick. Collard was also a performer with his own specialty. One he performed well, by all accounts."

"What specialty, for heaven's sake?"

Quincannon said, "Ventriloquism."

♦ ♦ ♦

Sheriff Beadle and his deputies arrived without further delay, anticlimactically, on the noon train from Fresno. By this time, even though Collard was still maintaining his innocence, Nora Zacks had admitted her part in her husband's murder. She claimed the entire plan had been Collard's and that he had coerced her into it—a falsehood, to be sure, but one she had already begun to play well with tears and lamentations. She was a comely woman; Quincannon had little doubt that she would be able to convince a jury to be lenient.

That evening he left Delford on the same train the two conspirators had intended to take, the six o'clock Limited for Stockton. He was in a fine humor. In his wallet was the balance of his fee, plus a bonus from a somewhat chastened O.H. Goodland; and in his coat pocket was a telegram from Sabina, which he had picked up at the Western Union office shortly before Beadle's arrival.

As the train rattled its way north through sun-browned wheat fields, he took out the wire and read it again.

```
EAGERLY  AWAIT  YOUR  RETURN  AND  DETAILS  OF
BRILLIANT DETECTIVE WORK STOP HEART AFLUTTER
WITH   ANTICIPATION   OF   GLORIOUS   WEEKEND
CELEBRATION STOP DID MY HERO COLLECT BALANCE
OF FEE QM
```

A roguish smile split his freebooter's beard. Sabina's sarcasm didn't fool him, not for a minute. Her defenses were definitely crumbling . . .

LADY ONE-EYE

Behind the long, brass-trimmed bar in McFinn's Palace Saloon and Gaming Parlor, Quincannon drew two more draughts from the lager keg, sliced off the heads with the wooden paddle, and slid the glasses down the bar's polished surface. The Irish hardrock miner who caught them flipped him a two-bit piece in return. "Keep the nickel change for yourself, laddie," he said.

Quincannon scowled as he rang up the 20¢ sale. A whole nickel for himself, finally, after six hours of hard work. He debated leaving it in the register, but his Scot's blood got the best of that; he pocketed the five-cent coin. The lot of a bartender was neither an easy nor a profitable one, a fact he hadn't fully realized until the past two days. Nor was it a proper undertaking for a man who no longer drank strong waters of any kind. He cursed himself for a rattlepate. Adopting the guise of a mixologist had been his blasted idea, not Amos McFinn's.

For the moment there were no more customers at his station. Most of the miners and sports lining the mahogany were watching the square raised platform in the center of the cavernous room, where the two women faced each other across a green baize, green-skirted poker table. The play between the pair had been going on for nearly three hours now. At first the other gaming tables —poker, faro, roulette, chuck-a-luck, vingt-et-un—had had their usual heavy clutch of players. But the spectacle of the two lady gamblers engaged in a moderately high-stakes stud-poker challenge was too enticing. The number of kibitzers around the platform, watching the flash of cards reflected in the huge overhead mirrors, doubled when it became apparent that Lady One-Eye's opponent, the Saint Louis Rose, was a formidable mechanic in her own right. Now the crowd had swelled so large that some of the nearby tables had been shut down for the duration.

The fact that the two women were complete opposites added to the appeal of their match. The older by ten years, Lady One-Eye was dark-haired, dark-complected; her dress was of black velvet and encased her big-boned body so totally that only her head and her long-fingered white hands were revealed.

The black velvet patch covering her blind left eye gave her a faintly sinister aspect. She sat quiet and played quiet, seldom speaking, but she was nonetheless a fierce competitor who asked no quarter and granted none. The only times her steely one-eyed gaze left the cards was when she glanced at the tall, handsome gent who sat at a nearby table—her gambler husband, John Diamond, who called himself Jack O'Diamonds.

The Saint Louis Rose cut a slimmer and far gaudier figure. Too gaudy by half, in Quincannon's judgment. She wore a fancy sateen dress of bright scarlet, fashioned low across the bosom and high at the knee so that a great deal of creamy skin was exposed. A lemon-yellow wig done in ringlets, half a pound of rouge and powder, false eyelashes the size of Daddy Longlegs, and a mouth painted blood-crimson completed her outlandish image. She laughed often and too loud and was shamelessly flirtatious with the kibitzers. Even Jack O'Diamonds now and then let his gaze stray from his wife—and from the sultry presence of Lily Dumont, at whose faro bank he sat—to rest on the Rose's swelling bosom.

Quincannon was one of the few people in the hall not paying attention to the game. As they had all evening, even while he was serving customers, his eyes roamed the packed room in search of odd or furtive behavior. No weapons were permitted inside the Palace, but none of the patrons would have stood still for enforced searches by McFinn's bouncers. Quincannon was willing to wager that there were a score of hideout guns in the hall on any given night.

Movement to his left caught the edge of his vision and turned his head. But it was only Amos McFinn once more slipping around behind the plank. He was a nervous little gent, McFinn, even at the best of times; on this night he hopped and twitched like a man doused with itching powder. Sweat gleamed on his bald dome. The ends of his mustache curled around his downturned mouth as if they were pincers.

He drew Quincannon to the backbar and asked in a hoarse whisper, "Anything suspicious?" It was the fifth or sixth time he'd come to voice the question. He had spent most of the evening shuttling back and forth among the half dozen bouncers spotted around the hall and Quincannon behind the bar.

"Only two small things, Mr. McFinn. Your actions being one of them."

"Eh? *My* actions?"

"Stopping by to chat every half hour or so. Someone might wonder why the owner of this establishment is so interested in his new mixologist."

"No one is paying any attention to us."

"Not at the moment. At least not overtly."

"Well, I can't help worrying that he's here tonight," McFinn said. "Not that I expect he'll make an attempt in front of so many witnesses, and yet . . ."

Quincannon was silent, his gaze roaming again. McFinn knew as well as he did that a packed room was an ideal place for an attempted murder. Especially if the person was deranged enough not to have much fear for his own safety.

McFinn sighed and said, "All right, I'll leave you be." He started to do this and then stopped and leaned close again. "Two small things, you said. What's the other?"

"Jack O'Diamonds."

"Eh?"

"Have you noticed his interest in Lily Dumont?"

"No. Lily Dumont?"

"They've been thick at her table for more than an hour."

"You mean you think they—?"

"More than likely, yes."

"I don't believe it. Why, Jack is devoted to Lady One-Eye. I'd stake my life on it."

Then your life, Quincannon thought wryly, is worth less than a plugged nickel.

One of the reasons he'd chosen the guise of a bartender was that gaming-hall employees were far more likely to pass along private knowledge to a fellow drone than to a detective or even a customer. A bouncer and one of the other bartenders had both confided that Lily and Jack O'Diamonds had spent time alone at her cottage on more than one occasion. They had also told him Lily's swain, a Nevada City saloon owner named Glen Bonnifield, knew about the affair and was in a rage over it. Quincannon had had proof of this: Bonnifield, a tall thin gent in a flowered vest, was in the crowd tonight, and the look in his eye as he watched Lily and Jack O'Diamonds was little short of murderous.

Lily seemed not to care that she was being observed by either Bonnifield or Lady One-Eye. Several times she had pressed close to Diamond and whispered in his ear, and she did so again now. From the look on the gambler's face, she had passed a comment of a highly intimate nature. He nodded and smiled at her—a rather lusty smile—and touched the three-carat diamond stickpin in his cravat, his trademark and good-luck charm. His wife's single eye was on her cards; she didn't seem to notice. But Bonnifield did and his smoldering look kindled and flared. He took a step toward them, changed his mind and held his ground.

McFinn was saying, "Even if there *is* something between Jack and Lily, what does it have to do with the reasons—either of the reasons—I hired you?" He paused and then blinked. "Unless you think one of them—?"

"I don't think anything at this point," Quincannon said.

This was an evasion, but McFinn accepted it and let the matter drop. As he twitched away, a ripple passed through the crowd. Lady One-Eye had won another hand, this time with a spade flush over the Saint Louis Rose's high two pair. Someone at the bar said that it was the fifth pot in a row she'd taken. Quincannon glanced up at the ceiling mirrors. Early on, the pile of red and blue chips had been tall in front of the Rose; in the past hour it had begun to dwindle there, to grow on Lady One-Eye's side. One or two more large pots and she would have picked the Rose clean.

Lady One-Eye shuffled the cards for another deal, her long fingers manipulating them with practiced skill. According to the story she'd told McFinn, a buggy accident eight years ago had claimed her left eye and damaged her left hip so that she was unable to walk without the aid of her gold-knobbed cane. But she considered herself fortunate because her hands were her livelihood and both had come through the accident unscathed. Her handicap, in fact, had won her sympathy and support among the sports who frequented gaming halls such as the Palace. Even hardbitten professional gamblers, who considered it bad luck to play against a one-eyed man, had been known to sit at a poker table with Lady One-Eye. Only once, though, in most cases, since their luck with a one-eyed woman generally turned out to be just as bad.

Five-card stud was her game, the only game she would permit at her table. And the table here *was* hers: she rented it from McFinn, paying a premium because alone on the raised platform it was the Palace's central attraction. She had occupied it for eight weeks now, ever since she and Jack O'Diamonds had arrived in Grass Valley from Tombstone, by way of Sacramento. Already word of her skill and phenomenal luck had spread wide. She never refused a game, even for low stakes; and so far she had not lost a single high-stakes match, once taking $8,000 from a Rough and Ready placer miner and on another occasion relieving a Sacramento brewer of $2,000 on a single hand of stud. Some said she was a better mechanic than such sporting queens as Poker Alice, Madame Moustache, Lurline Monte Verde, and Kitty the Schemer. A few claimed she was the equal of King Fisher, Luke Short, even Dick Clark.

At least one thought she might be a cheat to rival George Devol, the legendary Mississippi River skin-game artist.

That lone skeptic was not a victim of her talents, fair or foul. He was the one person, other than the Lady and her husband, who had benefitted most from her presence in the Palace: Amos McFinn.

McFinn ran a clean establishment. He had to in order to remain in business. Grass Valley—and its close neighbor, Nevada City—were no longer the wide-open, hell-roaring mining camps they'd once been. Now, five years from the new century, they were settled communities with schools, churches, and Civic Betterment Leagues. There was a move afoot to ban gambling in both towns. So far McFinn and the other gaming parlor operators had managed to forestall the efforts of the bluenoses; but if it came out that a female tinhorn had been working the Palace with impunity for eight weeks, it might just give the anti-gambling faction enough ammunition to shut down McFinn and the others along with him.

This was one reason why McFinn had hired Carpenter and Quincannon, Professional Detective Services. Lady One-Eye had increased the number of his customers and thereby his profits; he couldn't afford to send her packing on a fearful hunch, without proof. He had to know, one way or the other, before he could act—and as quickly as possible.

The other reason he'd sought the help of detectives was just as urgent and potentially even more disastrous. Four days ago an anonymous note written in green ink had been slipped under the door of the room Lady One-Eye shared with Jack O'Diamonds in the Holbrooke Hotel. She'd found it and taken it to McFinn, who in turn had brought it to Sheriff Jeremiah Thorpe. But there was little the law could do. The note might well have been the work of a crackpot, all blather and bunkum. On the other hand, it might be just what it seemed: a thinly veiled death threat. Quincannon had examined the note in Thorpe's office shortly after the Nevada County Narrow Gage Railway deposited him in Grass Valley. It read:

WARNING TO LADY ONE EYE AND J DIAMOND

The good citizens of Grass Valley don't want your kind. We have got rid of bunko steerers, confidence sharks, sure thing men, thimble riggers and monte throwers and we will get rid of wommen card sharps and there men too. Leave town in 48 hours or you will pay the price and pay dear when you least expec it. I mean what I say. I have fixed your kind befor, permanent.

Crude language and spelling, and poor penmanship as well. It might have been written by a near-illiterate with a misguided moral streak; this was McFinn's assessment. But Quincannon wondered. It could also have been written by someone educated and clever, with a motive for wanting the pair dead that had little or nothing to do with their professions. In any case, they had ignored the warning and the 48-hour period had passed. If the note-writer carried out his threat, particularly if he carried it out inside the Palace, McFinn would be ruined as effectively as if Lady One-Eye were exposed as a cheat—

"Three fives! The pot's mine, dearie!"

The Saint Louis Rose's loud, coarse voice echoed through the hall. Quincannon frowned and glanced up at the mirror above the poker table; the Rose was dragging in a small pile of red and blue chips. Lady One-Eye watched her stoically.

"Two in a row now and more to come," the Rose said to a knot of bearded miners close on her left. "My luck is changing for fair, gents. It won't be long before all the red and blue pretties are mine to fondle."

The knot of miners sent up a small cheer of encouragement. Most of the onlookers, however, remained Lady One-Eye's champions. Like them, Quincannon wished the Rose would close her mouth and play her game in silence. Listening to her plume herself was an irritation and a distraction.

The deal was Lady One-Eye's. Without speaking she picked up the deck. Again, Quincannon studied her dexterous fingers as they manipulated the deck, set it out to be cut, then dealt one card face down and one face up to the Rose and herself. If she was a skin-game artist, he reflected, she was in a class by herself.

The professionals she'd cleaned over the past eight weeks would have caught her out if she had been doing anything as obvious as dealing seconds, dealing off the bottom, switching hole cards, or using a mirror or other reflective surface to reveal the faces of the cards to her as she dealt them. She wasn't using advantage cards: the house provided sealed decks, which were opened in plain view at the table, and switching them for marked decks hidden in her clothing was next to impossible for a woman who wore a highcollared dress with long, tight-fitting sleeves. Nor could her gaff be table bags or any of the other fancy contraptions manufactured by the likes of Will & Fink, the notorious San Francisco firm that specialized in supplying gimmicks to crooked gamblers. Because of the raised platform, and the fact that a woman played upon it, the table wore its floor-length green skirt; but the skirt was drawn up until Lady One-Eye took her chair, thus allowing potential players to examine both it and the table if they chose to. Table tricks were the cheap grifter's ploy anyway. And Lady One-Eye was anything but a cheap grifter.

The Rose's up card was the jack of clubs, the Lady's the four of hearts. Both women checked their hole cards; then the Rose winked at her admirers, bet twenty dollars. Lady One-Eye called and dealt a ten of diamonds to go with the jack, a deuce of spades for herself. This time the Rose bet fifty dollars. Again, silently, Lady One-Eye called.

The fourth round of cards brought the Rose a spade jack, the Lady a five of diamonds. The challenger grinned at her high pair and said, "Jacks have never let me down," a remark that caused Lady One-Eye to cast an almost imperceptible sidelong glance at her husband. "One hundred dollars on the pair of 'em, dearie."

Quincannon wondered if the remark was deliberate—if the Rose, too, had noticed the intimacy between Jack O'Diamonds and Lily Dumont. Lady One-Eye was aware of it, of that he was fairly certain.

Without another glance at her hole card, the Lady called. Slowly she dealt the fifth and final cards. Jack of hearts. And for herself, the three of clubs.

The onlookers began to stir and murmur. Play at the few other open tables suspended for the moment. Everyone in the Palace stood or sat watching the two women. Even McFinn, leaning against one of the roulette layouts, was motionless for the time being.

"Well, dearie," the Rose said, "three pretty little jacks to your possible straight." She tapped her hole card. "Is this the fourth jack I have here? It may well be. What do you think, Lady, of my having the jack of diamonds?"

To Quincannon, the innuendo was plain. But whatever Lady One-Eye thought of it, she neither reacted nor responded.

"Or it may be another ten. A full house beats a straight all to hell, dearie. If you've even got a six or an ace to fill."

"Bet your jacks," Lady One-Eye said coldly.

The Rose's sly smile faded. She separated four blue chips from her small remaining stack, slid them into the pot. "Two hundred dollars says you don't have a six or an ace and it doesn't matter if you do."

"Your two hundred, and raise another two."

Voices created an excited buzzing, ebbed again to total silence. Neither of the women seemed to notice. Their gazes were now fixed on each other.

"A bluff, dearie?" the Rose said.

"Call or raise and you'll soon know."

"Four hundred is all I have left."

"Call or raise."

"Your two hundred, then, and raise my last two hundred."

"Call."

The pile of red and blue chips bulged between them. The crowd was expectantly still as the Rose shrugged and turned over her hole card.

The queen of hearts. No help.

"Three jacks," she said. "Beat 'em if you can."

Her one good eye as icy as any Quincannon had ever seen, Lady One-Eye flipped her hole card. And when it was revealed in the glistening mirrors, a triumphant shout went up from her admirers.

Ace of clubs to fill the straight.

The pot and all of the Rose's table stakes were hers.

♦ ♦ ♦

For the next half hour Quincannon was busy attending to the reborn thirst of the customers. But not so busy that he was unable to maintain his observations.

The Saint Louis Rose, after fending off a pair of drunken sports who considered her fair game, slipped quietly out of the hall. Lady One-Eye gathered her winnings and cashed them in, all the while keeping watch on her husband and Lily Dumont. Jack O'Diamonds didn't stay long at Lily's faro bank; nor did he approach his wife. Instead he stepped up to the bar and called for forty-rod whiskey. The Nevada City saloonkeeper, Glen Bonnifield, took this opportunity to stalk to Lily's table, lean down with his face close to hers. Their conversation was brief and heated. Then Bonnifield slapped the table hard with his open hand—as a substitute for slapping Lily, Quincannon thought—and swung away, back past the bar. His gaze met Diamond's in the mirror; the two struck sparks, but neither man made a move toward the other. Bonnifield stalked to the front entrance and was gone.

Quincannon served Jack O'Diamonds his whiskey. "Your wife had a fine run of luck tonight, Mr. Diamond."

"My wife's luck is always fine." The gambler didn't sound pleased about it. Jealousy? Compared to Lady One-Eye's skill with the pasteboards, honest or not, his own was mediocre.

"And your luck with Lily? Has that been fine too?"

The comment produced a tight-lipped glower. "What do you mean by that?"

"No offense, sir," Quincannon said blandly. "Mr. Bonnifield seemed to think it was, that's all."

"I don't give a damn what Bonnifield thinks," Jack O'Diamonds said. He fingered his flashy diamond stickpin, downed his whiskey at a gulp. Then he too left the Palace—alone, and still without speaking to his wife.

Lady One-Eye took her leave five minutes later, in the company of the two burly bouncers assigned by McFinn as escorts. But first she approached Lily Dumont and engaged her in a brief, heated discussion, just as Bonnifield had. Lily's reaction to whatever was said to her was to call the Lady an unladylike name, in a voice loud enough to turn heads. Lady One-Eye responded by making a warning gesture with her gold-knobbed cane.

Quincannon decided he'd had enough of bartending, for tonight if not for the rest of his life. He hung up his apron, donned his coat and derby hat, helped himself to half a dozen cheroots from a cigar vase on the bar, and went to pay Lily a visit himself.

She was shuffling and cutting a full deck of cards for placement in her tiger-decorated faro box; the cards made angry snapping sounds in her slim fingers. She, too, was a complete opposite of Lady One-Eye. She had flaming red hair, a volatile temper to match, and the hot sparking eyes of a gypsy. Fire to the Lady's ice.

"Trouble with Her Majesty?" Quincannon asked sympathetically.

"Her Majesty. Hah. I'll tell you what that female is." Which Lily proceeded to do in language that would have made a hardrock miner blink.

"A cold and jealous one, all right," he agreed.

"Threaten me, will she? I'll fix her first. I'll rip out her other eye and turn her into Lady Blind."

"Why did she threaten you?"

"Never mind about that."

Quincannon shrugged. "What does Jack O'Diamonds see in her?"

"Money, of course. But maybe not for much longer."

"Oh? He wouldn't be planning to leave her, would he?"

"That's none of your business."

"Is it any of yours, Lily?"

"Miss Dumont to you. My business is mine, no one else's."

"Not even Glen Bonnifield's?"

"Damn Glen Bonnifield. Damn Lady One-Eye. And damn *you*."

As Quincannon made his way toward the front entrance, he spied Amos McFinn moving hurriedly through the crowd to intercept him. He pretended not to see the Palace's owner; he had no interest in answering the "Anything suspicious?" question yet again. He managed to make good his escape before McFinn got close enough to ask it.

It was some past midnight now, and the mountain air was chill. Even though June was not far off, snow still mantled the Sierras' higher elevations. Grass Valley's hilly streets were deserted; the only sounds were the faint throb of a piano in one of the nearby saloons, the continual beat of the stamps at the big Empire Mine southeast of town. A far cry from the boom years of Grass Valley and Nevada City, following the 1851 discovery of gold in quartz ledges buried beneath the earth, when thousands of goldseekers, camp followers, and Cornish and Irish hardrock miners had clogged the streets day and night. Even on Quincannon's first visit here, more than a dozen years ago, the town had still retained some of its Gold Rush flavor. Now nearly all the rough edges had been buffed down and rounded off. This was fine if you were a law-abiding, church-going citizen with children to raise. But tame places were not for John Quincannon. He would rather walk the streets of a hell-roaring gold camp, or even those of the Barbary Coast.

He paused on the boardwalk to light one of the cheroots he had appropriated. He preferred a pipe to cigars, but free tobacco had a greater satisfaction than the paid-for kind. Then, instead of turning upstreet to the Holbrooke Hotel, where he had engaged a room, he walked downhill to the town's main thoroughfare, Mill Street. The only lighted building along there was the Empire Livery Stable. He saw the night hostler working inside as he passed—and no one else before or after he turned uphill on Neal Street.

The bouncer at McFinn's had told him that Lily Dumont's cottage was on Pleasant Street, just off Neal. He found it with no difficulty—a tiny frame building, of no more than three rooms, tucked well back from the street in the shade of a pair of live oaks. The neighborhood was a good one, and by the starlight he could tell that the cottage and its gardens were well set up. Much too well set up, he thought, for a woman who operated a faro bank to afford on her own. He wondered if Glen Bonnifield had an investment in the property.

The cottage's curtained windows were dark; so were those in the two nearest houses. He shed the remains of his cheroot and walked softly around to the rear. The back door was not locked. He entered, struck a lucifer to orient himself and to show him the way into the front parlor.

An oil lamp with a red silk shade sat atop a writing desk. He lit the wick, turning the flame low, and by this light he searched the desk. There was one bottle of ink, but it was blue, not green. Nothing else in the desk held any interest for him. He carried the lamp into Lily's bedroom, where he found further evidence of financial aid: satin dresses, a white fox capote, an expensive ostrich-feather hat. But that was all he found. If Lily had written the threatening note, she had either done it elsewhere or gotten rid of the bottle of ink she'd used.

Quincannon returned the lamp to the writing desk, snuffed the wick, then followed the flicker of another match to the rear door. He let himself out, shut the door quietly behind him.

He was just turning onto the path toward the front when the first bullet sang close past his right ear.

He went down instantly, a reflex action that saved his life: the second bullet slashed air where his head had been. The booming echo of the shots filled his ears. He reached under his coat for his Navy Colt, then remembered that he hadn't worn it because of his bartending duties; instead he'd armed himself with a double-barreled Remington derringer, an effective weapon at close quarters in a crowded room but with a range of no more than twenty feet. He rolled sideways, clawing the derringer free of his pocket, half expecting to feel the shock of a bullet. But there were no more shots. The thorny wood of a rose bush ended his roll; grimacing, he shoved away and then lay flat and still, the derringer up in front of him. He peered through the darkness, listening.

Running footsteps. Fading, then gone.

He pushed onto his knees. Lamplight suddenly brightened one of the windows in the house next door; its outspill showed him that the yard and the street in front were now deserted. He got quickly to his feet, careful to keep his head turned aside from the light. A face peered out through the lamplit window and a voice hollered, "What in tarnation's going on out there?" Quincannon didn't answer. Staying in the shadows, he ran ahead and looked both ways along Pleasant Street.

His assailant had vanished.

"Hell and damn!" he muttered angrily under his breath. He slid the derringer back into his pocket, hurried to Neal and around the corner before any of Lily's neighbors came out to investigate.

Grass Valley a tame place now, its streets safe at night? Bah! There was still plenty of hell left in this camp. The question was, was it hell directed at him or someone else?

♦ ♦ ♦

The Holbrooke, a two-story brick edifice on East Main, was Grass Valley's oldest and finest hostelry. Presidents Grant, Harrison, Cleveland, and Garfield had stayed there during visits to California; so had Gentleman Jim Corbett. And so had the notorious gold country highwayman, Black Bart—a fact that management chose not to advertise. If any of the hotel's distinguished guests had ever wandered uphill to Texas Tommy's Golden Gate Brothel, a nearby attraction in the old days, this fact was also held in discreet confidence.

The gaslit lobby was deserted when Quincannon entered. Gaslight flickered even more dimly in the upstairs hallways; electricity had yet to be installed here. He made his way, first, to the door of number 3, the room occupied by Lady One-Eye and Jack O'Diamonds. No light showed around its edges, and when he pressed his ear to the panel he heard nothing from within. From there he went around past number 8, his room, and stopped before number 11 at the rear. He knocked softly. It was no more than five seconds before the latch clicked and the door opened.

He said, "The Saint Louis Rose, I presume?"

"Hello, dearie." She caught hold of his coat sleeve, tugged him inside, and quickly shut the door. "You're late. I expected you an hour ago."

"I've been to Lily Dumont's cottage."

"Have you now. For what purpose?"

"Not the one you're thinking. She has too many admirers already."

"Jack Diamond, for one."

"So you noticed that too. I thought you had."

"Lady One-Eye is also aware of it."

He nodded. "Trouble there, do you think?"

"Of one kind or another. Lily Dumont is a dish to tempt any man, especially one with a block of ice for a wife."

"I prefer loud and bawdy blonds, myself." Quincannon gave her a broad wink. "Come over here, Rosie, and give us a kiss."

"I will not. Stand your distance."

"The Saint Louis Rose is no more likely than Lily Dumont to refuse a handsome man a kiss. Or anything else he might want."

"Perhaps not. But Sabina Carpenter *is* and you know it."

"To my great sorrow."

Quincannon sighed and went to sit on one of the room's plush chairs. He gazed wistfully at his partner in Carpenter and Quincannon, Professional Detective Services, and the object of his unrequited affections. She had removed all of the bawd's rouge and powder and false eyelashes, and shed the ridiculous ringlet wig. The transformation was amazing. In place of the hard, vulgar, blond Rose was a mature, well-bred, dark-haired woman with more than a dozen years of experience as a detective, six of those with the Pinkerton Agency's Denver office.

"What did you mean by loud and bawdy?" she demanded. "Do you think I overplayed my role tonight?"

"Perhaps a touch," he said tactfully.

"I thought my performance was rather good."

"It's too bad Lotta Crabtree wasn't here to see it. She might have offered you a new career as a stage actress."

"Don't make fun of me, John. I didn't strike a false note with Lady One-Eye, I'm certain of that."

"She was too busy plucking you like a chicken," Quincannon said. "How much did you lose, by the by? The entire fifteen hundred McFinn gave you?"

"Yes. Mostly on that last hand."

"A straight to your three jacks. Luck of the cards, or did she manufacture her own luck?"

"Oh, she's a skin-game artist, all right," Sabina said. "One of the best I've seen."

"Were you able to spot her gaff?"

"I think so. But she's so good at it that it took me most of the night. I wouldn't have seen it at all if I hadn't spent those weeks with Jim Moon at the Oyster Ocean in Denver a few years ago, learning his bag of tricks. It boils down to manipulating the cards so she knows her opponent's hole card on every hand she deals."

In gathering the cards for her deal, Sabina explained, Lady One-Eye dropped her own last hand on top of the deck, the five cards having been arranged so that the lowest was on top and the highest was second in line. As she did this she gave the five cards a quick squeeze, which produced a slight convex longitudinal bend. During the shuffle, she maneuvered the five-card slug to the top of the deck. Then, just before offering the deck for the cut, she buried the slug in the middle, at the point where her opponent tended to cut each time. The crimp in the cards ensured that the slug would be returned to the top. All she had to do then was to deal fairly, flexing the deck once or twice first to take out the slug's bend. The first card she dealt, which she knew from memory, was therefore the opponent's hole card. And her hole card, the second in line, was always higher.

"Clever," Quincannon said. "The advantage is small, but for a sharp it's enough to control almost any game."

Sabina nodded. "But I'd like to play her once more—or rather, the Rose would—to make absolutely sure I'm right about her gaff. An hour or so should do it. Will McFinn stake me to another five hundred, do you suppose?"

"Probably, but we needn't stretch his patience. I'll stake you, my dear. If you lose we'll add the sum to McFinn's bill."

"He might refuse to pay the extra charge."

"No matter. I'll accept your favors as reimbursement."

His boldness, as always, exasperated her. "You never give up, do you, John?"

"Never. You may as well say yes now and enjoy the consequences. I'll wear down your resistance sooner or later."

"No you won't. The answer is no and it always will be no. Why can't you accept the fact that we're business partners, nothing more?"

Quincannon sighed again, elaborately this time. But he wasn't daunted. He could be a very patient man when the situation warranted. He consoled himself with this, and with the pious thought that his intentions, after all, were honorable. Simple seduction had long ago ceased to be his primary motivation.

"To get back to business," Sabina said, "I don't intend to lose to Lady One-Eye tomorrow night. I know ways to counteract her gaff, thanks to Jim Moon."

"Either way, we'll have to put an end to the matter then. The sooner McFinn sends the Lady packing, the better off he'll be. It seems likely now that the threatening note is genuine."

"Now? Has something happened?"

"At Lily Dumont's cottage. Two rounds from a heavy revolver nearly took my head off."

"John! Someone tried to kill you? Who?"

"I didn't get a look at him. Too dark."

"Was there any light where you were?"

"No."

"Then whoever it was couldn't see you clearly either."

"Only my shape as I left the cottage. If you're thinking he might have mistaken me for someone else, you're right—he might well have."

"Jack O'Diamonds?"

"Or Glen Bonnifield. If it wasn't Bonnifield who did the shooting."

"Isn't he Lily Dumont's lover?"

"Evidently."

"Is he the reason you went to her cottage?"

"One of them," Quincannon said. "Lily's involvement with Jack O'Diamonds seems more than a simple dalliance. It occurred to me that she might have written the note, either in a foolish effort to drive Lady One-Eye out of town or as a clever ploy to pave the way for an attempt on the Lady's life."

"Did you find evidence to incriminate her?"

"None. No bottle of green ink."

Sabina nodded thoughtfully. "If Bonnifield is the jealous sort, *he* could be the author of the note."

"That he could. He was at the Palace tonight, glaring daggers at both Lily and Jack."

"Well. This business seems to be more complicated than we first believed."

"And more dangerous," Quincannon said. "Be on your guard tomorrow, Sabina. Take that little one-shot derringer of yours along to the Palace, just in case."

"It's already handy in my bag." She smiled impishly at him. "And knowing that, aren't you glad you didn't try to do more than just talk me into bed just now?"

♦ ♦ ♦

In the morning Quincannon hired a horse at the Empire Livery and rode the three miles to Nevada City. He spent the better part of four hours making the rounds of saloons—one of them Glen Bonnifield's Ace High—and local merchant establishments, pretending to be a patent medicine drummer and asking sly questions. He learned several things about Bonnifield and the saloonkeeper's relationship with Lily Dumont, a few of potential significance.

Bonnifield was in fact keeping Lily in her Grass Valley cottage and had been for two years. He was as hot-tempered as she and jealous to a fault; a year ago he had threatened to shoot a man who had been pestering her. And he carried a Buntline Special Colt with a twelve-inch barrel, a weapon with which he was reported to be an excellent shot.

A dangerous man, Bonnifield. But one of direct action, not devious design. Would such a man be likely to write a note forewarning both a rival and the rival's wife? Quincannon was left with the impression that the answer was a definite no.

When he returned to Grass Valley he went first to the Holbrooke. There was no message from Sabina at the desk, as there would have been if she'd learned anything important she felt he should know. Then he walked downstreet to the Palace.

By day, in the harsh glare of the sun, the gambling hall had an uninviting look. Like nearly all of the commercial buildings in Grass Valley, it was made of brick—the consequence of a disastrous fire in 1855 that had consumed the township's three hundred wooden structures, leaving nothing standing but Wells Fargo's brick and iron vault and a dozen scorched brick chimneys. The massive sign above the door had a warped and faded look. The brass fittings of the red-globed gaslights were pitted with rust. Little wonder, Quincannon thought, that the bluenoses were bent on closing it and its sisters down; some of the other gambling parlors here and in Nevada City had even tawdrier daylight appearances.

The Saint Louis Rose was not inside, nor was Lady One-Eye, Jack O'Diamonds, or Lily Dumont. McFinn was, however. He spied Quincannon, hurried up and plucked nervously at his sleeve.

"Well? Have you found out anything?"

"Nothing to be confided just yet, Mr. McFinn."

"That's just what your lady friend—"

"The Saint Louis Rose, you mean."

"Yes, yes, the Saint Louis Rose. That's just what she said when I spoke to her earlier. When will the two of you have something to confide? Eh?"

"Tonight, perhaps."

"When tonight?"

"After the Rose and Lady One-Eye have another game."

"Another game," McFinn said. "And another five hundred dollars of my money in the Lady's purse, I suppose."

"The Rose asked you for an additional stake, did she?"

"Yes, and I let her talk me into giving it to her."

"Pity. I was hoping she'd come to me instead."

"Are you sure she knows the game of poker?"

"Better than you or I, and as well as Lady one-Eye," Quincannon assured him. "Don't worry. Your money is being well spent."

"I'll consider it well spent if nothing calamitous happens," McFinn said mournfully. "I can't help feeling that disaster lurks close by."

"You're wrong, sir. It doesn't."

The one who was wrong, however, was John Quincannon.

♦ ♦ ♦

At five o'clock, in fresh clothing and with a plate of liver and onions residing comfortably under his vest, Quincannon returned to the Palace to resume his duties behind the bar. Lily Dumont appeared shortly afterward and began setting up her faro bank. She spoke to no one. She seemed preoccupied tonight —and almost as nervous as McFinn. Quincannon wondered if the cause of her agitation was that she'd gotten wind of the shooting last night.

Lady One-Eye and Jack O'Diamonds arrived together, but they soon parted without a word to each other. The Lady took her place at the platform table and was immediately challenged by a pair of whiskered gents who had the look of *nouveau riche* prospectors. Diamond made his way to the bar, where he drank two whiskeys in short order. Then he moved restlessly about the room, stopping for a while to play vingt-et-un and then again to play faro. But it was not Lily's bank that he chose. He avoided going anywhere near her, as if she were not even on the premises. Lily, likewise, paid not the slightest attention to him. A falling-out between them? Or was there another reason for their ignoring of each other?

The next to arrive was the Saint Louis Rose, wearing a purple dress that was even more revealing than last night's scarlet number. Where did she get such outfits? Quincannon wondered. Rent them or buy them? For all he knew Sabina had a closet full of such costumery and led a wanton double life, slipping out once or twice a week to Barbary Coast deadfalls. It made him feel testy to see the men in the hall ogling her bared flesh. As if he were a jealous husband. Which—and he might as well admit it—was what he wished he was.

The Rose joined Jack O'Diamonds at the faro table and attempted to engage him in conversation. He spurned her; he seemed as preoccupied as Lily Dumont. Three times in less than an hour he ordered whiskey from one of the percentage girls. But it seemed to have little or no effect on him.

Lady One-Eye made short work of the two prospectors, taking several hundred dollars from one and nearly a thousand from the other. They accepted their losses good-naturedly, offering to buy her a magnum of champagne as a token of their esteem for her skills. She declined. There was a tight set to her mouth tonight, a distracted mechanical quality to her movements. Trouble with her husband over Lily Dumont?

Shortly after the prospectors left her alone on the platform, Glen Bonnifield walked in. Or, more precisely, weaved in. His face was dark-flushed, his eyes bloodshot, his expression brooding: the look of a man who had spent a good part of the day in close company with a bottle of forty-rod, and not for pleasurable reasons. He lurched up to Quincannon's station, stood for a few seconds glowering in the direction of Lily Dumont. Then he called for whiskey.

Quincannon said politely, "Carrying a bit of a load tonight, eh, Mr. Bonnifield?"

"What if I am? No concern of yours."

"No, sir, except that you forgot to check your weapon."

"My what?"

"The Buntline Special poking out from under your coat."

"No damn concern of yours," Bonnifield growled. He spat into one of the knee-high cuspidors. "Pour my whiskey, barman, and be quick about it."

"Not until you check your weapon."

"Well now. Why don't you try checking it for me?"

His voice was loud, belligerent; some of the other patrons swung their heads to stare at him. So did Lily Dumont. When she saw the condition he was in, her nervousness evolved into visible fright.

"Let's not have any trouble, Mr. Bonnifield."

"There'll be plenty of trouble tonight, by God."

Abruptly Bonnifield shoved away from the rail, staggered over to Lily's faro bank. She shrank back while two of her customers scurried out of harm's way. Quincannon was on the run through the notch in the bar by then. He heard McFinn shout a warning to his bouncers; he also glimpsed Jack O'Diamonds jump up and start past the platform to Lily's defense.

What remained of Bonnifield's self-control had dissolved in drunken fury. He yelled, "You little tramp, I won't let you make a fool out of me!" and his hand groped under his coat for the Buntline Special.

Quincannon reached the saloonkeeper just as he drew the big-barreled gun, knocked his arm down before he could trigger a shot. Bonnifield swung wildly with his other hand, struck Quincannon's shoulder a glancing blow that drove him backward. Two of the bouncers muscled up; they caught hold of Bonnifield, tried to wrestle him into submission. He broke free and stumbled into a confused grouping of customers and Palace employees, still clutching his Buntline Special. Men shouted; a woman let out a shrill cry of alarm.

And in the midst of all this ferment, a single shot sounded, low and popping, like the explosion of a Fourth of July firecracker.

A man grunted loudly in pain. That and the shot ended the budding melee, parted the crowd in a fashion that was almost biblical. Quincannon saw a number of things in that instant. He saw the two bouncers drive Bonnifield to the floor and disarm him. He saw Lily rush out from behind her faro table. He saw Sabina running toward him. He saw Lady One-Eye seated at her table, one hand on the green baize and the other at the bodice of her dress. And in the cleared space where the mass of people had fallen back on both sides, he saw the victim of the gunshot lying supine and motionless, blood staining the right side of his coat at heart level.

Lily shrieked, "It's Jack! Oh no, it's *Jack!*"

She flung herself to the carpet beside Jack O'Diamonds, laid her flaming red head against his chest. When she lifted it again her eyes were wet with tears. "He's not breathing—he's dead."

Some of the men closed in and helped her to her feet. Immediately she shook a clenched fist at Glen Bonnifield, who was kneeling a few feet away. "You did it! Damn you, Glen, *you* killed him!"

Bonnifield was dazed from his scuffle with the bouncers; if he heard her he made no reply. One of the bouncers held the Buntline Special. Quincannon stepped over to him, took the weapon and felt and then sniffed the barrel. "Not with this, he didn't. It hasn't been fired."

McFinn came dancing up, his eyes as wide as a toad's. "Then who did shoot him? Quincannon, you blasted sorry excuse for a flycop, did you see who pulled the trigger?"

Quincannon admitted that he hadn't. He glanced at Sabina; her face told him she hadn't either.

"Did anyone see who fired that shot?" the little man roared over the babel of voices.

No one had. Or at least no one would own up to being a witness.

Beside himself now, McFinn bellowed to his bouncers to seal off the front and rear entrances, keep everybody inside the hall. No sooner had they rushed to obey than a new impassioned voice was raised above the others. This one belonged to Lady One-Eye, who had come down off the platform and was standing stock-still next to the remains of Jack O'Diamonds, pointing with her cane.

"Look at that!" she cried, her good eye blazing with cold fire. "Some black-guard not only murdered my husband in cold blood, he stole Jack's diamond stickpin too!"

She sounded more upset over the loss of his stickpin than she did over the loss of his life.

♦ ♦ ♦

Sheriff Jeremiah Thorpe was a man in his early thirties, with muttonchop whiskers and an efficient, no-nonsense manner. He took charge as soon as he and two of his deputies arrived with the bartender McFinn had dispatched to bring them. The answers to a few terse questions allowed him to separate the principal players in the drama from the extras and onlookers. These, with one exception, he herded into McFinn's private quarters at the rear, while his deputies remained in the main hall to question the others. The exception was Glen

Bonnifield. One of the bouncers had fetched him a crack on the head with a bungstarter in order to subdue him, and Bonnifield still hadn't regained his wits. He was being administered to by a town doctor.

Suspense crackled among the small group. Lily Dumont continued to shed tears and Lady One-Eye was once again coldly stoic, hiding her emotions behind her poker face; but it was plain that neither was happy to learn that a pair of San Francisco detectives had been operating in their midst, even though the reasons had yet to be divulged. McFinn was still in a lather. He kept glaring at Quincannon with open hostility.

Both Quincannon and Sabina had met Thorpe on their arrival in Grass Valley; he'd been friendly enough then, but the friendliness was in abeyance now. There was an edge to his voice as he said, "Well, Mr. Quincannon? Can you sort out what took place here tonight?"

"He couldn't sort out a handful of poker chips," McFinn said, glaring. "Neither him nor his lady partner. I hired them to keep disaster from my door and they failed miserably. I'll be ruined— "

"Amos, hold your tongue."

"I still say Glen Bonnifield shot poor Jack," Lily said. "He hated him, he made no bones about that. And last night . . . there were shots fired at my cottage. That must have been Glen, too, after Jack."

"Diamond was at your cottage last night?"

"No. I wasn't either when it happened. But Glen must've thought we were there together."

"Why would he fire shots at an empty cottage?"

Quincannon said carefully, "It may be that he was hiding outside and mistook a shadow for a man." Declaring that *he* was the mistaken target would serve no purpose except to vex the sheriff. He had, after all, entered Lily's home illegally; and he had also failed to report the shooting.

Thorpe asked him, "So then you agree that Bonnifield killed Diamond?"

"No. It was Bonnifield last night but not tonight."

"How do you know it wasn't?"

"He carries a Buntline Special. I examined it before you came and it hadn't been fired. Also, the report of a Buntline is loud, booming. The shot that folded Jack O'Diamonds was low and popping, like a firecracker."

"A small caliber weapon, then."

"Yes. A derringer or a pocket revolver."

"Does Bonnifield carry a hideout weapon, Miss Dumont?"

"No. I've never seen one."

"Then who did shoot Diamond?"

"And who," Lady One-Eye said, "stole his stickpin?"

Quincannon said, "Lily Dumont did that."

"Her! I should've known." The Lady jabbed menacingly at the younger woman with her cane. "You damned murdering husband-stealer—!"

Lily shrank away from her. "It's a lie! I didn't kill Jack, I swear I didn't kill him."

"But you did steal his stickpin," Quincannon insisted. "Slipped it out of his cravat when you flung yourself down beside his body, before you announced that he was dead. You were the only person close enough to've managed it without being noticed."

Sabina said wryly, "Jack O'Diamonds' handsome face wasn't his only lure for her. Money and the promise of more to come was at least part of the reason she was going away with him."

"What's that?" Thorpe said. "She was going away with Diamond?"

"All right," Lily cried, "all right, I was. And yes, I took his stickpin—why shouldn't I? He was dead and he would've wanted me to have it. He loved me and I did love him."

Lady One-Eye uttered a coarse word well known to the breeders of cattle.

"But I *didn't* shoot him. You have to believe me. I don't own a handgun, I don't even know how to fire one."

The sheriff turned to Quincannon. "Is she telling the truth or not?"

This was the moment Quincannon had been avoiding. For once his deductive prowess had failed him: he had no clear-cut idea of who had fired the fatal shot. He resisted an impulse to tug at his shirt collar, which now seemed a little snug.

"Ah, perhaps she is," he hedged, "and then again perhaps she isn't."

"What the devil does that mean?"

"It means," McFinn said scornfully, "he doesn't know either way. He doesn't have a clue to the identity of Jack's murderer."

There was a small uncomfortable silence.

Sabina broke it by saying, "Of course he does. We both know the murderer's name and how the crime was done. Don't we, John?"

He blinked at her. Her smile was faint but reassuring. By Godfrey, he thought, she *does* know. Dear Sabina, the love of my life, the savior of my reputation—she knows!

"Well?" Thorpe demanded. "Who was it?"

"Lady One-Eye, of course."

Heads swung toward the recent widow. Lady One-Eye stood in her usual ramrod-stiff posture, one hand resting on the gold knob of her cane, her good eye impaling Sabina. The only emotion it or her expression betrayed was contempt.

"How dare you accuse me? I might've been shot too tonight, the same as my husband. Have you forgotten the note that threatened both our lives?"

"I haven't forgotten it. The fact is, you wrote that note yourself."

"*I* wrote it?"

"When we were playing stud last night," Sabina said, "I noticed a fading smudge of green on your left thumb—green ink, the same color as the note. Chances are you didn't bother to dispose of the bottle and the sheriff will find it in your hotel room."

"Suppose she did write the note," Thorpe said. "What was her purpose?"

Lady One-Eye said, "Yes, Rose or whatever your name is. What possible reason could I have for threatening myself and then shooting my husband?"

"He was going to leave you, that's why!" Lily shouted. The shift of suspicion from her to Lady One-Eye had relieved her and made her bold again. "He was tired of you and your cold and stingy ways. And you knew it."

"I knew nothing of the kind."

"Yes you did. You as much as said so last night at my table. You warned me against trying to take him away from you."

"Liar. It's your word against mine."

"Oh, you knew, Lady," Sabina said. "And you planned to kill Jack if he tried to go through with it. He must have let something slip earlier today that convinced you he was leaving soon, perhaps as soon as tonight. With Lily and no doubt with some or all of the gambling winnings you accumulated. That's why you acted when you did. As for the note, you wrote that to divert suspicion from yourself—to make it seem as though you were also an intended victim. I'll warrant, too, that if you'd had enough time to complete your plan, you would've hidden the weapon you used at Lily's faro table or in her cottage, to frame her as the guilty party. That way, you'd have gotten your revenge on both of them."

"Sheriff," Lady One-Eye said to Thorpe, "I won't stand for any more of these outrageous accusations. How could I possibly have shot my husband? I was sitting at my table on the platform, in plain sight of the room. My hands were in plain sight too. If I had drawn a gun and fired it, someone would surely have seen me do it."

"That's right," McFinn said, "*I* would have. I glanced at her table just before the shot and again just afterward and she was sitting as she said, with her hands in plain sight."

"Yes she was," Sabina agreed. "I saw her myself. One hand on the table, the other at her bosom."

"Well then?"

"Lady One-Eye is a mistress of sleight of hand. She has been cheating her opponents at poker with it—that's right, Mr. McFinn, she *is* a skin-game artist —and tonight she used the same principle to shoot Jack O'Diamonds. Only in this case the sleight of hand only indirectly involved her hand."

"Don't talk in riddles, Mrs. Carpenter. How the devil did she do it?"

Sabina said, "Remember, there was general confusion at the time; no one was looking closely at her. Remember, too, that the lower half of her body was mostly hidden by the skirt of her dress and the table skirt." And before Lady One-Eye could stop her, Sabina leaned down, took the hem of the woman's black velvet dress, and hoisted the skirt straight up over the knee.

Quincannon, who was seldom surprised by anything any more, gawped and said, "Hell and damn!" in utter amazement. There were similar astonished outcries from the others.

Lady One-Eye was also Lady One-Leg.

Her left leg from the knee down and her shoe-encased left foot were made of wood.

And fastened with tape to the joining of foot and leg was a pearl-handled .32 caliber revolver, a long length of twine leading from its trigger up inside the dress to its bodice.

♦ ♦ ♦

"Apparently she lost her leg in the same buggy accident that claimed her eye," Sabina said to Quincannon later, in her room at the Holbrooke. "She had two reasons for hiding the fact, I expect. One was vanity. The other was pro-fessional fear. Most sports didn't mind too much playing a woman with one eye; it added an element of spice to their games. But a woman with one eye and one leg might well have made them uneasy. You know how superstitious gamblers are. Too many would've considered a double-handicapped lady gambler to be bad luck."

"So they would," he agreed. "Now tell me how you knew the leg was wooden."

"I bumped her foot accidentally last night, while we were in the midst of our game. She wore a shoe over it, as you saw, and she drew it back quickly, but the feel of the contact was odd enough to linger in my memory."

"How did you deduce the revolver fastened to it—the fact she'd literally shot him with her raised leg?"

"Two things," Sabina said. "One was a glimpse of the trigger string between two dress buttons. That was just after the shooting; she hadn't quite pushed it all the way inside yet."

"It might have been a thread."

"Yes, but then I remembered a man I knew once in Denver, when I was with the Pinks. He had a wooden leg and used to keep a hideout gun strapped to it. He fired it with a spring mechanism, but it struck me that a length of twine would do just as well."

Quincannon said admiringly, "You're a clever woman, my dear. Yes, and better than I am at the detecting game more often than I'd like to admit."

"Amos McFinn doesn't consider either of us much of a detective. And with some justification, at least from his point of view."

"Poor McFinn. But Lady One-Eye's devious actions were none that we could have foreseen or prevented."

"True. Still, I feel sorry for him. He may well be ruined by tonight's events."

Quincannon was philosophical. "Ah well, it was only a matter of time before the bluenoses had their way. Gambling parlors such as the Palace are doomed to extinction, I fear, at least in small towns like this one."

"Perhaps, but . . . John, he'll refuse to pay the balance of our fee. You know that as well as I do. What would you say to us forfeiting it, rather than suing to collect? As a gesture of good will."

" Forfeit the balance?" Now he was aghast. "Do you mean it?"

"Yes. From a practical standpoint it would also enhance our reputation. Results guaranteed at no risk to our clients."

"My father would have been appalled." Thomas L. Quincannon, in fact, would have had any member of his Washington detective agency horsewhipped for suggesting such a thing. "So would Allan Pinkerton."

"The new century is almost upon us, John. New business practices are necessary in a new age."

"Well, I suppose we can discuss the matter. In the morning, when we're both rested."

"Yes, in the morning."

At the door she said, "Did you really mean it that I'm often better at the detecting game than you?"

"I did. Though just how often I wouldn't care to say."

"Quite an admission for the likes of you." She favored him with a smile that was almost tender. And to his surprise and pleasure she leaned up to press her lips against his cheek.

Always one to seize an opportunity, Quincannon gathered her into his arms and kissed her soundly on the mouth. At first she struggled; then, for a few seconds, she softened and returned the kiss. Only for a few seconds, but a distinctly passionate few they were.

Sabina pushed him away and stepped back. Her cheeks were flushed. She fanned herself with one hand. A little breathlessly she said, "Well! Good night, Mr. Quincannon."

"Good night, my dear."

He stepped into the hallway. "You can just forget any notions that kiss may have given you," she said then. "It . . . wasn't me who responded. It was the Saint Louis Rose."

Quincannon stood grinning as the door closed between them. The Saint Louis Rose indeed, he thought.

And then he thought: Oh, that Rose!

CONEY GAME

Quincannon said, "I've never seen a better counterfeit hundred, Mr. Boggs. Nearly perfect."

"Perfect enough to have fooled more than one bank teller." Boggs licked his Havana cigar from one corner of his mouth to the other—a habitual gesture of concern and irritation. "Recognize the coney work?"

"Not offhand, no."

"Take another look."

The hundred-dollar note, a series 1891 silver certificate bearing the portrait of James Monroe, lay on Quincannon's desk blotter. Sunlight slanting in through the agency window highlighted one corner of the bill; he moved it over until it lay entirely in the sun patch. As he took up his magnifying glass, Sabina rose from her desk and came to lean over his shoulder.

The counterfeit had been made, he judged, using one of the new processes of photolithography or photoengraving. The latter, most likely: the quality of reproduction was excellent, though not remarkably so, and the note bore the rich dark lines of genuine government bills. There was a certain loss of detail, too, of the sort caused by the erratic biting of acid during the etching process. The loss of detail was one thing that marked the hundred as bogus. He had noted others: the Treasury seal was lightly inked and looked pink instead of carmine; the bill's dimensions were a fraction of an inch too small in both width and length; and the formation of the letters spelling "James" under President Monroe's portrait showed evidence of either poor etchwork or acid burn. All of these flaws were minor enough to escape the naked eye, even a well-trained one. A glass was necessary to spot them.

The paper appeared to be genuine, carrying both the "U.S." watermark in several places and the large, prominent colored silk threads used by the government's official papermaker, Crane & Co. of Dalton, Massachusetts. This would have been startling, given the rigid Treasury Department safeguards against the theft of banknote paper, except for two things. One was that the bogus note was a bit too thick. The other was that crisscrossing the engraved scroll lines were fine, colorless marks which ran in seeming confusion—the imprints of previous engraving.

Quincannon raked fingers through his thick freebooter's beard, cudgeling his memory. "Long Nick Darrow," he said at length.

"You haven't lost your eye," Boggs said, nodding. "No koniaker has ever done a better job of bleaching and bill-splitting than Darrow. This is his work or I'll eat my hat."

Sabina said, "Bleaching and bill-splitting?"

"An old trick," Quincannon explained. "The counterfeiter slices a one-dollar note lengthwise down the center, giving him two thin sheets. Then he bleaches each half to transparency with chemicals, places colored silk threads in the zone systems between the layers to resemble the authentic variety, pastes the halves back together, and reprints each side from his bogus hundred-dollar plates. A slight thickness from the paste is the giveaway. With a glass you can also make out the pressure marks from the original scroll work on the one-dollar bill—the colors can be bleached out but not those marks."

"I see. And Long Nick Darrow?"

"A koniaker I arrested in Montana twelve years ago, when I was with the Secret Service. One of the slipperiest coney men west of the Mississippi at that time." He looked at Boggs, head of the Service's San Francisco field office and his former chief. A round, graying man with a bulbous nose, Boggs had once been likened to a keg of whiskey with the nose as its bung—an apt description. "When did Darrow get out of prison?"

"Four months ago."

"Have you been able to trace his movements since?"

"No. He dropped out of sight as soon as he was released."

Quincannon tapped the phony hundred. "Where did this turn up?"

"Here in the city. Along with sixteen others, so far."

"The first one when?"

"Just last week. The president of First Western Bank spotted it and brought it to us. It wasn't until we'd rounded up the others that I began to suspect Darrow."

"So that's why you've come to us. You think Darrow has traveled here to run his new coney game."

"It would seem so. I felt you should know."

"Why, Mr. Boggs?" Sabina asked. "If this man Darrow is working at his old trade, it's a matter for your office, not a private agency. What can John and

I do?"

"Be on your guard, Mrs. Carpenter."

"I don't understand."

"Long Nick Darrow swore to have his revenge on John when he was sent to prison," Boggs said. "Swore to track him down and shoot him dead. It wasn't an idle threat."

"But one made a dozen years ago . . ."

"A dozen years in which to nurse his hatred. That's the kind of man Darrow is."

"Then why hasn't he made an attempt on John's life? You said he's been free for four months. Surely if he meant to carry out his threat he'd have done so by now."

"Not necessarily. For one thing, Darrow worships money and all the fine vices it can support. Even revenge would become secondary to the care and feeding of his greed—and making and shoving queer is the only fast-money job he knows. For another thing, he isn't one to act rashly. He'll bide his time and savor his revenge."

"Savor it? You mean . . . he may already have been stalking John on the sly?"

"Just his sort of sport, yes."

Quincannon, silent through all of this, had been studying the note again. He lowered his glass now and sat back. "The plates that made this were photoengraved, wouldn't you say, Mr. Boggs?"

"I would. Every letter and line cut into the metal by hand, following the tracings of the photographic image—the same process used in the Bureau of Printing and Engraving. Except that Darrow didn't have the advantage of using a geometric lathe."

"But the process hadn't been perfected yet when Darrow went to prison. If I remember correctly, anastatic printing was his transfer method then." For Sabina's benefit Quincannon added, "He placed a genuine hundred on a zinc plate and transferred its ink to the metal with a solvent. Then he engraved the plate by following the inked lines and letters."

Boggs said, "A long, slow, and imperfect method. Photoengraving is faster and more certain—a boon to the koniakers and a headache for the Service. It's no surprise that Darrow would take advantage of the new, improved technique."

"You've had your operatives canvassing printing and engraving shops in the city and outlying areas?"

"Of course. But there are a damned lot of them, and as usual we're short-handed."

"The shop would have to have a fairly large printing press to produce bills of this caliber," Quincannon mused. "That should narrow the field a bit."

"There are still more than two dozen to be checked, and better than half of those are outside the city. If we only had some sort of lead to follow . . ."

"What about the man who has been passing the queer? Or have there been more than one?"

"Two, evidently," Boggs said. "None of the bank tellers or merchants who accepted the notes could give a useful description of either one."

Quincannon took out his pipe, began to load it from the glass jar of tobacco on his desk. "Sabina and I may be able to provide some assistance. We have certain sources of information not available even to you."

"I've no doubt of that." Boggs licked his dead cigar back to the other side of his mouth, pushed his bulk upright, and reclaimed the counterfeit certificate. "Until we talk again, my friend, I'd advise you to keep a sharp eye on your backside."

"I'd rather keep a sharp eye on my partner's backside," Quincannon said wolfishly, a remark that at any other time would have aroused Sabina's indignation. It was a measure of her concern that she seemed not even to have heard it. He found this heartening. Underneath her reserve and her determination to keep their relationship strictly professional, there lurked a fondness for him that he was sure was almost as strong as his for her. They would be more than partners one day. He was as devoted to this end as she was to the opposite.

When Boggs was gone Sabina asked, "John, are you convinced this man Darrow is the maker of that bogus hundred?"

"It seems likely."

"And are you also convinced he plans to murder you?"

"Not so much of that, no. Boggs tends to leap to conclusions." He shrugged. "Besides, rougher men than Long Nick Darrow have sworn to bump me off, and a few have made the attempt. I'm a hard man to fit for a coffin."

"I've known others who felt the same. Each ended up wearing a headstone before his time."

"Not John Quincannon. I intend to remain above ground a long while—

at least long enough to convince you to share my bed and board."

"Then you'll live to ninety and still die frustrated."

Quincannon laughed. Without haste he went to put on his derby hat and Chesterfield. Sabina watched him narrowly, her hands fisted on slender hips. Her back was to the Market Street window; sun light made the jeweled comb she wore in her sleek black hair shine as if with an inner fire.

"Where are you off to?" she asked.

"A walk on the Barbary Coast."

"I thought as much. While you're gone, I believe I'll try to find out if Long Nick Darrow has any known associates in the Bay Area—just in case. Which prison was he in?"

"Leavenworth."

"Good. I've dealt with the warden there before."

"You might also wire the Pinkerton office in Missoula. They had a file on Darrow twelve years ago."

"I'll do that. The Denver office too." She followed him to the door. "You're an observant man," she said then. "If Darrow has been watching you, you'd have noticed the surveillance, wouldn't you?"

"Of course."

"And you haven't?"

"No, my dear, I haven't."

But the truth was, he had. More than once during the past two weeks he'd been followed—not by Darrow himself but a youngish, carrot-topped man who had given him the slip when he'd tried to accost him. He had withheld this from Sabina to spare her more worry. Now, despite what he'd said about Boggs leaping to conclusions, there was no question in his own mind of who had sent the carrot-top. Or that Long Nick Darrow was in San Francisco and did in fact plan to carry out his twelve-year-old threat.

♦ ♦ ♦

The Barbary Coast had been infamous for nearly half a century as the West's seat of sin and wickedness, a "devil's playground" equaled by none other in the country and few in the world. There was a good deal of truth in this, as Quincannon well knew, but on a bright spring afternoon the area appeared relatively tame and not a little tawdry. As he made his way along Stockton Street he passed Cheap John clothing stores, rundown hotels and lodging houses, deadfalls, cheap dance halls, and a variety of cribs, cowyards, and parlor houses. One of the last sported a sign that never failed to bring a wry smile to his mouth:

MADAME LUCY
YE OLD WHORE SHOPPE

The streets were crowded: seamen, sports, gay blades; gamblers, pick-pockets, swindlers, and roaming prostitutes. Quincannon was propositioned twice by painted women in the first two blocks. But for all of this, things were quiet at this hour, almost orderly. It was not until darkness settled that a man's valuables—and in some parts of the Coast, his life—were in jeopardy.

The center of the district was the three-block-square area between Broadway and Washington, Montgomery and Stockton streets. Ezra Bluefield's Scarlet Lady saloon was here, an evil-looking building in an alley off Pacific Avenue. Until a short time ago, Bluefield had operated a crimping joint on these premises—a saloon where seamen were served doctored drinks composed of whiskey and gin and laced with laudanum or chloral hydrate, and then sold to shanghai shipmasters in need of crews. But the Sailor's Union of the Pacific had put an end to that, forcing the temporary closure of the Scarlet Lady. When enough bribes had been paid and Bluefield reopened the place, it was as a simple deadfall where customers were relieved of their cash by "pretty waiter girls," bunco ploys, and rigged games of chance. Knockout drops were used only when all other methods failed.

There had been three known murders in the Scarlet Lady, and any number of unknown ones, and brawls were common. But Bluefield himself remained aloof from it all. He employed several bouncers and vanished into his private office whenever trouble broke out. It wasn't that he was a coward; he'd had his share of fistfights and cutting scrapes. He considered himself above such rowdiness these days, having aspirations to own a better class of saloon in a reputable neighborhood. As a result he cultivated the company of respectable citizens, among them a reasonably honest private investigator, the city's finest, who had once saved him from assassination at the hands of a rival saloon owner.

Quincannon found Bluefield in his office, partaking of a huge plate of oysters on the half-shell. He was a big man, Bluefield, with an enormous handlebar mustache the ends of which were waxed to saber points. He waved Quincannon to a chair, slurped in one last oyster, washed it down with a draught of lager, and belched contentedly as he leaned back in his chair.

"Well, John, my lad, what can I do for you?" Small talk was not one of Bluefield's vices, a quality Quincannon found laudable.

"Supply the answers to a few questions, if you can."

"Gladly. If I can."

"Have you heard anything of a new coney game recently set up in the Bay Area? A major operation, evidently, involving hundred-dollar silver certificates."

"Not a whisper," Bluefield said. "Coney game, eh? Don't tell me you're working with old Boggs again?"

"Yes, but not officially. The gent we suspect of running the game swore to kill me when I sent him to prison a dozen years ago."

"Not a whisper of that, either. What's this scruff's name?"

"Long Nick Darrow."

Bluefield shook his head. "Description? Age?"

"Tall, long-necked, thin as a rail. Twelve years ago he wore a mustache and goatee and favored fancy suits and brocade vests. He'll be close to fifty now."

"Not familiar. Habits?"

"Women, roulette, French food and wine. In that order of preference."

"If he's indulging himself on the Barbary Coast, or anywhere else in the city, I'll know it within forty-eight hours. But if he's lying low to work his game . . ." Bluefield shrugged and spread his hands.

"One other thing: It's likely he has a gent with carroty hair working for him, youngish and well set up."

"Right. I'll do what I can, lad."

Quincannon left Bluefield to his oysters and lager, and continued on his rounds of the Barbary Coast. He found and spoke with a Tar-Flat hoodlum named Luther James, a bunco steerer who went by the moniker of Breezy Ned, and a "blind" newspaper vendor known as Slewfoot—all of whom had sold him information in the past for cash or favors. As with Ezra Bluefield, none of the three had yet picked up a whisper about Long Nick Darrow and his coney game. Each promised to go on the earie, and to spread the word that Quincannon would pay handsomely for a proper tip.

There was little else he could do then except to wait. A visit to the Hall of Justice would have been wasted: the San Francisco police disliked private detectives in general and Quincannon in particular, since he was far more successful at catching crooks than they were. Besides which, the city's minions of the law were openly corrupt, more corrupt that Long Nick Darrow and Ezra Bluefield combined; they would be too busy collecting graft to know or care that a notorious koniaker was operating in their bailiwick. The only ones who could put an end to Darrow's game were Boggs and his handful of Secret Service operatives, and/or John Quincannon.

♦ ♦ ♦

The next two days were uneventful. There was no word off the Barbary Coast; and Sabina's telegrams produced negative results. Quincannon went about his business, and was satisfied that he wasn't followed and that no one was watching the agency offices or his rooming house. The carrot-topped gent had either been frightened off, or Darrow had already learned all he felt necessary about his quarry's habits and activities.

On the afternoon of the second day, a Friday, Quincannon paid a call on Boggs at the Service's cubbyhole field offices at the San Francisco Mint. The branch chief had nothing new to report.

"We've nearly finished checking all printing and engraving shops in and out of the city," he said. "None seems to be even a mild candidate for Darrow's operation."

"He's a sly fox," Quincannon said. "It could be that he arranged to ship in a dismantled press and have it set up in a warehouse or abandoned building. And brought along an out-of-state printer to run it."

Boggs nodded gloomily and tongue-rolled his perpetual dead cigar. "Expensive ploy, but it wouldn't surprise me. If that's the case, it might take weeks to track down the location."

"Darrow won't stay that long. He'll get wind soon, if he hasn't already, that you've tumbled to his bogus silver certificates. Once his gang has difficulty passing them, he'll cut and run."

"But first, he'll have his try at you."

" 'Try' is the word, Mr. Boggs. If it comes to that, it'll be his downfall."

That evening Quincannon dined alone at Pop Sullivan's Hoffman Café, one of his favorite haunts during his drinking days and still a lure now and then. He'd asked Sabina to join him, but she declined; she had another engagement, she said. Whether the engagement was with a gentleman or a lady friend, she refused to confide. Her reticence aroused both his frustration and his jealousy. She was a strict guardian of her private life; he knew little enough about it. But she was a healthy and attractive young widow, and doubtless she had male suitors by the score. The thought that she might allow one of them to spend a passionate few hours in her Russian Hill flat was maddening—almost as maddening as the possibility that she would say yes to a marriage proposal from someone other than John Quincannon.

After dinner he went straight to his rooms on Sutter Street, where he made an attempt to read from Wordsworth's *Poems in Two Volumes*. Usually poetry relaxed him; on this night, however, it did nothing to ease his restlessness. He was on the verge of going out again, for a long walk this time, when the knock sounded on his door.

He answered it warily, one hand on his Navy Colt. But the caller was a welcome one: a runner for Ezra Bluefield, bearing a sealed envelope. The contents of the envelope, a brief note in the saloon owner's bold hand, brightened his mood considerably.

John, my lad—

You may find it enlightening to have a talk with Bob Podewell, 286 Spear Street. He is a young and well set up carrot-top and he has been heard to brag while in his cups of an affiliation with "a clever blackleg who is taking the Treasury Department for a ride." The blackleg himself appears to be saving the public indulgence of his vices for a later time.

Quincannon made a mental note to send Bluefield a bottle of good Scotch whiskey. Then he checked the loads in his Navy, donned his Chesterfield, and hurried out into a roiling fog that had robbed the city of its daytime warmth.

♦ ♦ ♦

The section of Spear Street where Bob Podewell resided was close to the Embarcadero and the massive bulk of the Ferry Building. Flanking its dark length was a mix of warehouses, stores operated by ship's chandlers and outfitters, and lodging houses that catered to seamen, laborers, and shop workers. Whoever Podewell was, he had been in pinched circumstances before hooking up with Long Nick Darrow—if in fact he had hooked up with Darrow—and was still too little paid, or perhaps too miserly, to move to better quarters.

There was no one abroad as Quincannon turned onto Spear from Mission Street. Or at least no one visible to him. He hadn't been followed from his rooming house, he was certain of that, but the waterfront was a rough place at night; a man alone, particularly a man who was rather nattily dressed, was fair prey for footpads. He walked swiftly, his gaze probing the swirls of mist. Out on the Bay foghorns moaned in ceaseless rhythm. As he crossed Howard he had glimpses of pier sheds and the masts and steam funnels of anchored ships, gray-black and indistinct like disembodied ghosts.

Number 286 took shape ahead—a three-story firetrap built of warping wood, never painted and sorely in need of carpentry work. Smears of electric light showed at the front entrance, illuminating a sign that grew readable as he neared: *Drake's Rest—Rooms by Day, Week, Month.*

Inside he found a narrow lobby that smelled of salt-damp and decay. Behind the desk, a scrawny harridan was feeding crackers to an equally scrawny parrot in a cage. It was even money as to which owned the more evil eye, the woman or the bird. Hers ran Quincannon up and down in a hungry fashion, as if she would have liked nothing better than to knock him on the head and steal his valuables.

He greeted her and then gave Bob Podewell's name.

"What about him?"

"I've business with the gent. Is he in?"

"No. What business would a swell like you have with the likes of Bob Podewell?"

"Mine and his, madam. Where might I find him?"

"Madam," she said. "Faugh! How would I know?"

Quincannon took a silver dollar from his pocket, flipped it high so that it caught the light from the ceiling globe. The woman's greedy eye followed its path up and back down into his palm. She licked her thin lips.

"Now then," he said. "Where does Bob spend his evenings?"

"The Bucket of Blood saloon, I hear tell, when he's not working late at his miserable job." Her gaze was still fixed on the coin.

"He works late some nights, does he?"

"Didn't used to. Does now."

"What's his job?"

"Picture-taker's assistant."

"For which picture-taker?"

"Name of Drennan."

"Address of Mr. Drennan's shop?"

"Fremont Street, near Mission. Brick 'un next to the rope-and-twine chandler's."

"Storefront? Or does Mr. Drennan own the entire building?"

"Entire. So I hear tell."

Quincannon tossed her the silver dollar. She caught it expertly, bit it between snaggle teeth. The parrot cackled and said, "Ho, money! Ho, money!" She glared at the bird, then cursed it as Quincannon turned for the door. She seemed genuinely concerned that the parrot might break out of its cage and take the coin away from her.

Outside Quincannon allowed his lips to stretch in a humorless grin. Photographer's assistant, eh? Well, well. Unless he missed his guess, a showdown with Long Nick Darrow was closer at hand than either of them had anticipated.

♦ ♦ ♦

The brick building on Fremont Street was long and narrow, flanked on its north side by the rope-and-twine chandler's and on the south side by a pipe yard. Alleyways and tall board fences gave it privacy from its neighbors. No lights showed behind the plate glass window in front. Quincannon stepped up to the window, read the words *Matthew Drennan, Photographer* painted there, then laid his ear against the cold, fog-damp glass. He could just make out a steady sound—part metallic thud and part hiss-and-hum—that came from the rear. The sound was percussive enough to cause the window to vibrate faintly against his ear.

He drew his Colt, went around and into the strip of blackness along the south wall. He felt his way along the rough brick, sliding his feet so as not to trip over any hidden obstacles. Toward the rear the thud-and-hiss became audible again, muffled by the thick wall. Then it grew louder still—and his groping fingers discovered a recess in the bricks, touched the wood of a door.

He shouldered in close, located the latch. It was unlocked and the door unbarred. When he eased it inward a few inches, pale lamplight illuminated the opening—and the throbbing rhythm increased two-fold. But its source was still some distance away, behind another closed door in the bowels of the building.

Quincannon raised his weapon, pushed the alley door the rest of the way inward. Storage room. The light came from a hanging lantern, revealing a clutter of photographic equipment: cameras and tripods, printing frames, lenses, chemicals, boxes labeled *Mr. Eastman's Instantaneous Dry Plates*. That was all the room contained: no one had been stationed here to watch over the alley entrance.

Carefully Quincannon moved inside, shut the alley door, and crossed to the inner one. He inched it free of its jamb. The machinery noise, then, was almost deafening. When he laid an eye to the opening he saw exactly what he'd expected to see, across a dusty expanse of warehouse floor lit by electric ceiling bulbs.

The printing press took up the entire far half of the open room. No wonder Darrow's bogus hundred-dollar notes were of such high quality: the press was not one of the old-fashioned single-plate, hand-roller types, but rather a small steam-powered Milligan that would perform the printing, inking, and wiping simultaneously through the continuous movement of four plates around a square frame. It was being operated at the moment by a middle-aged man wearing a green eyeshade and a leather apron, a hired printer or perhaps Matthew Drennan himself. A second man, young and orange-haired, stood at a long wooden bench laden with tools and chemicals and tins of ink: Bob Podewell. There was no one else in sight.

Long Nick Darrow was a sly fox, all right, Quincannon thought with grudging admiration. No one would think to look for a steam press in a photographer's warehouse, even though a picture-taker was a likely member of Darrow's coney gang. An expert photographic reproduction of a genuine government bill was an essential ingredient in the photoengraving process he was now using.

Quincannon debated. Should he arrest these two himself, or report to Boggs and let him do the honors? Darrow was the man he wanted; if Darrow were present, he wouldn't hesitate. Still—two birds in hand. And chances were, the birds would know where Long Nick could be found—

With a clank and a hiss, the Milligan press shut down abruptly. The silence that followed the racket was acute—and in that silence Quincannon heard a small, new sound behind him.

Someone was opening the alley door.

He wheeled in a half-crouch. In the lantern glow he saw a man framed in the doorway, at the same instant the man saw him. There was a frozen brace of seconds as they recognized and stared at each other. Then Long Nick Darrow flung himself backward and sideways, and the foggy darkness swallowed him before Quincannon could trigger a shot.

He ran across the storage room, out into the alley. It was like hurling himself into a vat of India ink; wet black closed around him and he could see nothing but vague shapes beyond ragged tendrils of mist. He listened, heard only silence, took two steps toward the rear—

Something swung out of the murk, struck him squarely across the left temple, and knocked him over like a ninepin.

It was not the first time he had been hit on or about the head, and his skull had withstood harder blows without serious damage or loss of consciousness. He didn't lose consciousness now, though his thoughts rattled around like pebbles in a tin can. He rolled over onto his knees and forearms, then hoisted himself unsteadily to his feet. Pain throbbed in his temple; there was a ringing in his ears. He realized he still held his revolver—and realized a second later that he was now standing in the faint out-spill of light from the storage room. He had just enough time to dodge forward, in tight against the wall, before the gun crashed from a short distance away.

The bullet struck high above his head, showering him with brick dust. He fired at the muzzle flash, missed in the dark; a moment later, the sound of running steps penetrated the fading buzz in his ears. An oath swelled his throat. He bit it back, set out blindly after the retreating footfalls.

He ran in close to the wall, headless of obstacles now, shaking his head to clear it. Blood trickled warm and sticky down over his right cheek, adding fuel to his outrage. The fleeing steps veered off to the right, were replaced by scraping sounds, then commenced again at a greater distance. Quincannon's mental processes steadied. There must be a second, north-south alley intersecting this one behind Drennan's building. He slowed, saw the intersection materialize through the fog, and swung himself around the corner into the new passage.

Where, after six paces, he ran into a wooden fence.

He caromed off, staggering. The oath once more swelled his throat and this time two of its smoky words slipped out. He plunged back to the fence, caught the top and scaled its six-foot height. When he dropped down on the far side he could hear Darrow's steps more clearly. The fog was patchier here; he was able to see all the way to the dull shine of an electric streetlamp on Howard Street beyond. A running shadow was just blending into other shadows there, toward the Embarcadero.

When he reached the corner he skidded to a halt, breathing in thick wheezes. Visibility was still good: he could make out the counterfeiter's tall, thin shape less than half a block away. He ran again, lengthening his strides, and he was fifteen rods behind when Darrow crossed Beale Street. Gaining on him, by God. He dashed across Beale. But as he came up onto the sidewalk on the opposite side, the koniaker disappeared once more.

Another alleyway, this one dirt-floored, Quincannon saw as he reached its mouth. He turned into it cautiously. No ambush this time: Darrow was still on the lammas. He rushed ahead, managed to reach the far end without blundering into anything. He slowed there long enough to determine that the footsteps were now coming from the right, in the direction of Folsom Street. He went that way, spotted Darrow some distance ahead—and then, again, didn't see him. Nor were his footfalls audible any longer.

The fog was thick-pocketed that way; the shimmery lamps of a hansom cab at the far intersection were barely visible. At a walk now, Quincannon continued another ten paces. Close by, then, he heard the nervous neighing of a horse, followed by a similar sound from a second horse. A few more paces, and the faint glow of a lantern materialized. Another, slender wedge of yellow came from the right. One of the horses nickered again, and harness leather creaked. He heard nothing else.

He kept moving until he could identify the sources of the light. One came from a lantern mounted on a wagon drawn by two dray animals which filled the width of the alley, and the other from a partially open door to the building on the right—a two-story brick structure with an overhanging balcony at the second level. Above the door was a sign that was just discernible: *McKenna's Ale House.*

The wagon was laden with medium-sized kegs, which indicated a late delivery to the saloon. There was no sign of anyone human. Quincannon drew closer, peering to the right because that direction offered the largest amount of space for passage around the wagon.

The hurled object came from the left. Quincannon saw it—one of the kegs —in time to pitch his body sidewise against the ale house wall. The keg sailed past his head, missing him by precious little, slammed into the bricks above and broke apart. He threw his arm up to protect his head as staves and metal strapping and the contents of the keg rained down on him.

Beer. A green and pungent lager.

The foamy brew drenched him from head to foot, got into his eyes and mouth and nose. Spluttering, he pawed at his face and shook his head like a bewildered bull—and Darrow's revolver banged again from behind the wagon.

The shot was wild. Quincannon recoiled backward, slipped in the beer mud and nearly fell. The slip was fortunate because it took him out of the way of a second bullet. He staggered, righted himself, started to rush forward— and was almost brained by a plunging hoof on one of the frightened dray horses. Again he dodged, again he slipped. There were shouts from inside McKenna's Ale House, and, then, audible among them, the resumed pound of Darrow's running steps.

The saloon's rear door opened and a pair of curious heads poked out. Quincannon, recovering, brandished the Navy and the heads disappeared so quickly they might never have been there at all. He slid along the bricks, rubbing at his beer-stung eyes. The dray horses were still shuffling around in harness, though neither was plunging any longer. He pushed past them and the wagon, ran out to Folsom Street.

The fog rolling up from the waterfront was as thick as Creole gumbo. All he could hear was the ever-present clanging of fogbells. All he could see was empty damp-swirled darkness.

Long Nick Darrow had vanished again. And this time there was no picking up his trail.

♦ ♦ ♦

Quincannon's humor was black and smoldering as he made his way back to Fremont Street. Darrow had not only gotten away, but twice had narrowly missed killing shots with a handgun. And he, Quincannon, had suffered the added indignities of a mushy and painful wound on his temple where the koniaker had clubbed him, a knot on his forehead from his collision with the fence, torn and beer-drenched clothing, and the lingering scent of a derelict. If he could lay hands on Darrow this minute, he'd tear him limb from limb.

And where *was* Darrow now? Gone to wherever he'd been living, to hatch a new plan? It was unlikely that he would risk returning to the warehouse of Matthew Drennan, Photographer. Or that either Bob Podewell or the middle-aged gent who had been operating the Milligan press would still be there; the shot fired by Darrow in the alley would surely have panicked them and sent them on the lammas. But Quincannon had nowhere else to go. The warehouse was his only link to the koniaker.

From the street in front, the building still wore its dark cloak. He disdained the alley this time; with his Navy in hand he approached the front entrance, listened, heard nothing, and proceeded to open the rather flimsy door lock with one of his burglar picks. No sounds came to him as he stepped inside. He struck a lucifer, and by its pale light he found his way into the rear warehouse section.

The overhead electrics still burned there, but as he'd expected, the place was now abandoned. Darrow's accomplices had stayed long enough to gather up most of the already printed counterfeit notes; several bills lay scattered across the floor, testimony to the haste of their departure.

Quincannon went to have a look at the press. And smiled grimly when he found the counterfeit plates still attached to the machine. Fear had dominated the two accomplices, kept them from tarrying even the extra few minutes it would have taken to remove the plates and carry them away too. Darrow would be livid when he found this out. The plates were far more valuable to a coney man than a few hundred bogus certificates.

Quincannon detached the plates, wrapped them in a piece of burlap and slid them into his sodden Chesterfield pocket. Then he commenced a rapid search of the rest of the building, looking for some clue that might lead him to Darrow.

He found one almost immediately, and it disconcerted as well as enlightened him. A small room off the warehouse section had been outfitted with a cot, worktable, and a variety of foodstuffs and potables. There was French paté in an ice chest, along with three bottles of expensive French wine. And hanging from a water pipe were three good, rather flashy cheviot suits and three equally flashy brocade vests.

Long Nick Darrow had been living here. Made his counterfeit plates here, distributed the queer from here, holed up here the entire time he'd been in San Francisco.

And now he was on the run, without his plates, without most of his bogus notes, and with only the clothes on his back.

Where would he go?

A thought wormed its way into Quincannon's mind—an ugly and fearful thought that raised the hackles on his nape. After the chase through the foggy streets, Darrow would be filled with as much hatred for his nemesis as Quincannon felt for him. One thing he might do was to make for Sutter Street, set up an ambush at Quincannon's rooming house. But there was also another, even more devilish plan of action that his sly brain might lead him to take.

Sabina. Suppose he'd gone after Sabina?

◆ ◆ ◆

The hansom cab let Quincannon off half a block uphill from Sabina's Russian Hill flat. He had already paid the driver on Market Street; the hackie, chary of Quincannon's appearance and ripe lager smell, had refused to permit him inside the cab until he'd handed over his money in advance. He hurried away from the hansom now without a backward glance, keeping to the shadows cast by shade trees and hedges.

The house in which Sabina lived was one of a row of smallish, two-flat buildings set back from the sidewalk behind iron picket fences. Her flat, upstairs, showed light behind drawn front curtains. As late as it was—after midnight—this might have been unusual except for the fact of her unexplained engagement. She might be entertaining her companion, damn his eyes if it was a man. Or she might have just arrived home, alone, and hadn't yet prepared for bed.

The other possibility was Long Nick Darrow.

Quincannon moved to the front gate. Shrubbery and cypress hedges choked the yard within, offering plenty of cover. The fog was thinner here on the hillside, torn and driven high by an icy wind off the ocean; he shivered in his still-wet clothing as he drifted through the gate, crossed to the stairs. No sounds came to him other than the wind, the distant, muffled clanging of cable-car bells, the fog warnings from the buoys on the bay. The house's stillness seemed almost funereal.

He considered climbing to the foyer, picking the lock on the front door. Then he remembered that there was an outside stairway at the rear that led straight up to a landing outside Sabina's kitchen—a more direct access and only a single lock to deal with. A branch of the gate path hooked around on the building's east side. He started that way, only to stop again, abruptly, after half a dozen steps.

The light in Sabina's front window had just gone out.

To bed, now? Alone, he fervently hoped, if so. He listened—still nothing from the house—and then went ahead along the path, pacing carefully in the clotted darkness.

The rear yard extended back some thirty rods, to where a woodshed and a small carriage barn marked the end of the property. Half a dozen fruit trees threw thick puddles of shadow, their bloomheavy branches clicking and rattling in the wind. This noise kept him from hearing the footfalls on the outside rear stairs until he reached the corner.

He froze for three heartbeats, then craned his neck and upper body forward so he could peer around toward the stairs. Two shapes were descending, neither fast nor slow, one below the other. He couldn't see them clearly until they reached the yard and moved away from the staircase. Then his lips flattened in tight against his teeth; fury inflated his chest like a bellows.

The shape in the lead, walking stiff-backed, was Sabina.

And the man behind her was Darrow.

Quincannon had to restrain himself from taking rash action. In the windy dark he didn't dare risk firing a shot that might miss Darrow and strike Sabina instead. Or one that might miss both and cause the counterfeiter to shoot Sabina in retaliation; the elongated blob in his right hand was surely a gun. And the grass was too wet, the footing too uncertain to chance gliding up on him from behind, unseen and unheard. Quincannon held his ground, chafing at the necessity to watch and wait, as Darrow herded Sabina toward the carriage barn.

At first he thought they were bound for the barn. But as they neared it, they veered off to a gate in the boundary fence nearby. Heavy tree shadow swallowed them. He couldn't wait any longer; as soon as they vanished he stepped out from the house wall and passed as swiftly as he dared among the fruit trees, at an angle that brought him up against the barn's side wall.

He could hear them then, out in the carriageway that bisected the block. Heard, too, the faint whicker of a horse and the rattle of a bit chain. Darrow had some kind of conveyance waiting there, no doubt one that he'd recently stolen.

Quincannon went to the rear corner, looked out into the carriageway. The conveyance, standing only a few rods off, was an open buggy drawn by a single horse. Darrow stood at the driver's step, gesturing for Sabina to climb up to the seat.

"No balking now." The koniaker's voice carried distinctly on the wind. "Climb up and sit down, if you know what's good for you."

"Where are you taking me?"

"You'll find that out soon enough."

"And when we get there? What will you do then?"

Darrow made a chuckling sound. "Your virtue is safe with me, if that's worrying you."

"It isn't." Sabina sounded calm and unruffled, which came as no surprise to Quincannon. She was as fearless and as capable in a crisis as any man he'd ever known. "Kidnapping is a serious crime, Mr. Darrow."

"So is counterfeiting. But neither is as serious as one other."

"Murder, you mean. Are you planning to murder me?"

"That depends on you, Mrs. Carpenter."

"You won't get away with it if you do. John will hound you to the ends of the earth."

"Your man John won't be alive to hound anyone."

"So that's your scheme, is it? Use me to lure John so you can kill him."

"I should have killed him weeks ago, when I first came to this wretched city. And I damned well should have seen him dead earlier tonight. Twice I came within inches of putting a bullet in his brain. Twice! He has more lives than an alley cat."

"Yes, and you won't take any of them."

"Won't I? Watch and see. Climb up, now, and be quick. I've no patience left for this."

Quincannon backed away from the corner. When he heard the buggy creak under Sabina's weight, the skittish movements of the horse, he hurried around to the front of the barn and across to its far corner. From there he could see that the fence gate was still open. He stepped out, his boots sliding noiselessly through the tall grass. Darrow was still facing toward the buggy, waiting for Sabina to settle into the seat. Quincannon kept going to the fence, turned through the opening, went straight and fast toward Darrow with his Navy at arm's length. He was still afraid to risk a shot from more than a short distance away.

There was twenty feet separating them when the counterfeiter heard or sensed his approach. Darrow swung around, bringing his weapon to bear. Quincannon had no choice but to fire then, and he did so without hesitation; but on the move as he was, his aim was off. The bullet struck Darrow—the man's yell of pain proved that—but it neither disarmed him nor put him on the ground. Quincannon would have fired a second time, and Darrow might have managed to trigger a round at him, if it hadn't been for the buggy horse's startled reaction to the first shot.

The animal frog-danced backward, causing the buggy to lurch and side-jump. The footboard caught Darrow's leg, pitched him off balance; and

Quincannon, in trying to dodge out of harm's way, slipped on the wet grass. He went down hard on his backside. The jarring impact robbed him of his grip on the Colt; the heavy weapon struck his boot, bounced into the grass. He scrambled onto one knee, groping for the revolver—and out of the tail of his eye he saw Darrow recover his balance. The koniaker still held his weapon and was raising it. Quincannon's fingers touched the butt of the Navy, but even as he gathered it into his hand he knew it was too late: Darrow would fire first and at this distance he wasn't likely to miss—

That was not what happened.

Long Nick Darrow had no chance to fire.

Sabina had managed to drop free of the buggy, and in that moment, from behind Darrow, she swung something long and thin at his head, in the fashion of a baseball player swinging at a pitched ball. It made the same sort of meaty smacking sound when it connected. The koniaker was upright and aiming one instant, and the next he was flat on his face in the grass, unmoving. He hadn't uttered a sound.

A little shakily, Quincannon gained his feet. He and Sabina asked each other if they were all right. Then he holstered his Colt, went to bend over Darrow and feel for his pulse.

Sabina said, "Is he alive?"

"Temporarily senseless. What did you hit him with?"

"The buggy whip. Reversed with the grip forward."

"A mighty blow, my dear. You saved my life."

"Just as you were about to save mine."

"True. We make a fine team, eh?"

"Professionally speaking, yes."

Professionally speaking. Bah. He straightened, turned to her, and gathered her against him in a tight embrace. She permitted the intimacy for no more than three seconds before she pushed him away.

"John, for heaven's sake! You smell like six nights in a brewery."

He nodded ruefully. "How well I know it."

"You haven't broken your vow of abstinence?"

"No. But this has been one of those nights," he said with feeling, "when I wish I'd never taken the pledge in the first place."

♦ ♦ ♦

Boggs said, "I invited you both to dinner not only as a token of my gratitude but to pass along more good news. Two of my operatives arrested Matthew Drennan and Bob Podewell this afternoon in Oakland. They were trying to pass one of the bogus hundreds at the railway station, for passage to Sacramento and points east. They've been holed up over there for the past four days."

"Did you recover the rest of the queer?" Sabina asked.

"Every last bill."

"How many others in the gang still at large?"

"None. Drennan worked as a printer before he became a photographer; got out of the printing game, in fact, after serving time in jail in Texas. He and Darrow once worked a coney game together in El Paso. Darrow got word that Drennan had relocated in San Francisco, approached him with his scheme, and talked him off the straight-and-narrow. Podewell was their helper and bill-passer—"

Quincannon interrupted Boggs' explanation by sneezing loudly. So loudly that conversations also ceased among the other diners—this was Coppa's Restaurant in the Montgomery Block, one of the city's tonier eateries—and a number of heads turned to stare at him. He paid no attention. He took out his handkerchief, blew his nose with a noise like a honking mallard.

Sabina asked, "John, do you feel all right?"

"As well as I've felt in four miserable days."

"Perhaps you should've spent another day in bed. That cold of yours seems to be lingering. If you're not careful it could turn into the grippe."

"I refuse to be an invalid. Besides, I've recovered my appetite. Where's our blasted food?"

Their blasted food was on the way to the table. When the waiter had distributed the steaming dishes and departed, Boggs said, "Well, to finish what I was saying, all the principals in the coney game are now behind bars. Neither of you will ever have to worry about Long Nick Darrow again. He'll get at least twenty years at hard labor, this time."

"All well and good," Quincannon said around a mouthful of Coppa's specialty, Chicken Pórtola, "but little enough satisfaction for me in the whole sorry business."

Boggs frowned. "Little enough satisfaction? Your life's no longer in jeopardy—isn't that enough?"

"Not as I see it. There's plenty of satisfaction for you, Mr. Boggs. A coney operation has been broken before much damage could be done and your superiors in Washington are singing your praises."

"I've given *you* full credit for capturing Darrow and confiscating his plates. The glory is yours, not mine."

"Glory. Bah. I was nearly killed three times Friday night, as well as drenched in beer and deprived of my favorite suit and Chesterfield, and then forced to spend three full days in bed with chills and fever. And what do I have to show for these indignities? Nothing."

"Show for them? I don't understand what you mean."

"He means," Sabina said, "that he wasn't and won't be paid a fee."

"That's right, not a red cent." Quincannon sneezed again. "I've no objection to being shot at or having my clothing and my health damaged, in exchange for a proper fee. But in this case I can't collect from you, Mr. Boggs, or from the government, or from Long Nick Darrow. The worst possible client a poor suffering detective can have is himself!"

THE DESERT LIMITED

Across the aisle and five seats ahead of where Quincannon and Sabina were sitting, Evan Gaunt sat looking out through the day coach's dusty window. There was little enough to see outside the fast-moving Desert Limited except sun-blasted wasteland, but Gaunt seemed to find the emptiness absorbing. He also seemed perfectly comfortable, his expression one of tolerable boredom: a prosperous businessman, for all outward appearances, without a care or worry, much less a past history that included grand larceny, murder, and fugitive warrants in three western states.

"Hell and damn," Quincannon muttered. "He's been lounging there nice as you please for nearly forty minutes. What the devil is he planning?"

Sabina said, "He may not be planning anything, John."

"Faugh. He's trapped on this iron horse and he knows it."

"He does if he recognized you, too. You're positive he did?"

"I am, and no mistake. He caught me by surprise while I was talking to the conductor; I couldn't turn away in time."

"Still, you said it was eight years ago that you had your only run-in with him. And at that you saw each other for less than two hours."

"He's changed little enough and so have I. A hard case like Gaunt never forgets a lawman's face, any more than I do a felon's. It's one of the reasons he's managed to evade capture as long as he has."

"Well, what *can* he be planning?" Sabina said. She was leaning close, her mouth only a few inches from Quincannon's ear, so their voices wouldn't carry to nearby passengers. Ordinarily the nearness of her fine body and the warmth of her breath on his skin would have been a powerful distraction; such intimacy was all too seldom permitted. But the combination of desert heat, the noisy coach, and Evan Gaunt made him only peripherally aware of her charms. "There are no stops between Needles and Barstow; Gaunt must know that. And if he tries to jump for it while we're traveling at this speed, his chances of survival are slim to none. The only sensible thing he can do is to wait until we slow for Barstow and then jump and run."

"Is it? He can't hope to escape that way. Barstow is too small and the surroundings too open. He saw me talking to Mr. Bridges; it's likely he also saw the Needles station agent running for his office. If so, it's plain to him that a wire has been sent to Barstow and the sheriff and a compliment of deputies will be waiting. I was afraid he'd hopped back off then and there . . . those few minutes I lost track of him shortly afterward . . . but it would've been a foolish move and he isn't the sort to panic. Even if he'd gotten clear of the train and the Needles yards, there are too many soldiers and Indian trackers at Fort Mojave."

"I don't see that Barstow is a much better choice for him. Unless . . ."

"Unless what?"

"Is he the kind to take a hostage?"

Quincannon shifted position on his seat. Even though this was October, usually one of the cooler months in the Mojave Desert, it was near-stifling in the coach; sweat oiled his skin, trickled through the brush of his freebooter's beard. Crowded, too, with nearly every seat occupied in this car and the other coaches. He noted again, as he had earlier, that at least a third of the passengers here were women and children.

He said slowly, "I wouldn't put anything past Evan Gaunt. He might take a hostage, if he believed it was his only hope of freedom. But it's more likely that he'll try some sort of trick first. Tricks are the man's stock-in-trade."

"Does Mr. Bridges know how potentially dangerous he is?"

"There wasn't time to discuss Gaunt or his past in detail. If I'd had my way, the train would've been held in Needles and Gaunt arrested there. Bridges might've agreed to that if the Needles sheriff hadn't been away in Yuma and only a part-time deputy left in charge. When the station agent told him the deputy is an unreliable drunkard, and that it would take more than an hour to summon soldiers from the fort, Bridges balked. He's more concerned about railroad timetables than he is about the capture of a fugitive."

Sabina said, "Here he comes again. Mr. Bridges. From the look of him, I'd say he's very much concerned about Gaunt."

"It's his own blasted fault."

The conductor was a spare, sallow-faced man in his forties who wore his uniform and cap as if they were badges of honor. The brass buttons shone, as did the heavy gold watch chain and its polished elk's-tooth fob; his tie was tightly knotted and his vest buttoned in spite of the heat. He glanced nervously at Evan Gaunt as he passed, and then mournfully and a little accusingly at Quincannon, as if he and not Gaunt was to blame for this dilemma. Bridges was not a man who dealt well with either a crisis or the disruption of his precise routine.

When he'd left the car again Sabina said, "You and I *could* arrest Gaunt ourselves, John. Catch him by surprise, get the drop on him . . ."

"He won't be caught by surprise, not now that he knows we're onto him. You can be sure he has a weapon close to hand and won't hesitate to use it. Bracing him in these surroundings would be risking harm to an innocent bystander."

"Then what do you suggest we do?"

"Nothing, for the present, except to keep a sharp eye on him. And be ready to act when he does."

Quincannon dried forehead and beard with his handkerchief, wishing this were one of Southern Pacific's luxury trains—the Golden State Limited, for instance, on the San Francisco-Chicago run. The Golden State was ventilated by a new process which renewed the air inside several times every hour, instead of having it circulated only slightly and cooled not at all by sluggish fans. It was also brightly lighted by electricity generated from the axles of moving cars, instead of murkily lit by oil lamps; and its seats and berths were more comfortable, its food better by half than the fare served on this southwestern desert run.

He said rhetorically, "Where did Gaunt disappear to after he spied me with Bridges? He gave me the slip on purpose, I'm sure of it. Whatever he's scheming, that's part of the game."

"It was no more than fifteen minutes before he showed up here and took his seat."

"Fifteen minutes is plenty of time for mischief. He has more gall than a roomful of senators." Quincannon consulted his turnip watch; it was nearly two o'clock. "Four, is it, that we're due in Barstow?"

"Four-oh-five."

"More than two hours. Damnation!"

"Try not to fret, John. Remember your blood pressure."

Another ten minutes crept away. Sabina sat quietly, repairing one of the grosgrain ribbons that had come undone on her traveling hat. Quincannon fidgeted, not remembering his blood pressure, barely noticing the way light caught Sabina's dark auburn hair and made it shine like burnished copper. And still Evan Gaunt peered out at the unchanging panorama of sagebrush, greasewood, and barren, tawny hills.

No sweat or sign of worry on *his* face, Quincannon thought with rising irritation. A bland and unmemorable countenance it was, too, to the point where Gaunt would all but become invisible in a crowd of more noteworthy men. He was thirty-five, of average height, lean and wiry; and although he had grown a thin mustache and sideburns since their previous encounter, the facial hair did little to individualize him. His lightweight sack suit and derby hat were likewise undistinguished. A human chameleon, by Godfrey. That was another reason Gaunt had avoided the law for so long.

There was no telling what had brought him to Needles, a settlement on the Colorado River, or where he was headed from there. Evan Gaunt seldom remained in one place for any length of time—a predator constantly on the prowl for any illegal enterprise that required his particular brand of guile. Extortion, confidence swindles, counterfeiting, bank robbery . . . Gaunt had done them all and more, and served not a day in prison for his transgressions. The closest he'd come was that day eight years ago when Quincannon, still affiliated with the U.S. Secret Service, had led a raid on the headquarters of a Los Angeles-based counterfeiting ring. Gaunt was one of the koniakers taken prisoner after a brief skirmish and personally questioned by Quincannon. Later, while being taken to jail by local authorities, Gaunt had wounded a deputy and made a daring escape in a stolen milk wagon—an act that had fixed the man firmly in Quincannon's memory.

When he'd spied Gaunt on the station platform in Needles, it had been a much-needed uplift to his spirits: he'd been feeling less than pleased with his current lot. He and Sabina had spent a week in Tombstone investigating a bogus mining operation, and the case hadn't turned out as well as they'd hoped. And after more than twenty-four hours on the Desert Limited, they were still two long days from San Francisco. Even in the company of a beautiful woman, train travel was monotonous—unless, of course, you were sequestered with her in the privacy of a drawing room. But there were no drawing rooms to be had on the Desert Limited, and even if there were, he couldn't have had Sabina in one. Not on a train, not in their Tombstone hotel, not in San Francisco—not anywhere, it seemed, past, present or future. Unrequited desire was a maddening thing, especially when you were in such close proximity to the object of your desire. His passion for his partner was exceeded only by his passion for profitable detective work; Carpenter and Quincannon, Lovers, as an adjunct to Carpenter and Quincannon, Professional Detective Services, would have made him a truly happy man.

Evan Gaunt had taken his mind off of that subject by offering a prize almost as inviting. Not only were there fugitive warrants on Gaunt, but two rewards totaling five thousand dollars. See to it that he was taken into custody and the reward money would belong to Carpenter and Quincannon. Simple enough task, on the surface; most of the proper things had been done in Needles and it seemed that Gaunt was indeed trapped on this clattering, swaying iron horse. And yet the man's audacity, combined with those blasted fifteen minutes—

Quincannon tensed. Gaunt had turned away from the window, was getting slowly to his feet. He yawned, stretched, and then stepped into the aisle; in his right hand was the carpetbag he'd carried on board in Needles. Without hurry, and without so much as an eyeflick in their direction, he sauntered past where Quincannon and Sabina were sitting and opened the rear door.

Close to Sabina's ear Quincannon murmured, "I'll shadow him. You wait here." He adjusted the Navy Colt he wore holstered under his coat before he slipped out into the aisle.

The next car back was the second-class Pullman. Gaunt went through it, through the first-class Pullman, through the dining car and the observation lounge into the smoker. Quincannon paused outside the smoker door; through the glass he watched Gaunt sit down, produce a cigar from his coat pocket, and snip off the end with a pair of gold cutters. Settling in here, evidently, as he'd settled into the day coach. Damn the man's coolness! He entered as Gaunt was applying a lucifer's flame to the cigar end. Both pretended the other didn't exist.

In a seat halfway back Quincannon fiddled with pipe and shag-cut tobacco, listening to the steady, throbbing rhythm of steel on steel, while Gaunt smoked his cigar with obvious pleasure. The process took more than ten minutes, at the end of which time the fugitive got leisurely to his feet and started forward again. A return to his seat in the coach? No, not yet. Instead he entered the gentlemen's lavatory and closed himself inside.

Quincannon stayed where he was, waiting, his eye on the lavatory door. His pipe went out; he relighted it. Two more men, a rough-garbed miner and a gaudily outfitted drummer, came into the smoker. Couplings banged and the car lurched slightly as its wheels passed over a rough section of track. Outside the windows a lake shimmered into view on the southern desert flats, then abruptly vanished: heat mirage.

The door to the lavatory remained closed.

A prickly sensation that had nothing to do with the heat formed between Quincannon's shoulder blades. How long had Gaunt been in there? Close to ten minutes. He tamped the dottle from his pipe, stowed the briar in the pocket of his cheviot. The flashily dressed drummer left the car; a fat man with muttonchop whiskers like miniature tumbleweeds came in. The fat man paused, glancing around, then turned to the lavatory door and tried the latch. When he found it locked he rapped on the panel. There was no response.

Quincannon was on his feet by then, with the prickly sensation as hot as a fire-rash. He prodded the fat man aside, ignoring the indignant oath this brought him, and laid an ear against the panel. All he could hear were train sounds: the pound of beating trucks on the fish-plates, the creak and groan of axle play and the whisper of the wheels. He banged on the panel with his fist, much harder than the fat man had. Once, twice, three times. This likewise produced no response.

"Hell and damn!" he growled aloud, startling the fat man, who turned quickly for the door and almost collided with another man just stepping through. The newcomer, fortuitously enough, was Mr. Bridges.

When the conductor saw Quincannon's scowl, his back stiffened and alarm pinched his sallow features. "What is it?" he demanded. "What's happened?"

"Evan Gaunt went in here some time ago and he hasn't come out."

"You don't think he—?"

"Use your master key and we'll soon find out."

Bridges unlocked the door. Quincannon pushed in first, his hand on the butt of his Navy Colt—and immediately blistered the air with a five-jointed oath.

The cubicle was empty.

"Gone, by all the saints!" Bridges said behind him. "The damned fool went through the window and jumped."

The lone window was small, designed for ventilation, but not too small for a man Gaunt's size to wiggle through. It was shut but not latched; Quincannon hoisted the sash, poked his head out. Hot, dust-laden wind made him pull it back in again after a few seconds.

"Gone, yes," he said, "but I'll eat my hat if he jumped at the rate of speed we've been traveling."

"But . . . but he must have. The only other place he could've gone—"

"Up atop the car. That's where he did go."

Bridges didn't want to believe it. His thinking was plain: If Gaunt had jumped, he was rid of the threat to his and his passengers' security. He said, "A climb like that is just as dangerous as jumping."

"Not for a nimble and desperate man."

"He couldn't hide up there. Nor on top of any of the other cars. Do you think he crawled along the roofs and then climbed back down between cars?"

"It's the likeliest explanation."

"Why would he do such a thing? There's nowhere for him to hide *inside*, either. The only possible places are too easily searched. He must know that, if he's ridden a train before . . ."

"We'll search them anyway," Quincannon said darkly. "Every nook and cranny from locomotive to caboose, if necessary. Evan Gaunt is still on the Desert Limited, Mr. Bridges, and we're damned well going to find him."

♦ ♦ ♦

The first place they went was out onto the platform between the lounge car and the smoker, where Quincannon climbed the iron ladder attached to the smoker's rear wall. From its top he could look along the roofs of the cars, protecting his eyes with an upraised arm: the coal-flavored smoke that rolled back from the locomotive's stack was peppered with hot cinders. As expected, he saw no sign of Gaunt. Except, that was, for marks in the thin layers of grit that coated the tops of both lounge car and smoker.

"There's no doubt now that he climbed up," he said when he rejoined Bridges. "The marks in the grit are fresh."

The conductor's answering nod was reluctant and pained.

Quincannon used his handkerchief on his sweating face. It came away stained from the dirt and coal smoke, and when he saw the streaks his mouth stretched in a thin smile. "Another fact: No matter how long Gaunt was above or how far he crawled, he had to be filthy when he came down. Someone may have seen him. And he won't have wandered far in that condition. Either he's hiding where he lighted, or he took the time to wash up and change clothes for some reason."

"I still say it makes no sense. Not a lick of sense."

"It does to him. And it will to us when we find him."

They went to the rear of the train and began to work their way forward,

Bridges alerting members of the crew and Quincannon asking questions of selected passengers. No one had seen Gaunt. By the time they reached the first-class Pullman, the urgency and frustration both men felt were taking a toll: preoccupied, Quincannon nearly bowled over a pudgy, bonneted matron outside the women's lavatory and Bridges snapped at a white-maned, senatorial gent who objected to having his drawing room searched. It took them ten minutes to comb the compartments there and the berths in the second-class Pullman: another exercise in futility.

In the first of the day coaches, Quincannon beckoned Sabina to join them and quickly explained what had happened. She took the news stoically; unlike him, she met any crisis with a shield of calm. She said only, "He may be full of tricks, but he can't make himself invisible. Hiding is one thing; getting off this train is another. We'll find him."

"He won't be in the other two coaches. That leaves the baggage car, the tender, and the locomotive; he has to be in one of them."

"Shall I go with you and Mr. Bridges?"

"I've another idea. You have your derringer with you or packed away in your grip?"

"In here." She patted her reticule.

"Backtrack on us, then; we may have somehow overlooked him. But don't take a moment's chance if he turns up."

"I won't," she said. "And I'll warn you the same."

♦ ♦ ♦

The baggage master's office was empty. Beyond, the door to the baggage car stood open a few inches.

Scowling, Bridges stepped up to the door. "Dan?" he called. "You in there?"

No answer.

Quincannon drew his revolver, shouldered Bridges aside, and widened the opening. The oil lamps were lighted; most of the interior was visible. Boxes, crates, stacks of luggage and express parcels . . . but no sign of human habitation.

"What do you see, Mr. Quincannon?"

"Nothing. No one."

"Oh, Lordy, I don't like this, none of this. Where's Dan? He's almost always here, and he never leaves the door open or unlocked when he isn't.

Gaunt? Is he responsible for this? Oh, Lordy, I should've listened to you and held the train in Needles . . ."

Quincannon shut his ears to the conductor's babbling. He eased his body through the doorway, into an immediate crouch behind a packing crate. Peering out, he saw no evidence of disturbance. Three large crates and a pair of trunks were belted in place along the near wall. Against the far wall stood a wheeled luggage cart piled with carpetbags, grips, warbags. More luggage rested in neat rows nearby; he recognized one of the larger grips, pale blue and floral-patterned, as Sabina's. None of it appeared to have been moved except by the natural motion of the train.

Toward the front was a shadowed area into which he couldn't see clearly. He straightened, eased around and alongside the crate with his Navy at the ready. No sounds, no movement . . . until a brief lurch and shudder as the locomotive nosed into an uphill curve and the engineer used his air. Then something slid into view in the shadowy corner.

A leg. A man's leg, bent and twisted.

Quincannon muttered an oath and closed the gap by another half-dozen paces. He could see the rest of the man's body then—a sixtyish gent in a trainman's uniform, lying crumpled, his cap off and a dark blotch staining his gray hair. Quincannon went to one knee beside him, found a thin wrist and pressed it for a pulse. The beat was there, faint and irregular.

"Mr. Bridges! Be quick!"

The conductor came running inside. When he saw the unconscious crewman he jerked to a halt; a moaning sound vibrated in his throat. "My God, Old Dan! Is he—?"

"No. Wounded but still alive."

"Shot?"

"Struck with something heavy. A gun butt, like as not."

"Gaunt, damn his eyes."

"He was after something in here. Take a quick look around, Mr. Bridges. Tell me if you notice anything missing or out of place."

"What about Dan? One of the drawing-room passengers is a doctor . . ."

"Fetch him. But look here first."

Bridges took a quick turn through the car. "Nothing missing or misplaced, as far as I can tell. Dan's the only one who'll know for sure."

"Are you carrying weapons of any kind? Boxed rifles, handguns? Or dynamite or black powder?"

"No, no, nothing like that."

When Bridges had gone for the doctor Quincannon pillowed the baggage master's head on one of the smaller bags. He touched a ribbon of blood on the man's cheek, found it nearly dry. The assault hadn't taken place within the past hour, after Gaunt's disappearance from the lavatory. It had happened earlier, during his fifteen-minute absence outside Needles—the very first thing he'd done, evidently, after recognizing Quincannon.

That made the breaching of the baggage car a major part of his escape plan. But what could the purpose be, if nothing here was missing or disturbed?

♦ ♦ ♦

The doctor was young, brusque, and efficient. Quincannon and Bridges left Old Dan in his care and hurried forward. Gaunt wasn't hiding in the tender; and neither the taciturn engineer nor the sweat-soaked fireman had been bothered by anyone or seen anyone since Needles.

That took care of the entire train, front to back. And where the bloody hell was Evan Gaunt?

Quincannon was beside himself as he led the way back down-train. As he and Bridges passed through the forward day coach, the locomotive's whistle sounded a series of short toots.

"Oh, Lordy," the conductor said. "That's the first signal for Barstow."

"How long before we slow for the yards?"

"Ten minutes."

"Hell and damn!"

They found Sabina waiting at the rear of the second coach. She shook her head as they approached: her backtracking had also proven fruitless.

The three of them held a huddled conference. Quincannon's latest piece of bad news put ridges in the smoothness of Sabina's forehead, her only outward reaction. "You're certain nothing was taken from the baggage car, Mr. Bridges?"

"Not absolutely, no. Every item in the car would have to be examined and then checked against the baggage manifest."

"If Gaunt did steal something," Quincannon said, "he was some careful not to call attention to the fact, in case the baggage master regained consciousness or was found before he could make good his escape."

"Which could mean," Sabina said, "that whatever it was would've been apparent to us at a cursory search."

"Either that, or where it was taken from would've been apparent."

Something seemed to be nibbling at her mind; her expression had turned speculative. "I wonder . . ."

"What do you wonder?"

The locomotive's whistle sounded again. There was a rocking and the loud thump of couplings as the engineer began the first slackening of their speed. Bridges said, "Five minutes to Barstow. If Gaunt is still on board—"

"He is."

"—do you think he'll try to get off here?"

"No doubt of it. Wherever he's hiding, he can't hope to avoid being found in a concentrated search. And he knows we'll mount one in Barstow, with the entire train crew and the authorities."

"What do you advise we do?"

"First, tell your porters not to allow anyone off at the station until you give the signal. And when passengers do disembark, they're to do so single-file from one exit only. That will prevent Gaunt from slipping off in a crowd."

"The exit between this car and the next behind?"

"Good. Meet me there when you're done."

Bridges hurried away.

Quincannon asked Sabina, "Will you wait with me or take another pass through the cars?"

"Neither," she said. "I noticed something earlier that I thought must be a coincidence. Now I'm not so sure it is."

"Explain that."

"There's no time now. You'll be the first to know if I'm right."

"Sabina . . ." But she had already turned her back and was purposefully heading forward.

He took himself out onto the platform between the coaches. The Limited had slowed to half speed; once more its whistle cut shrilly through the hot desert stillness. He stood holding onto the handbar on the station side, leaning out to where he could look both ways along the cars—a precaution in the event Gaunt tried to jump and run in the yards. But he was thinking that this was another exercise in futility. Gaunt's scheme was surely too clever for such a predictable ending.

Bridges reappeared and stood watch on the offside as the Limited entered the railyards. On Quincannon's side the dun-colored buildings of Barstow swam into view ahead. Thirty years ago, at the close of the Civil War, the town —one of the last stops on the old Mormon Trail between Salt Lake City and San Bernardino—had been a teeming, brawling shipping point for supplies to and high-grade silver ore from the mines in Calico and other camps in the nearby hills. Now, with Calico a near-ghost town and most of the mines shut down, Barstow was a far tamer and less populated settlement. In its lawless days, Evan Gaunt could have found immediate aid and comfort for a price, and for another price, safe passage out of town and state; in the new Barstow he stood little enough chance—and none at all unless he was somehow able to get clear of the Desert Limited and into a hidey hole.

A diversion of some sort? That was one possible gambit. Quincannon warned himself to remain alert for anything, anything at all, out of the ordinary.

Sabina was on his mind too. Where the devil had she gone in such a hurry? What sort of coincidence—

Brake shoes squealed on the sun-heated rails as the Limited neared the station platform. Less than a score of men and women waited in the shade of a roof overhang; the knot of four solemn-faced gents standing apart at the near end was bound to be Sheriff Hoover and his deputies.

Quincannon swivelled his head again. Steam and smoke hazed the air, but he could see clearly enough: No one was making an effort to leave the train on this side. Nor on the offside, else Bridges would have cut loose with a shout.

The engineer slid the cars to a rattling stop alongside the platform. Quincannon jumped down with Bridges close behind him, as the four lawmen ran over through a cloud of steam to meet them. Sheriff Hoover was burly and sported a tobacco-stained mustache; on the lapel of his dusty frock coat was a five-pointed star, and in the holster at his belt was a heavy Colt Dragoon. His three deputies were also well-armed.

"Well, Mr. Bridges," the sheriff said. "Where's this man Evan Gaunt? Point him out and we'll have him in irons before he can blink twice."

Bridges said dolefully, "We don't have any idea where he is."

"You don't— What's this? You mean to say he jumped somewhere along the line?"

"I don't know what to think. Mr. Quincannon believes he's still on board, hiding."

"Does he now." Hoover turned to Quincannon, gave him a quick appraisal. "So you're the flycop, eh? Well, sir? Explain."

Quincannon explained, tersely, with one eye on the sheriff and the other on the rolling stock. Through the grit-streaked windows he could see passengers lining up for departure; Sabina, he was relieved to note, was one of them. A porter stood between the second and third day coaches, waiting for the signal from Bridges to put down the steps.

"Damn strange," Hoover said at the end of Quincannon's recital. "You say you searched everywhere, every possible hiding place. If that's so, how could Gaunt still be on board?"

"I can't say yet. But he is—I'll stake my reputation on it."

"Well, then, we'll find him. Mr. Bridges, disembark your passengers. All of 'em, not just those for Barstow."

"Just as you say, sheriff."

Bridges signaled to the porter, who swung the steps down and permitted the exodus to begin. One of the first passengers to alight was Sabina. She came straight to where Quincannon stood, took hold of his arm and drew him a few paces aside. Her manner was urgent, her eyes bright with triumph.

"John," she said, "I found him."

He had long ago ceased to be surprised at anything Sabina said or did. He asked, "Where? How?"

She shook her head. "He'll be getting off any second."

"Getting off? How could he—?"

"There he is!"

Quincannon squinted at the passengers who were just then disembarking: two women, one of whom had a small boy in tow. "Where? I don't see him—"

Sabina was moving again. Quincannon trailed after her, his hand on the Navy Colt inside his coat. The two women and the child were making their way past Sheriff Hoover and his deputies, none of whom was paying any attention to them. The woman towing the little boy was young and pretty, with tightly curled blond hair; the other woman, older and pudgy, powdered and rouged, wore a gray serge traveling dress and a close-fitting Langtry bonnet that covered most of her head and shadowed her face. She was the one, Quincannon realized, that he'd nearly bowled over outside the women's lavatory in the first-class Pullman.

She was also Evan Gaunt.

He found that out five seconds later, when Sabina boldly walked up and tore the bonnet off, revealing the short-haired male head and clean-shaven face hidden beneath. Her actions so surprised Gaunt that he had no time to do anything but swipe at her with one arm, a blow that she nimbly dodged. Then he fumbled inside the reticule he carried, drew out a small-caliber pistol; at the same time he commenced to run.

Sabina shouted, Quincannon shouted, someone else let out a thin scream; there was a small scrambling panic on the platform. But it lasted no more than a few seconds, and without a shot being fired. Gaunt was poorly schooled in the mechanics of running while garbed in woman's clothing: the traveling dress's long skirt tripped him before he reached the station office. He went down in a tangle of arms, legs, petticoats, and assorted other garments that he had wadded up and tied around his torso to create the illusion of pudginess. He still clutched the pistol when Quincannon reached him, but one well-placed kick and it went flying. Quincannon then dropped down on Gaunt's chest with both knees, driving the wind out of him in a grunting hiss. Another well-placed blow, this one to the jaw with Quincannon's meaty fist, put an end to the skirmish.

Sheriff Hoover, his deputies, Mr. Bridges, and the Limited's passengers stood gawping down at the now half-disguised and unconscious fugitive. Hoover was the first to speak. He said in tones of utter amazement, "Well, I'll be damned."

Which were Quincannon's sentiments exactly.

♦ ♦ ♦

"So that's why he assaulted Old Dan in the baggage car," Bridges said a short while later. Evan Gaunt had been carted off in steel bracelets to the Barstow jail, and Sabina, Quincannon, Hoover, and the conductor were grouped together in the station office for final words before the Desert Limited continued on its way. "He was after a change of woman's clothing."

Sabina nodded. "He devised his plan as soon as he recognized John and realized his predicament. A quick thinker, our Mr. Gaunt."

"The stolen clothing was hidden inside the carpetbag he carried into the lavatory?"

"It was. He climbed out the window and over the tops of the smoker and the lounge car to the first-class Pullman, waited until the women's lavatory was empty, climbed down through that window, locked the door, washed and shaved off his mustache and sideburns, dressed in the stolen clothing, put on rouge and powder that he'd also pilfered, and then disposed of his own clothes and carpetbag through the lavatory window."

"And when he came out to take a seat in the forward day coach," Quincannon said ruefully, "I nearly knocked him down. If only I had. It would've saved us all considerable difficulty."

Hoover said, "Don't chastise yourself, Mr. Quincannon. You had no way of suspecting Gaunt had disguised himself as a woman."

"That's not quite true," Sabina said. "Actually, John did have a way of knowing—the same way I discovered the masquerade, though at first notice I considered it a coincidence. Through simple familiarity."

"Familiarity with what?" Quincannon asked.

"John, you're one of the best detectives I've ever known, but honestly, there are times when you're also one of the most unobservant. Tell me, what did I wear on the trip out to Arizona? What color and style of outfit? What type of hat?"

"I don't see what that has to do with—" Then, as the light dawned, he said in a smaller voice, "Oh."

"That's right," Sabina said, smiling. "Mr. Gaunt plundered the wrong woman's grip in the baggage car. The gray serge traveling dress and Langtry bonnet he was wearing are mine."

THE HORSESHOE NAIL

The High Sierra sawmill camp was spread out on a flat along the Truckee River south of Verdi, just across the Nevada state line. It was larger than Quincannon had expected: several barns and corrals, storehouse, cookhouse, a pair of bunkhouses, blacksmith's shop, lumberyard, string of rough-log cabins for the foreman and crew bosses, and the huge steam-powered mill built back into the mouth of a canyon rimmed by high volcanic cliffs. A railroad spur cut through the camp, as did a pair of rutted wagon roads, one from Verdi that followed the rail line and the other connecting the sawmill with its logging camp higher up in the mountains.

The place was a swarm of activity: teamsters, swampers, and handlers working with horses and oxen, freighters shunting mule-drawn wagons laden with supplies, men working with long pike-poles on the logs that clogged the pond alongside the mill, men stacking and cutting and loading rail cars with lumber and cordwood. The air rang and hummed with the steady metallic whine of the circular saws. The mill cut better than thirty thousand feet of lumber each day in peak season—and there was a rush on now, as autumn lengthened, to maintain a high production pace before the snows came and shut down operations for the winter.

There was no taste yet of snow in the air; the woods scent mixed with the sharp tang of fresh-cut logs was almost summery. The sun lay warm on Quincannon's face as the bullwhacker beside him drove the big Studebaker freight wagon down the Verdi road into camp. It was a fine day to be in the mountains, he thought. An early frost had colored the leaves of the cottonwoods fringing the river, and far up on the mountainside he could see patches of shimmering gold where quaking aspens grew among the pine. Fall days like this one reminded him of his youth. And of the season he had spent working in a sawmill camp in the Oregon woods. That season would make the job that had brought him here easier; once he took his bearings, he would neither look nor feel out of place.

He glanced down at the rough timber-cruiser's outfit he wore. With his thick freebooter's beard, he even *looked* like a lumberman. A smile bent the corners of his mouth. Ah, if Sabina could see him now, a fine Bunyanesque figure of a man, steely-eyed, with the mountain wilderness all around him and the hot blood raging in his veins . . . would she finally weaken, find herself overcome with uncontrollable passion? She wouldn't succumb to wit, sophistication, or clever subtleties; perhaps raw earthiness was the secret route to her heart and her bed. He would have to find out when he returned to San Francisco, riding yet another triumph as the mighty Bunyan rode Babe the Blue Ox . . .

The bullwhacker brought his mules to a stop at the rear of the cookshack. Two men waited there, a long-queued Chinese cook in a white apron and a shaggy-bearded beanpole of about fifty dressed in congress shoes and a pair of high-topped pants. The cook's interest was in the wagonload of stores; the beanpole's was in Quincannon. He approached as Quincannon swung down, warbag in hand, and looked him over with a blearily critical eye.

"You the new cheater?" he demanded in a rusty-file voice.

"Cheater?" Quincannon's memory jogged. "Timekeeper and scaler—that's right. But only an assistant and only temporary."

"How temporary?"

"No more than a week. I won't be needed past then."

"Too bad for you. This here's a highball camp, best in the Sierras. I ought to know. What's your name?"

"John Quincannon."

"Scot, eh? I got nothing against Scots." He scratched at a scrawny neck as wrinkled as an old pair of logger's tin pants. His own trousers were stiff with dirt and held up by the most enormous galluses Quincannon had ever seen. Oddments such as twists of baling wire decorated the galluses; a miscellany of hand tools hung from a belt around his waist. "Mine's Ned Coombs. Nevada Ned, they call me. I'm the bullcook here—best damn bullcook in this or any other camp. What do you say to that?"

Quincannon shrugged. A bullcook was a camp chore boy, usually a super-annuated logger and often enough a souse suffering from locomotor ataxia. Despite the name, a bullcook had nothing to do with the preparation of food; his workday consisted of sweeping out the bunkhouses, cutting and bringing in fuel, washing lamps, and the like. "If you say you're the best, I'll take your word for it."

"Damn well better," Nevada Ned said. "You got any drinkin' likker in your kick?"

"No."

"No? How come?"

"I don't use it."

"Hell you say. A cheater that don't use likker." He spat on the ground at Quincannon's feet and then produced a four-ounce bottle from a pants pocket, yanked out the cork, and took a long draught. After which he made a face and said, "Jakey. Can't afford better, and now I'm almost out. Sure you ain't got any good likker?"

"I'm sure. Where do I find Jack Phillips?"

"Camp office." Nevada Ned had lost interest in him. "Ask anybody," he said and turned his back and disappeared around the corner of the cookshack.

Quincannon found his way to the camp office, a cottonwood-shaded building near the lumberyard. Jack Phillips, High Sierra's foreman, turned out to be a burly gent in his late thirties, with a black beard almost as thick and piratical as Quincannon's. An unlit corncob pipe jutted at an authoritative angle from the midst of all the facial brush. When they were alone in the foreman's private cubicle, Quincannon presented him with the letter of introduction he'd been given in Sacramento. Phillips scowled as he read it, and when he was finished he slapped it down on his desk and transferred the scowl to his visitor.

"How is it a flycop has such pull with Cap Fuller?" he asked. Cap Fuller was the head of the High Sierra Logging Company and Phillip's boss.

"I don't know Mr. Fuller," Quincannon said. "It so happens he's a friend of Senator Johannsen, and the senator—"

"—is a friend of yours."

"Satisfied former client would be more accurate."

Phillips grunted. "Well, I'll cooperate because I've been ordered to. But I don't mind telling you, I don't like it."

"Why is that, Mr. Phillips?"

"Flycop sneaking around my camp, pretending to be somebody he's not, putting the arm on one of my men—it's bad for morale."

"If all goes according to plan, no one but you and me and Mr. Fuller need ever know about it."

Another grunt. "Besides, Guy DuBois is my best sawyer. I hate like hell to lose him this late in the season."

"He's also a thief."

"You sure about that? No doubt he's the one stole that woman's jewelry?"

"None," Quincannon said.

"Rich San Francisco widow taking up with a French Canadian logger—don't make much sense to me."

"DuBois's sister was one of Ida Bennett's maids. Mrs. Bennett was the one who sent the wire notifying him when the sister died unexpectedly two weeks ago. She met him at the funeral, felt sorry for him, and invited him to her home for dinner. Matters evidently progressed rapidly from that point."

"Talked her out of her drawers, eh?"

"Not that she admitted, but I suspect so. It wasn't until after DuBois left the city that she discovered the three valuable items of jewelry were missing."

"A brooch, a pendant, and a ring worth fifty thousand dollars?"

"Diamonds, rubies, and platinum gold, Mr. Phillips."

"Well, what makes you think he brought them back here with him?"

"A strong hunch backed by facts. I traced his movements from San Francisco; he went straight to Sacramento and straight from there to Verdi."

"Could've stashed the loot somewhere along the way, couldn't he?"

"He could, but where? He's a timber beast—no permanent home, no relatives now that his sister has passed on, no safe deposit box that I've been able to locate. I like the odds that the booty is still in his possession."

"Why in hell would he do such a fool thing as to come back and resume his work as a sawyer, if he has fifty thousand in jewelry in his kick? If it were me, I'd've kept right on traveling east."

Quincannon said, "My guess is that his motive is a fool's mix of cleverness and uncertainty. The widow Bennett knows he was working here; he might believe it's the last place anyone would look for him. And because he's not a professional thief, it's likely he hasn't a clear idea of how to dispose of the swag. By continuing at his job until the camp shuts down he can finance a winter search for a fenceman, one who'll give him top dollar."

"All well and good," Phillips said, "but I still don't see why you can't just arrest him now instead of skulking around on the sly first."

"The safe return of the jewelry is Mrs. Bennett's paramount concern," Quincannon explained. "Punishment for DuBois is secondary."

"So? If he has the goods with him, he'd tell you where they are or you'd find them on your own."

"Not necessarily. He may have found a clever hiding place in all this wilderness that will elude my searches. And thieves in his position, once caught, sometimes develop the sly notion of remaining silent so they can return for the swag when they get out of prison."

"Beat the hiding place out of him, then. That's what I'd do."

"A last resort, Mr. Phillips. I prefer to use my wiles rather than my fists." Particularly with a client as rich as Mrs. Ida Bennett, who was paying Carpenter and Quincannon, Professional Detective Services, a handsome daily retainer.

"No more than a week of you and your wiles?"

"No more than that, and with any luck, considerably less. If I haven't recovered the jewelry by this time next week, I'll arrest DuBois—quietly, of course—and adopt the persuasive approach."

"Well, I still don't like it, but since I don't have a vote in the matter . . ." Phillips lit his corncob with a sulphurous lucifer and puffed up a cloud of acrid smoke. "Where do you want to be quartered, bunkhouse or private cabin?"

"Where does DuBois hang his hat?"

"He has a cabin."

"I'd prefer one near his, then, if that can be arranged."

"It can. Anything else?"

"Names of his friends, and something about his habits."

"He has no friends. DuBois isn't well liked—he's a loner and owns a surly disposition, the more so when he's been drinking. We don't permit the public consumption of alcohol, and drunkenness is grounds for dismissal, but some of the men . . ." Phillips shrugged. "Sawmill camps are rough-and-tumble places. As I assume you know, since Cap Fuller's letter says you're familiar with the business."

Quincannon nodded. "Is drinking DuBois's only vice?"

"No. Stud poker's another."

"Ah. Does he play with a core group?"

"Ben Irons, his setter at the mill. Okay King, the blacksmith. Hank Ransome, one of the teamsters. No one else on a regular basis."

"How often?"

"Most nights for a few hours after supper."

"His cabin?"

"No. Usually Okay King's."

"Good," Quincannon said, smiling. "Very good."

"If you say so." The foreman squinted at him through tendrils of smoke. "One more thing I'd like to know, Quincannon. Do you intend to just prowl around camp all day, taking up space, or will you make yourself useful in your sham role?"

"Useful?"

"You're supposed to be an assistant timekeeper. There's plenty of work to be done by the man holding that position. I'd feel better about your presence if you'd do your share between skulks and searches. Assuming you'll be here more than one day, that is. And assuming you can handle the job."

"Oh, I can handle it," Quincannon told him. "For the standard assistant's wages, of course."

"Wages?" Phillips was indignant at first; then his mouth shaped into a crooked smile. "By God, you've got gall, I'll give you that. Wages! All right, then—wages paid for work done. Agreed?"

"Agreed, Mr. Phillips. And you'll not regret it. No man works harder for an honest dollar than John Quincannon."

◆ ◆ ◆

The cabins, some ten in all, were arranged in a staggered row, some shaded by tall pines, others afforded a measure of privacy by elderberry and chokecherry bushes. All were small, single-room affairs, and the one Quincannon was given was as monastic as a monk's cell: sheet-iron stove, puncheon table, wall bench, and a pole bunk mattressed with finely cut fir boughs and covered with wool blankets. That was all, save for a lantern hanging from a wall peg. A small glass-paned window admitted tree-filtered shafts of sunlight. The only means of protection against intruders was a pair of iron brackets mounted one on each side of the door, into which a heavy wooden crossbar could be fitted.

Quincannon stowed his warbag under the bunk and took himself to the cabin three away from his that Phillips had pointed out to him as Guy DuBois's. There was no one else in the vicinity; he slipped around to the side to have a look through the window. The interior was similar to his, except that it was considerably more cluttered. DuBois's duffel, jammed under the bunk, bulged invitingly.

Back at the front, he made sure he was still alone and unobserved and then quickly slipped inside and shut the door again behind him.

The cabin stank of unwashed clothing, woodsmoke, and alcohol. The ripe blend of odors set him to breathing through his mouth as he knelt beside the bunk.

The duffel was not the only item wedged underneath. Pushed back behind the bag was a small wooden case. He checked the case first. It contained half a dozen identical dark-brown bottles; the label on one he lifted out bore a steel-engraved photograph of a healthy looking gent and the words Perry Davis's Pain Killer. Quincannon was familiar with the product—a patent medicine which claimed to have great thaumaturgic powers, good for man and beast, but whose main ingredient was pure alcohol. It was more potent, in fact, than most lawfully manufactured whiskies.

He turned his attention to the duffel and its contents. Wads of soiled shirts, socks, and union suits. A new sealed deck of playing cards. A torn dime novel featuring the exploits of a character named Mexican Bill, the Cowboy Detective. And a leather drawstring pouch which clinked and rattled when he shook it. The pouch, however, turned out to be a disappointment. All it contained was a collar button, a woman's corset stay, two Indian Head pennies, the nib of a pen, and half a dozen other odds and ends of value only to DuBois.

He replaced the pouch and the rest of the items, pushed the duffel and the case of Pain Killer back under the bunk. Then he searched the remainder of the room, beginning with the pair of calked boots, coil of rope, and other logger's paraphernalia littering the floor against the wall under the window. He even went so far as to feel in among the fir boughs lining the bunk and to check the stove's ash box and flue.

There was no sign anywhere of the stolen jewel-work.

Well, he thought philosophically, he hadn't really expected to find the swag so easily, had he? Time was on his side—time, and a handsome fee and day wages besides. He cracked the door open, peeked out. A foraging jay had the area to itself; it flew off squawking and scolding when Quincannon emerged and sauntered away along the river bank.

Before returning to the camp office to begin his assistant timekeeper's duties, he detoured to the sawmill for a gander at Guy DuBois in the flesh. The widow Bennett had described the French Canadian to a bitter T, but Quincannon preferred to take the measure of an adversary himself—well in advance, if possible, of any sort of face to face confrontation.

The huge circular saws were quiet when he stepped inside the cavernous enclosure. This was because a fresh log, just winched up from the pond below, was being rolled into place on the saw carriage and clamped down by means of iron "dogs." The setter—Ben Irons, he assumed, a keg of a man with drooping, tobacco-stained mustaches—used his levers to move the log into position for the first cut. The sawyer, DuBois, then stepped in close to the two blades, one set directly above the other, their sharp teeth almost touching. When he started the carriage, steadying its progress as the saws bit deep into the wood, streams of sawdust flew high and the screech of steel against wood was deafening.

Quincannon watched DuBois as he and Irons sliced off a slab of rough bark and wood that would be chopped up into firewood, then commenced reducing the log to thinner strips of board lumber. The French Canadian was a much less imposing figure than Ida Bennett had led him to believe; in fact, DuBois was anything but a "handsome little devil." Short, long-necked, knobby-armed, with a nose like a cant hook, a sullen mouth, and eyes sunk deep under wire-brush brows—altogether an unlovely specimen, in Quincannon's estimation. Mrs. Bennett must have been lonelier than he'd thought, and with poorer eyesight, to have taken DuBois into her home and bed.

He was smiling as he left the mill. He had six inches in height and fifty pounds in solid weight on the sawyer, not to mention years of experience in the niceties of handling felons; he would have no trouble with DuBois when the time came to make his arrest. This job was looking better all the time—a veritable lark, compared to some he'd had in recent months. The only challenge was locating the whereabouts of the stolen jewelry, and for a detective with his talents he didn't see how he could fail to meet it successfully, sooner or later.

♦ ♦ ♦

Supper was served in the cookshack, at a single table that ran the length of the room and was flanked by wooden benches. Quincannon contrived to find a seat across from DuBois, the better to observe him and to listen in on his conversations. A good plan, except that it produced no results. DuBois sat along-side Ben Irons and a barrelchested gent with a lion's mane of blond hair— Okay King, the blacksmith—but spoke to neither of them nor to anyone else. He kept his eyes on his plates of boiled potatoes, corned beef, baked beans, and cornstarch pudding, ate hurriedly and wolfishly, and then left the table, alone, before any of the other men were finished.

When DuBois was gone, Quincannon tried to strike up conversations with both Irons and King. Neither man showed more than a cursory interest in him. Loggers and sawmill camp workers could be standoffish with newcomers until they got to know them, and Quincannon, despite his gregarious nature, was no exception. It would take some doing to cultivate Irons and King to the point where he could ask them probing questions about DuBois and expect straight-forward answers. He could begin the cultivation, he thought, at the stud game tonight.

But he was wrong. The game, in Okay King's cabin, was already in progress when he arrived and all six places were filled. And they stayed filled for the next hour, forcing him into a passive kibitzing role. Conversation among the players was desultory; DuBois, again, had almost nothing to say to anyone. The stakes were low—coins rather than greenbacks—but the French Canadian played as if he were in a cutthroat, high-stakes game, betting conservatively, keeping his hole cards close to his chest and studying them, the cards face up on the table, and the faces of his opponents with a brooding concentration.

His luck was poor tonight; he lost steadily, often with second best hands. His expression darkened into a sullen glower and he began nipping at a bottle of Perry Davis's Pain Killer without offering it to any of the others. Not a good loser, DuBois. When his nine-high straight was beaten by Okay King's queens full, he slammed his fist down on the table and growled, "*Sacre Dieu!* If I do not know better, *mon ami*, I think maybe you make your own luck."

King glared back at him. "But you do know better, don't you, Frenchy?" he said in a deceptively mild voice.

"Perhaps. But the cards are yours."

"Same cards we always play with."

"I say we play with a new deck."

"And I say we don't. Anybody else think there's something wrong with this one?"

Headshakes. Irons said, "Whose deal is it? Mine?"

DuBois's eyes were still on the blacksmith. He said angrily, "*J'en ai plein le cul!*"

"You want to cuss me," King said, laying his massive hands flat on the table, "by God do it in English."

"Bah! I am sick of this game, that's what I tell you."

"Then quit, why don't you?"

DuBois bounced to his feet, kicking over the box he'd been sitting on, and scraped up his few remaining coins. "So!" he said. "I quit!" And he stormed out of the cabin and banged the door behind him.

Quincannon moved over to right the upended box. "Mind if I sit in, lads?"

The men around the table looked him over. Okay King shrugged and said, "Sit. Your money's good as anybody's."

"New cheater, ain't you?" the teamster, Hank Ransome, asked.

"Assistant. And a more honest cheater you'll never meet."

The men liked that; all of them except Okay King laughed. The humorless blacksmith asked him, "What's the name again?"

"Quincannon. John Quincannon."

"Scot, eh? Well, I reckon a Scot's got a better chance than most of being honest."

"He has for a fact. And I'm not half so feisty as the former occupant of this seat. That French Canadian has a fine temper."

"You don't know the half of it," Irons said. "Ought to work with him on a saw carriage all day long."

"Difficult fellow?"

"Difficult? Grizzly bear's got a better disposition."

"What's the source of his bile?"

"Born with it, and it's eating his vitals."

"Along with that Perry Davis he's so fond of," Ransome said.

"Is that what makes him such a poor loser?"

"Among other things. Fact is, he don't like losing at nothing. Don't trust nobody either, that Frenchy. Anything goes wrong for him, he figures it's somebody else's fault—somebody out to do him dirt. Only one doing him dirt's his ownself."

"To hell with DuBois," Okay King said. "We're here to play stud and time's growing short. Deal the cards, Ben, and let's get on with it."

They played until ten o'clock, with Quincannon winning more hands than he lost. He tried twice more to steer the sporadic table talk around to DuBois, but the others wanted no more of the French Canadian tonight. He counted the evening a success, nonetheless. He'd learned enough about his quarry and the men's feelings toward the man to discard the notion that any of them, or anyone else in the camp, was in cahoots with him; DuBois was too much of a loner and too suspicious of others to have let on to anyone about the stolen jewelry. Nor would he have hidden the swag anywhere it was likely to be found by accident. He would have it close at hand, where he could check on it regularly to make sure it was safe.

Quincannon whistled a jaunty tune as he walked back to his cabin. Not only was he one step closer to finding the loot, but he had won twelve dollars at stud—another little bonus to add to his accumulating pile. Today had been profitable in more ways than one. Tomorrow might be even more so.

DuBois's cabin, he noticed as he passed by, was dark and not even a dribble of smoke came from its stovepipe chimney. No fire to ward off the night's chill? Well, loggers in general and French Canadians in particular were a hardy lot. Sleep well, *mon ami*, he thought cheerfully. Your time is about up.

He didn't know until morning how right he was.

DuBois's time was up, for a fact. Permanently.

♦ ♦ ♦

It was the bullcook, Nevada Ned, who brought the news. When Quincannon trudged sleepily through the frosty five a.m. darkness to the cookshack, summoned by the cook's bell, there was no sign of the sawyer; and when DuBois still hadn't arrived by the middle of breakfast, an annoyed Jack Phillips sent Ned to find out what was keeping him. The bullcook came rushing back inside of ten minutes, as the men were finishing the last of their boiled coffee, waving his arms and shouting at the top of his voice.

"He's dead! By grab, he's deader than a boiled owl!"

Phillips, sitting near Quincannon, was on his feet first. He called over the general commotion, "What're you babbling about, Ned? Who's dead?"

"DuBois. Frenchy. Lyin' on the floor of his cabin, deader than a boiled owl."

"The devil you say! How? What happened to him?"

"Side of his head's busted in. Looks like he tripped on a coil of rope and cracked his skull wide open on the stove."

The cookshack emptied swiftly, Phillips leading the rush of men and Quincannon, muttering "Hell and damn!" under his breath, close behind. Pale dawnlight had begun to seep into the eastern sky, but the shadows were still long and thick in the surrounding woods and across ground so heavy with frost it looked snow-patched; Phillips carried a lantern he'd claimed from Nevada Ned, and several of the others had lighted their lamps as well. When they arrived at DuBois's cabin, the foreman reached out for the latch.

"Can't get in that way," Ned told him. "Barred inside—I tried it before I come running."

They hurried around to the side window. Phillips held the lantern up close to the dusty glass; Quincannon crowded in next to him. The lamplight threw wavery shadows over the dark interior, over the figure of DuBois sprawled face down in front of the stove, his arms drawn back against his sides. Dried blood gleamed faintly on the raw wound above his left temple.

Phillips half turned to scan the faces behind him. "Ned," he said to the bullcook, "you're not much wider than a fence pole. Think you can squeeze through here?"

"Sure thing, once I shuck my mackinaw. Want me to bust out the glass?"

"I'll do it. Give me your hammer."

Ned slipped the hammer free of its belt loop, handed it over, and Phillips broke the window and cleaned shards from the frame. Then the bullcook wriggled his beanpole body through the opening, went to unbar the door. Quincannon made sure he was the first man inside after Phillips, the first to kneel down for a close look at the dead man. Caught around DuBois's left ankle was a loop of hemp from the coil against the wall under the window. Blood was smeared on a lower corner of the stove, as well as on DuBois's hair and cracked skull. Quincannon touched an edge of it with his forefinger: dried to a crust. When he grasped one of the backflung arms he found it stiff and unyielding: the early stages of rigor mortis.

Dead since sometime last night, he thought. Eight or nine hours. Dead, by God, when I walked by at ten o'clock.

Behind him Okay King said, "Drunk, likely. Drunk on Perry Davis and staggering around in the dark."

"Damn fool," Phillips agreed disgustedly.

"Ain't much of a loss, you ask me."

"Poor excuse for a man, I'll grant you that, but good at his job. It's too late in the season to find another sawyer. That means extra shifts for everyone at the mill, same as when he was in Frisco."

During this exchange, and while the millhands were grumbling at the foreman's words, Quincannon made a quick, deft search of DuBois's clothing. If the brooch, pendant, and diamond ring had been on the body, he'd have found them. And he didn't.

Veritable lark, eh? Minor challenge? Faugh!

As Quincannon straightened Ben Irons said, "Blasted Frenchy, makin' trouble dead as well as alive. If he had to have a freak accident, why couldn't he wait until we shut down for the winter?"

Wrong, Mr. Irons, Quincannon thought darkly. Not a freak accident. Not on your tintype.

Murder.

Murder plain and simple.

♦ ♦ ♦

On Phillips' orders, three of the men removed DuBois's corpse and carried it to the loading dock, where it was to be held for shipment to Verdi on the morning train. The rest, except for Quincannon, dispersed to begin their day's work. He faded away to his own cabin, so as to avoid, for the time being, another private talk with Phillips in the camp office. The foreman would want to know his intentions now that DuBois was dead, and he wasn't ready yet for that discussion, or to reveal the truth about his quarry's demise.

He waited fifteen minutes, ruminating over a pipeful of shag tobacco. Then he transferred his Navy Colt from his warbag to his belt, buttoned his shirt over it, and returned to DuBois's cabin.

It was deserted now. He let himself inside. Sunrise was only a few minutes away, but little of the morning light penetrated the broken window; he lighted DuBois's lantern. In its glow he first examined the stove and the floor around it. Next he studied the door, the iron brackets mounted on either side of it, and the wooden crossbar. There was a tiny hole, almost a gouge, high up on the door. And near one end of the bar he found a fresh, five-inch vertical furrow.

He lowered the lantern and searched the floor here. Among the boot-crushed remains of window glass he spied a horseshoe nail, two inches long and slightly bent. It hadn't been there long; it was shiny new, free of dust. He nodded in satisfaction and dropped the nail into his shirt pocket.

Only one question remained now.

Had DuBois been killed for the stolen jewel-work or for some other reason?

He continued his search, leaving no corner of the room and nothing in it uninspected. He felt along the underside of the table, probed the walls and floor for loose boards and the legs of the table and the bunk poles for hollows. He reexamined the stove and its flue, the logger's boots and other items strewn under the window. He sifted once more through the four bottles of Perry Davis's Pain Killer, through the clothing and other contents of DuBois's duffel.

"Hell and damn!" he muttered aloud when he was done.

He had the answer to his question of motive. But what he still didn't have was Ida Bennett's expensive baubles.

♦ ♦ ♦

The blacksmith shop stood on the bank of a shallow creek that flowed into the Truckee, not far from the teamster's barn and corrals. Made of unbarked logs like the other camp buildings, it had a steep shed roof but neither doors nor windows. As Quincannon approached the wide entrance he saw Okay King and another man working at a heavy wooden crib set alongside the forge and bellows. Inside the crib, slung from a windlass-drawn harness fashioned of heavy bands of leather and rope, its four legs tied to the corner timbers, was a wild-eyed and bellowing ox.

The second man, a bullwhacker from the looks of him, was saying to the ox, "Quit your hollerin', Tex. This ain't hurtin' you none," as Quincannon entered.

King was hunched over by the animal's near hind foot, trimming off the rough edges of the hoof and cleaning it with a sharp knife. Finished with that, he laid one half of a new shoe against the hoof. The fit wasn't right; he took the shoe to the forge, thrust it under the coals with a pair of tongs, and pumped the bellows until the coals flared a smoky red. When he stepped back to wait for the heat to soften the iron he spied Quincannon. His sweating face pinched into a scowl.

"What is it *you* want?"

"Two minutes of your time."

"You've got eyes, man, you can see I'm busy."

"It's important," Quincannon told him. "Did you know DuBois long enough and well enough to make a guess as to where he might have hidden something of value?"

"Hidden something? Hidden *what*? What the devil are you gabbling about?"

"There's no time to explain now. Can you make a guess?"

"No," King said. "All I know about Frenchy is that I didn't like him any more'n a horse's hind end. He went his way, I went mine. Stud poker's all we had in common, and damn little there. Talk to Ben Irons and Hank Ransome —they knew him better than I did."

Quincannon produced the horseshoe nail and held it up for King to see. "One of yours, I'll warrant."

The blacksmith squinted at it, wiping his hands on a fire-blackened leather apron. "Looks like. Why?"

"It was on the floor of DuBois's cabin. Would he have had any reason to keep horseshoe nails?"

"A sawyer? Not hardly. Somebody might've tracked it in on a boot-sole this morning. Anyhow, what's a blasted nail got to do with anything?"

"A great deal," Quincannon said. "Oh, a great deal, Mr. King."

He asked two more questions, the answers to which were just as he'd expected. By this time the caged ox had begun to toss its head in a frenzy, hurling flecks of slobber all the way over to where Quincannon stood. Its bawling increased in volume.

King growled to the bullwhacker, "Hell's fire, Joe, can't you shut that critter up?"

"Tex ain't never took well to a shoein', you know that."

"He ain't the only one."

Joe prodded the animal with his goad, and when that had no effect, he commenced to swearing at it. If anything, this caused the ox's complaints to grow even more frantic.

The 'smith glared at Joe, at the ox, and then at Quincannon. "No damn peace in this camp since you showed up," he said aggrievedly. He stalked back to the forge, yanked out the glowing shoe, laid it on his anvil, and began hammering it with a vengeance, as if trying to drown out both the ox's bellows and Joe's steady cussing.

♦ ♦ ♦

Hank Ransome was away from the settlement, delivering a load of supplies to the logging camp higher up in the mountains. Quincannon went from the teamster's barn to the mill, avoiding the camp office on the way. Inside the mill, he watched Ben Irons and DuBois's tow-headed replacement saw a massive redwood log into board lumber. When they were done and a fresh log was being winched up, he approached Irons and drew him aside.

The setter frowned at his question about DuBois. "What would that Frenchy have that's valuable enough to hide?"

"Something he stole in San Francisco."

"Stole? Well, that don't surprise me none. Money, is it?"

"Expensive jewelry. Three small pieces."

"Don't say. How come you know so much about it?"

"It's a long story and time is short. I'll explain later. In or near his cabin, would you guess? Or somewhere else in camp?"

"No place else DuBois spent much time, except Okay's cabin and right here in the mill."

"Would he have chanced hiding it here?"

"No spot safe enough. My pick is his cabin."

"Mine, too, but I've searched it twice."

"Maybe he buried it somewhere outside . . ." Irons paused and then shook his head. "No, not him. He'd be afraid somebody'd see him do it. Got to be inside. He'd play that hand like he played his cards—close to the vest, no risks. Hide valuables where he could keep a close eye on 'em, particularly if they was stolen goods."

Cards, Quincannon thought.

Cards!

Half to Irons and half to himself he said, "Last night DuBois all but accused Okay King of doctoring the deck. Not for the first time when he lost?"

"Hell, no. He was always tryin' to blame somebody."

"Did he ever bring his own cards to the game?"

"Time or two."

"Recently?"

"Not since he come back from his sister's funeral."

"Yet he called for a new deck last night."

"Yeah, he did. What—?"

Quincannon said, "That's the answer, then," and spun on his heel and hurried out of the mill.

For the third time that morning he entered DuBois's cabin. He went straight to the bunk, hauled out the duffel and rummaged around inside until he located the sealed box of playing cards. It had the feel of a brand-new deck, and at a casual glance it had the look of one. But on closer inspection he found that the original seal had been pried loose, probably with a knife blade, and then carefully reglued. He slit the seal with his thumbnail, opened the box.

It contained no more than two dozen cards, separated into two halves to help create the illusion of a full deck; and sandwiched tightly between the cards, in a wrapping of tissue paper, were the widow Bennett's brooch, pendant, and diamond ring.

Quincannon offered himself congratulations and at the same time cursed himself for a rattlepate, a difficult feat even for him. An ingenious hiding place, to be sure, but he should have inspected the card box more closely on his first search, or at least his second. After all, he was no stranger to the ploy of card mechanics bilking suckers with resealed decks—

Sounds outside. Someone was approaching the cabin.

Swiftly and silently he stood and moved to the wall behind the door.

He had just enough time to pocket both the card box and the jewelry, and to unbutton his shirt above the handle of his Navy, before the door swung inward.

The man who entered kicked the door shut behind him without turning. As Quincannon had done minutes earlier, he made straight for DuBois's bunk and knelt beside it. But it wasn't the duffel that he was after. Eager fingers drew out the case containing the four remaining pint bottles of Perry Davis's Pain Killer. He put one of these into the pocket of his mackinaw, was lifting out a second when Quincannon made his presence known.

"Hello, Ned," he said. "Come after the rest of the spoils, have you?"

The bullcook twisted around on one bony knee. His expression in that instant was one of surprise and trapped fear; but in the next, as he recognized Quincannon, he managed to reclaim some of his usual arrogance and bluster. He gained his feet, still clutching the pint of Pain Killer.

"Oh, it's you. The cheater. What're you doin' here?"

"Same as you, Ned. Only it's altogether different spoils that interest me."

"I don't know what you're talkin' about. Foreman sent me down to gather up DuBois's gear. This here Perry Davis ain't gonna do him no good, so I figured I might as well help myself."

"Just as you helped yourself last night, eh?"

"Last night? Wasn't nowhere near here last night."

"Around nine or so," Quincannon said. "Helping yourself to a pint of Pain Killer while DuBois was away playing stud."

"That's a damn lie!"

"Fact. One of several. You told me yesterday you were almost out of jakey and you're a man who sorely needs Demon Rum in one form or another to keep his bones together. You knew DuBois brought a case of Pain Killer back with him from San Francisco; saw him unloading it, likely. And you thought he might not miss one bottle, or wouldn't know for certain who'd pilfered it if he did. But you picked the wrong night, Ned. DuBois left the stud game early and caught you at the job. A brief struggle, perhaps, and you sent him to his reward."

"I never did no such thing."

"Hit him with that hammer of yours, I'll wager, and down he went. If he wasn't dead then, you made sure he was by thumping his cranium against the stove."

Nevada Ned's seamed face had lost its color. The look of trapped fear was back in his eyes. "You're crazy as a one-winged jay. DuBois was drunk, he tripped on that coil of rope and fell against the stove and busted his own skull—"

"No, that's how you made it look. After which you took two pints of Pain Killer instead of one and went on your merry way. There were six bottles in the case when I was here yesterday, looking for my spoils, and only four when I searched again earlier."

"The door," Ned said desperately, "the door was barred on the *inside*. You was here when we busted in, you saw that same as everybody else. Wasn't nobody but DuBois could have barred it. Nobody!"

"Except you," Quincannon said. "You and your trusty hammer and one little horseshoe nail—"

Ned threw the pint of Pain Killer at him. Launched it in one sudden, fluid motion, with not even a flicker of his eyes as warning. Quincannon was caught off guard. The bottle fetched him a glancing blow on the cheekbone—if he hadn't twisted his head at the last second it would have struck him squarely between the eyes—and staggered him backwards into the wall. The impact was jarring enough to upset his balance; his right foot slid, then his left, and he toppled to one knee. By the time he lunged upright again, Ned was past him and out the door.

Quincannon wasted breath on a smoldering six-jointed oath, shook his head to clear out the cobwebs, drew his revolver, and gave chase. The bullcook had a fifty-yard lead, running spraddle-legged along the riverbank to the north. Quincannon mowed down an elderberry shrub, but the shrub paid him back by scratching his hands and chin. It also slowed him enough for Ned to add ten more yards to his lead.

"Stop or I'll shoot, you damned blackguard!" Quincannon bellowed, wasting more breath. Nevada Ned threw a look over his shoulder but not even sight of the big revolver broke his stride. Whether he realized it or not, however, he had nowhere to go. The river ran too fast here for swimming, if in fact Ned could swim, and the terrain offered neither a hidey hole nor an escape route.

Younger and in better physical condition, Quincannon soon closed the gap between them to thirty yards. Ahead was the mill pond, pole-wielding men wearing steel-calked boots balanced on the floating logs; he couldn't risk a shot that might miss the bullcook and hit one of them. Catch up and tackle him, that was the best way to end the chase. But before he could gain any more ground, Ned veered away from the river at an angle toward the lumberyard and loading dock.

Men working there stopped to watch as Nevada Ned and Quincannon pounded toward them. One shouted something that was lost in the screaming whine of the mill saws, the chuffing of a yard engine on the spur track. The bullcook stumbled around a huge cone of sawdust, and when he dodged between stacks of board and slab lumber, Quincannon lost sight of him. Hell and damn! He put on a burst of speed, reached the stacks, cut through them —and then skidded to a halt.

Ned had pulled up next to a jumble of cut firewood. And in his hands now, drawn up menacingly, was a double-bitted ax.

Quincannon sleeved sweat from his eyes. Both he and Ned were panting like dray horses in the thin mountain air. "Put the ax down," he managed, "and give yourself up. Don't make me shoot you."

"Hell I will! Stay away from me, you heathen murderer!"

Half a dozen burly lumbermen were closing in around them. One called, "What's this all about, Ned?"

"DuBois . . . he didn't die accidental. Cheater here killed him and now he's tryin' to blame it on me."

"So that's your game, is it?" Quincannon said. "Well, it won't work." He drew another ragged breath and said to the others, "I'm not a timekeeper, lads, I'm a detective from San Francisco. Come here undercover to arrest DuBois for theft."

A surprised muttering greeted this pronouncement. Two lumbermen who had been edging closer to Quincannon stopped and held their ground.

"He's lying!" Nevada Ned shouted. "He's the thief. He killed DuBois for his stash of Perry Davis's Pain Killer."

Quincannon shifted the Navy to his left hand, and with his right fished the brooch and pendant from his pocket. When he held them high, sunlight glinted off the diamonds and rubies and gold settings. Sharp exclamations came from the gathering men this time.

"These are what DuBois stole. Ned's the one who murdered him—not for these but for the Pain Killer. One of you fetch Jack Phillips. He'll vouch for who I am."

"No need to fetch me, I'm already here." The foreman appeared at a trot from behind a stack of redwood burls. "Quincannon is who he says he is, all right, a flycop from—"

Phillips didn't finish the sentence because Nevada Ned, trapped and lost and impelled by hate, chose that moment to attack the flycop with his ax.

Again without warning, he rushed forward and swung the weapon in a vicious horizontal arc, as if he were about to fell a sapling. Quincannon twisted aside just in time; the blade sliced air two inches from his jugular. He didn't dare fire the Navy with the workers milling around. Instead, as the bullcook pivoted back toward him, lifting the ax for another swipe, he drove the toe of his boot into Ned's shin, staggering him; then he slammed the Colt's barrel against his knobby wrist. The bone snapped with a dry, brittle sound, like the crack of an old pine cone under a heavy tread. Ned screamed in pain. And the ax dropped harmlessly at his feet.

Phillips shoved up next to Quincannon as some of the others dragged the moaning bullcook away. "By God, that was close. He nearly sliced that blade clean through your neck. Are you all right?"

"Never better," Quincannon lied. "Close, true, but history was on my side, Mr. Phillips."

"History?"

He smiled ruefully. "No member of the Quincannon clan has ever lost his head in a fight."

♦ ♦ ♦

A short while later, in Phillips' private cubicle, he was feeling his old self again. This was due in large part to the grudging mix of awe, admiration, and respect now being accorded him by the foreman—a mix that grew richer still as he made his explanations.

"When did I first suspect DuBois had been murdered?" he said, leaning back comfortably in his chair. "Why, from the first moment you held the lantern up to his cabin window. I knew it for certain as soon as we were inside."

"Even though the door was barred?"

"Even though."

"But how, man? How?"

Quincannon applied a fresh match to the tobacco in his pipe. When he had it drawing to his satisfaction he said, "From the position of the body. If DuBois had tripped and fallen against the stove, drunk or sober, he would not have been lying as he was."

"I don't see what—"

"His arms, Mr. Phillips. When a man trips and falls, his instinctive reaction is to throw his arms out in front of him to break the fall. DuBois's should have been outflung *toward* the stove, or at least caught under his body, but they weren't. They were drawn back *along his sides*. Therefore, he hadn't died where he lay—his body had been moved."

"Of course. Now why didn't I notice that myself?"

"You haven't the trained eye of a master detective."

"What else did your trained eye notice?"

"The location of the coil of rope," Quincannon told him. "It was against the wall next to the window, a placement where it was unlikely to snare the foot of even a drunkard who was familiar with his surroundings. But much more telling is the fact that in the darkness this morning, even with the aid of your lantern, I couldn't see the coil from outside the window. Nor the loop of rope caught around DuBois's ankle. The angle was wrong and the shadows inside too thick."

"Ah."

"Ah, indeed. When Ned burst into the cookshack he told you it looked as though DuBois had 'tripped on a coil of rope and cracked his skull wide open on the stove'—his exact words. But he couldn't have seen the rope from outside the window any more than I could; he had to've been inside the cabin. And if he was inside, then he must be the one who killed DuBois and rearranged the position of the body."

"And the barred door? How did he manage that trick?"

"Oh, it wasn't difficult," Quincannon said. "The trick likely isn't original with him; he's not clever enough to devise spur-of-the-moment subterfuges. I'll wager that somewhere in his travels he saw it done or heard of it being done, and since it takes very little time to arrange and he had all the tools he needed on his person, he seized on it as a way to ensure that DuBois's death would be taken as accidental."

"What tools?" Phillips asked.

"The hammer in his toolbelt. And a horseshoe nail, which I later found, slightly bent, on the cabin floor. Okay King told me Ned sometimes helped him around the blacksmith's shop; and a bullcook by nature fills his pockets with all manner of miscellaneous items gathered on his rounds."

"True enough. But a hammer and a horseshoe nail . . . that's all he used?"

"That's all," Quincannon said. "He drove the nail into the door high up near its outer edge—no more than a quarter-inch deep. Then he set one end of the crossbar into the bracket on the hinge side, and rested the bar's other end on the nail. The door could still be opened inward with the bar in that diagonal position. Not far, only a few inches, but far enough for a man as thin as Ned to squeeze through. I found a vertical gouge in the bar where the bracket had cut into it during the squeeze. Once Ned was outside, he had only to pull the door closed with enough force to dislodge the nail—once or at the most twice. When the nail bent and fell, the upper end of the bar dropped into the second bracket and completed the seal. As simple as that."

Phillips was shaking his head. "You're a marvel, Quincannon, you really are. How many other detectives could've done what you've done here, and in such a short time?"

Quincannon smiled modestly around the stem of his briar. "None, Mr. Phillips," he said. "Not even Allan Pinkerton himself."

♦ ♦ ♦

Later that day, after he had returned to Verdi and handed Nevada Ned over to the sheriff there, Quincannon sent a wire to Sabina in San Francisco.

ARRIVING HOME SIX P.M. TRAIN TOMORROW STOP
DUBOIS MURDERED BUT BAFFLING CRIME SWIFTLY
SOLVED AND CULPRIT ARRESTED AFTER FIERCE
STRUGGLE STOP ALL BENNETT JEWELRY RECOVERED
STOP MASTER DETECTIVE AND DOTING PARTNER
SURELY DESERVING OF CELEBRATION AND SPECIAL
REWARD COMMA DON'T YOU AGREE QM

He had her reply in less than an hour. It said simply and eloquently:

NO

MEDIUM RARE

The night was dark, cold; most of San Francisco lay swaddled in a cloak of fog and low-hanging clouds that turned streetlights and house lights into ghostly smears. The bay, close by this residential district along lower Van Ness Avenue, was invisible and the foghorns that moaned on it had a lonely, lost-soul sound. Bitter-sharp, the wind nipped at Quincannon's cheeks, fluttered his thick piratical beard as he stepped down from the hansom. A sudden gust almost tore off his derby before he could clamp it down.

A fine night for spirits, he thought wryly. The liquid kind, to be sure—except that he had been a temperance man for several years now. And the supernatural kind, in which he believed not one whit.

He helped Sabina alight from the coach, turned to survey the house at which they were about to call. It was a modest gingerbread affair, its slender front yard enclosed by a black iron-picket fence. Rented, not purchased, as he had discovered earlier in the day. Gaslight flickered behind its lace-curtained front windows.

No surprise there. Professor Vargas would have been careful to select a house that had not been wired for electricity; the sometimes spectral trembles produced by gas flame were much more suited to his purposes.

On the gate was a discreet bronze sign whose raised letters gleamed faintly in the outspill from a nearby streetlamp. Sabina went to peer at the sign as Quincannon paid and dismissed the hack driver. When he joined her he, too, bent for a look.

UNIFIED COLLEGE OF THE ATTUNED IMPULSES

Prof. A. Vargas

Spirit Medium and Counselor

"Bah. Hogwash," Quincannon said grumpily, straightening. "How can any sane person believe in such hokum?"

"Self-deception is the most powerful kind."

He made a derisive noise in his throat, a sound Sabina had once likened to the rumbling snarl of a mastiff.

She said, "If you enter growling and wearing that ferocious glare, you'll give the game away. We're here as potential devotees not ardent skeptics."

"Devotees of claptrap."

"John, Mr. Buckley is paying us handsomely for this evening's work. Very handsomely, if you recall."

Quincannon recalled; his scowl faded and was replaced by a smile only those who knew him well would recognize as greed-based. Money, especially in large sums, was what soothed his savage breast. In fact, it was second only in his admiration to Sabina herself.

He glanced sideways at her. She looked even more fetching than usual this evening, dressed as she was in an outfit of black silk brocade, her raven hair topped by a stylish hat trimmed in white China silk. His mouth watered. A fine figure of a woman, Sabina Carpenter. A man engaged in the time-honored profession of detective couldn't ask for a more decorous—or a more intelligent and capable—partner. He could, however, ask for more than a straightforward business arrangement and an occasional night on the town followed by a chaste handshake at her door. Not getting it, not even coming close to getting it, was his greatest defeat, his greatest frustration. Why, he had never even been inside Sabina's Russian Hill flat . . .

"John."

"Mmm?"

"Will you please stop staring at me that way."

"What way, my dear?"

"Like a cat at a bowl of cream. We've no time for dallying; we're late as it is. Mr. Buckley and the others will be waiting to begin the seance."

Quincannon took her arm, chastely, and led her through the gate. As they mounted the front stairs, he had a clear vision of Cyrus Buckley's bank check and a clear auditory recollection of the financier's promise of the check's twin should they successfully debunk Professor Vargas and his Unified College of the Attuned Impulses.

Buckley was a reluctant follower of Spiritualism, in deference to his wife who believed wholeheartedly in communication with the disembodied essences of the dead and such mediumistic doubletalk as "spiritual vibrations of the positive and negative forces of material and astral planes." She continually sought audiences with their daughter, Bernice, the childhood victim of diphtheria, a quest which had led them to a succession of mediums and cost her husband "a goodly sum." Professor Vargas was the latest and by far the most financially threatening of these paranormal spirit-summoners. A recent arrival in San Francisco—from Chicago, he claimed—Vargas evidently had a more clever, extensive, and convincing repertoire of "spirit wonders" than any other medium Buckley had encountered, and of course his fees were exorbitant as a result.

The Buckleys had attended one of Vargas' sittings a few days ago—a dark seance in a locked room in his rented house. The professor had ordered himself securely tied to his chair and then proceeded to invoke a dazzling array of bell-ringing, table-tipping, spirit lights, automatic writings, ectoplasmic manifestations, and other phenomena. As his finale he announced that he was being unfettered by his friendly spirit guide and guardian, Angkar, and the rope that had bound him was heard to fly through the air just before the lights were turned up; the rope, when examined, was completely free of the more than ten knots which had been tied into it. This supernatural flimflam had so impressed Margaret Buckley that she had returned the next day without her husband's knowledge and arranged for another sitting—tonight—and a series of private audiences at which Vargas promised to establish and maintain contact with the shade of the long-gone Bernice. Mrs. Buckley, in turn and in gratitude, was prepared to place unlimited funds in the medium's eager hands. "Endow the whole damned Unified College of the Attuned Impulses," was the way Buckley put it. Nothing he'd said or done could change his wife's mind. The only thing that would, he was convinced, was a public unmasking of the professor as the knave and charlatan he surely was. Hence, his visit to the Market Street offices of Carpenter and Quincannon, Professional Detective Services.

Quincannon had no doubt he and Sabina could accomplish the task. They had both had dealings with phony psychics before, Sabina when she was with the Pinkertons in Denver, and on two occasions since they had opened their joint agency here. But Cyrus Buckley wasn't half so sanguine. "You'll not have an easy time of it," he'd warned them. "Professor Vargas is a rare bird and rare birds are not easily plucked. A medium among mediums."

Medium rare, is he? Quincannon thought as he twisted the doorbell handle. Not for long. He'll not only be plucked but done to a turn before this night is over.

The door was opened by a tiny woman of indeterminate age, dressed in a flowing ebon robe. Her skin was very white, her lips a bloody crimson in contrast; sleek brown hair was pulled tight around her head and fastened with a jeweled barrette. Around her neck hung a silver amulet embossed with some sort of cabalistic design. "I am Annabelle," she said in sepulchral tones. "You are Mr. and Mrs. John Quinn?"

"We are," Quincannon said, wishing wistfully that it were true. Mr. and Mrs. John Quincannon, not Quinn. But Sabina had refused even to adopt his name for the evening's play-acting, insisting on the shortened version instead.

Annabelle took his greatcoat and Sabina's cape, hung them on a coattree. According to Buckley, she was Professor Vargas's "psychic assistant." If she lived here with him, Quincannon mused, she was likely also his wife or mistress. Seeking communion with the Afterworld did not preclude indulging in the pleasures of the earthly sphere, evidently; he had never met a medium who professed to be celibate and meant it.

"Follow me, please."

They trailed her down a murky hallway into a somewhat more brightly lighted parlor. Here they found two men dressed as Quincannon was, in broadcloth and fresh linen, and two women in long fashionable dresses; one of the men was Cyrus Buckley. But it was the room's fifth occupant who commanded immediate attention.

Even Quincannon, who was seldom impressed by physical stature, had to grudgingly admit that Professor A. Vargas was a rather imposing gent. Tall, dark-complected, with a curling black mustache and piercing, almost hypnotic eyes. Like his psychic assistant, he wore a long flowing black robe and a silver amulet. On the middle fingers of each hand were two enormous glittering rings of intricate design, both of which bore hieroglyphics similar to those which adorned the amulets.

He greeted his new guests effusively, pressing his lips to the back of Sabina's hand and then pumping Quincannon's in an iron grip. "I am Professor Vargas. Welcome, New Ones, welcome to the Unified College of the Attuned Impulses." His voice was rich, stentorian. "Mr. and Mrs. Quinn, is it not? Friends of the good Mr. Buckley? Your first sitting but I pray not your last. You are surrounded by many anxious friends in spirit-life who desire to communicate with you once you have learned more of the laws which govern their actions. Allow your impulses to attune with theirs and your spirit friends will soon identify themselves and speak with you as in earth-life . . ."

There was more, but Quincannon shut his ears to it.

More introductions followed the medium's windy come-on. Quincannon shook hands with red-faced, muttonchopped Cyrus Buckley and his portly, gray-haired wife, Margaret; with Oliver Cobb, a prominent Oakland physician who bore a rather startling resemblance to the "literary hangman," Ambrose Bierce; and with Grace Cobb, the doctor's much younger and decorous wife. Decorous, that is, if a man preferred an overly buxom and overly rouged blonde to a svelte brunette of Sabina's cunning dimensions. The Cobbs, like the Buckleys, had attended the professor's previous seance.

Margaret Buckley looked upon Vargas with the rapt gaze of a supplicant in the presence of a saint. Dr. Cobb was also a true believer, judging from the look of eager anticipation he wore. The blonde Mrs. Cobb seemed to find the medium fascinating as well, but the glint in her eye was much more predatory than devout. Buckley appeared ill at ease, as if he wished the evening's business was already finished; he kept casting glances at Quincannon which the detective studiously ignored.

Vargas asked Quincannon and Sabina if they would care for a refreshment —coffee, tea, perhaps a glass of sherry. They both declined. This seemed to relieve Buckley; he asked Vargas, "Isn't it about time to begin the seance?"

"Soon, Mr. Buckley. The spirits must not be hurried."

"Are they friendly tonight?" Mrs. Buckley asked. "Can you tell, dear Professor Vargas?"

"The auras are uncertain. I perceive antagonistic waves among the benign."

"Oh, professor!"

"Do not fear," Vargas said. "Even if a malevolent spirit should cross the border, no harm will come to you or to any of us. Angkar will protect us."

"But will my Bernice's spirit be allowed through if there is a malevolent force present?"

Vargas patted her arm reassuringly. "It is my belief that she will, though I cannot be certain until the veil has been lifted. Have faith, dear Mrs. Buckley."

Sabina asked him, "Isn't there anything you can do to prevent a malevolent spirit from crossing over?"

"Alas, no. I am merely a teacher of the light and truth of theocratic unity, merely an operator between the Beyond and this mortal sphere."

Merely a purveyor of pap, Quincannon thought.

Grace Cobb touched Vargas's sleeve; her fingers lingered almost caressingly. "We have faith in you, Professor."

"In Angkar, dear lady," Vargas told her, but his fingers caressed hers in return and the look he bestowed upon her had a smouldering quality—the same sort of cat-at-cream look, Quincannon thought, that Sabina had accused him earlier of directing at her. "Place your faith in Angkar and the spirit world."

Quincannon asked him, "Angkar is your spirit guide and guardian angel?"

"Yes. He lived more than a thousand years past and his spirit has ascended to one of the highest planes in the Afterworld."

"A Hindu, was he?"

Vargas seemed mildly offended. "Not at all, my dear sir. Angkar was an Egyptian nobleman in the court of Nebuchadnezzar."

Quincannon managed to refrain from pointing out that Nebuchadnezzar was not an Egyptian but the king of Babylon and conqueror of Jerusalem some six centuries B.C. Not that any real harm would have been done if he had mentioned the fact; Vargas would have covered by claiming he had meant Nefertitti or some such. None of the others, except Sabina perhaps, seemed to notice the error.

Sabina said, "Those rings are most impressive, Professor. Are they Egyptian?"

"This one is." Vargas presented his left hand. "An Egyptian Signet and Seal Talisman Ring, made from virgin gold. It preserves its wearer against ill luck and wicked influences." He offered his right hand. "This is the Ring of King Solomon. Its Chaldaic inscription stands as a reminder to the wearer that no matter what his troubles may be, they shall soon be gone. The inscription—here—translates as 'This shall also pass.' "

"Oh, Professor Vargas," Mrs. Buckley gushed, "you're so knowledgeable, so wise is so many ways."

Quincannon's dinner stirred ominously under his breastbone.

He was spared further discomfort, at least for the present, by the entrance of the psychic assistant, Annabelle. She announced, "All is in readiness, professor," and without waiting for a response, glided out again.

"Good ladies and gentlemen," Vargas said, "before we enter the spirit room may I accept your most kind and welcome donations to the Unified College of the Attuned Impulses, so that we may continue in our humble efforts to bring the psychic and material planes into closer harmony?"

Quincannon paid for himself and Sabina—the outrageous "New Ones" donation of $50 each. If he had not been assured of reimbursement from their client, he would have been much more grudging than he was in handing over the greenbacks. Buckley was tight-lipped as he paid, and sweat oiled his neck and the lower of his two chins; the look he gave Quincannon was a mute plea not to botch the job he and Sabina had been hired to do. Only Dr. Cobb ponyed up with what appeared to be genuine enthusiasm.

The medium casually dropped the wad of bills onto a table, as if money mattered not in the slightest to him personally, and led them out of the parlor, down the gloomy hallway, and then into a large chamber at the rear. The "spirit room" contained quite a few more accoutrements than the parlor, of greater variety and a more unusual nature. The floor was covered by a thick Oriental carpet of dark blue and black design. Curtains made of the same ebon material as the professor's and Annabelle's robes blotted the windows, and the gaslight had been turned low enough so that shadows crouched in all four corners. The overheated air was permeated with the smell of incense; Quincannon, who hated the stuff, immediately began to breathe through his mouth. The incense came from a burner on the mantel of a small fireplace—a horsey-looking bronze monstrosity with tusks as well as equine teeth and a shaggy mane and beard.

The room's centerpiece was an oval, highly polished table around which six straight-backed chairs were arranged; a seventh chair, larger than the others, with a high seat and arms raised on a level with that of the table top, was placed at the head. Along the walls were a short, narrow sideboard of oriental design, made of teak, with an intricately inlayed center top; a tall-backed rococo love seat; and an alabaster pedestal atop which sat a hideous bronze statue of an Egyptian male in full headdress—a representation, evidently, of the mythical Angkar. In the middle of the table was a clear-glass jar, a tiny silver bell suspended inside. On the sideboard were a silver tray containing several bottles of various sizes and shapes, a tambourine, and a stack of children's school slates with black wooden frames. Propped against the wall nearby was an ordinary looking three-stringed guitar. And on the high seat of the armchair lay a coil of sturdy rope Quincannon estimated as some three yards in length.

When the sitters were all inside and loosely grouped near the table, Vargas closed the door, produced a large brass key from a pocket in his robe, and proceeded with a flourish to turn the key in the latch. After which he brought the key to the sideboard and set it beside the tray in plain sight. While this was being done, Quincannon eased over in front of the door and tested it behind his back to determine if it was in fact locked. It was.

Still at the sideboard, Vargas announced that before they formed the "mystic circle" two final preparations were necessary. Would one of the good believers be so kind as to assist him in the first of these? Quincannon stepped forward just ahead of Dr. Cobb.

The medium said, "Mr. Quinn, will you kindly examine each of the slates you see before you and tell us if they are as they seem—ordinary writing slates?"

Quincannon examined them more carefully than any of the devotees would have. "Quite ordinary," he said.

"Select two, if you please, write your name on each with this slate pencil, and then place them together and tie them securely with your handkerchief."

When Quincannon had complied, Vargas took the bound slates and placed them in the middle of the stack. "If the spirits are willing," he said, "a message will be left for you beneath the signatures. Perhaps from a loved one who has passed beyond the pale, perhaps from a friendly sprite who may be in tune with your particular psychic impulses. Discarnate forces are never predictable, you understand."

Quincannon nodded and smiled with his teeth.

"We may now be seated and form the mystic circle."

When each of the sitters had selected and was standing behind a chair, Sabina to the medium's immediate left and Quincannon directly across from him, both by prearrangement, Vargas again called for a volunteer. This time it was Dr. Cobb who stepped up first. Vargas handed him the coiled rope and seated himself in the high chair, his forearms flat on the chair arms with only his wrists and hands extended beyond the edges. He then instructed Cobb to bind him securely—arms, legs, and chest—to the chair, using as many knots as possible. Quincannon watched closely as this was done. He caught Sabina's eye when the doctor finished; she dipped her chin to acknowledge that she too had spotted the gaffe in this phase of the professor's game.

Cobb, with Buckley's help, moved Vargas's chair closer to the table, so that his hands and wrists rested on the surface. Smiling, the medium asked the others to take their seats. As Quincannon sat down he bumped against the table, then reached down to feel of one of its legs. As he'd expected, the table was much less heavy than it appeared to be at a glance. He stretched out a leg and with the toe of his shoe explored the carpet. The floor beneath seemed to be solid, but the nap was thick enough so that he couldn't be certain.

Vargas instructed everyone to spread their hands, the fingers of the left to grasp the wrist of the person on that side; thus one hand of each person was holding and the other was being held. "Once we began," he said, "attempt to empty your minds of all thought, to keep them as blank as the table's surface throughout. And remember, you must not move either hands or feet during the seance—you must not under any circumstances break the mystic circle. To do so could have grave consequences. There have been instances where inattention and disobedience have been fatal to sensitives such as myself."

The professor closed his eyes, let his chin lower slowly to his chest. After a few seconds he commenced a whispering chant, a mixture of English and simulated Egyptian in which he called for the door to the spirit world to open and the shades of the departed to pass through and reveal their presence. While this was going on, the lights began to dim as if in phantasmical response to Vargas's exhortations. The phenomenon elicited a shivery gasp from Margaret Buckley, but Quincannon was unimpressed. Gaslight in one room was easily controlled from another—in this case by the assistant, Annabelle, at a pre-arranged time or on some sort of signal.

The shadows congealed until the room was in utter darkness. Vargas's chanting ceased abruptly; the silence deepened as it lengthened. Long minutes passed with no sounds except for the somewhat asthmatic breathing of Cyrus Buckley, the rustle of a dress or shuffle of a foot on the carpet. A palpable tension began to build. Sweat formed on Quincannon's face, not from any tension but from the overheated air. He was not a man given to fancies, but he was forced to admit that there was an eerie quality to sitting in total blackness this way, waiting for something to happen. Spiritualist mediums counted on this reaction, of course. The more keyed up their dupes became, the more eager they were to believe in the incredible things they were about to witness; and the more eager they were, the more easily they could be fooled by their own senses.

Someone coughed, a sudden sharp sound that made even Quincannon twitch involuntarily. He thought the cough had come from Vargas, but in such stifling darkness you couldn't be certain of the direction of any sound. Even when the medium spoke again, the words might have come from anywhere in the room.

"Angkar is with us. I feel his presence."

On Quincannon's left, Dr. Cobb stirred and their knees bumped together; Mrs. Buckley, on his right, brought forth another of her shivery gasps.

"Will you speak to us tonight, Angkar? Will you answer our questions in the language of the dead and guide us among your fellow spirits? Please grant our humble request. Please answer yes."

The silver bell inside the jar rang once, muted but clear.

"Angkar has consented. He will speak, he will lead us. He will ring the bell once for yes to each question he is asked, twice for no, for that is the language of the dead. Will someone ask him a question? Doctor Cobb?"

"I will," Cobb's voice answered. "Angkar, is my brother Philip well and happy on the Other Side?"

The bell tinkled once.

"Will he appear to us in his spirit form?"

Yes.

"Will it be tonight?"

Silence.

Vargas said, "Angkar is unable to answer that question yet. Please ask another."

There was a good deal more of this, with questions from Cobb, his wife, and Mrs. Buckley. Then Vargas called on Sabina to ask the spirit guide a question.

She obliged by saying, "Angkar, tell me please, is my little boy John with you? He was always such a bad little boy that I fear for his poor troubled soul."

Yes, he is one of us.

No, he is not here tonight.

"Has he learned humility and common sense, two qualities which he lacked on this earthly sphere?"

Yes.

"And has he learned to take no for an answer?"

Yes.

Quincannon scowled in the darkness. Although Sabina had been married once, she had no children. The "little boy John" was her doting partner, of course. Having a bit of teasing fun at his expense while at the same time establishing proof of Vargas's deceit.

"Mr. Quinn?" the professor said. "Will you ask Angkar a question?"

He might not have responded as he did if the heat and the sickly sweet incense hadn't given him a headache. But his head throbbed, and Sabina's playfulness rankled, and the words were out of his mouth before he could bite them back. "Oh yes, indeed," he said. "Angkar, will my dear wife ever consent to share my cold and lonely bed?"

Shocked murmurs, a muffled choking sound that might have come from Sabina, rose around him. The bell was silent. And then, without warning, the table seemed to stir and tremble beneath Quincannon's outstretched hands. Its smooth surface rippled; a faint creak sounded from somewhere underneath. In the next instant the table tilted sideways, turned and rocked and wobbled as if it been injected with a life of its own. The agitated movements continued for several seconds, stopped altogether—and then the table lifted completely off the floor, seemed to float in the air for another two or three heartbeats before finally thudding back onto the carpet.

Throughout all of this, the silver bell inside the jar remained conspicuously silent.

"Mr. Quinn, you have angered Angkar." The medium's voice was sharply reproachful. "He finds your question inappropriate, frivolous, even mocking. He may deny us further communication and return to the Afterworld."

Mrs. Buckley cried, "Oh no, please, he mustn't go!"

Cobb said angrily, "Damn your eyes, Quinn—"

"Silence!" Vargas, in a sibilant whisper. "We must do nothing more to disturb the spirits or the consequences may be dire. Do not move or speak. Do not break the circle."

The stuffy blackness closed down again. It was an effort for Quincannon to hold still. He regretted his question, though not because of any effect on Angkar and his discarnate legion; he was sure that the table-tipping and levitation would have taken place in any event. His regret was that he had allowed Sabina to glimpse the depth of his frustration, and unto the bargain added weight to her already erroneous idea of the nature of his passion. Seduction wasn't his game; his affection for her was genuine, abiding. Hell and damn! Now it might take him days, even weeks to undo the damage done by his profligate tongue—

A sound burst the heavy stillness, a jingling that was not of the silver bell in the jar. The tambourine that had been on the sideboard. Its jingling continued, steady, almost musical in an eerily discordant way.

Vargas's whisper was fervent. "Angkar is still present. He has forgiven Mr. Quinn, permitted us one more chance to communicate with the spirits he has brought with him."

Mrs. Buckley: "Praise Angkar! Praise the spirits!"

The shaking of the tambourine ended. And all at once a ghostly light appeared at a distance overhead, pale and vaporous; hovered and then commenced a swirling motion that created faint luminous streaks on the wall of dead-black. One of the sitters made an ecstatic throat noise. The swirls slowed, the light stilled again for a moment; then it began to rise until it seemed to hover just below the ceiling; and at last it faded away entirely. Other lights, mere pinpricks, flicked on and off, moving this way and that as if a handful of fireflies had been released in the room.

A thin, moaning wail erupted.

The pinpricks of light vanished.

Quincannon, listening intently, heard a faint ratchety noise followed by a strumming chord. The vaporous light reappeared, now in a different location closer to the floor; at the edge of its glow the guitar could be seen to leap into the air, to gyrate this way and that with no hand upon it. The strumming chord replayed and was joined by others—strange music that sounded and yet did not sound as though it were being made by the strings.

For three, four, five seconds the guitar continued its levitating dance, seemingly playing a tune upon itself. Then the glow once more faded, and when it was gone the music ceased and the guitar twanged to rest on the carpet.

Nearly a minute passed in electric silence.

Grace Cobb shrieked, "A hand! I felt a hand brush against my cheek!"

Vargas warned, "Do not move, do not break the circle."

Something touched Quincannon's neck, a velvety caress that lifted the short hairs there and bristled them like a cat's fur. If the fingers—they felt exactly like cold, lifeless fingers—had lingered he would have ignored the professor's remonstration and made an attempt to grab and hold onto them. But the hand or whatever it was slid away almost immediately.

Moments later it materialized long enough for it to be identifiable as just that—a disembodied hand. Then it was gone as if it had never been there at all.

Another period of silence.

The unearthly moan again.

And a glowing face appeared, as disembodied as the hand, above where Dr.

Cobb sat.

The face was a man's, shrouded as if in a bind of whitish drapery that ran right around it and was cut off at a straight line on the lower part. The eyes were enormous black-rimmed holes. The mouth moved, formed words in a deep-throated rumble.

"Oliver? It's Philip, Oliver."

"Philip! I'm so glad you've come at long last." Cobb's words were choked with feeling. "Are you well?"

"I am well. But I cannot stay long. The Auras have allowed me to make contact but now I must return."

"Yes . . . yes, I understand."

"I will come again. For a longer visit next time, Oliver. Next time . . ."

The face was swallowed by darkness.

More minutes crept away. Quincannon couldn't tell how many; he had lost all sense of time and space in the suffocating dark.

A second phantomlike countenance materialized, this one high above Margaret Buckley's chair. It was shimmery, indistinct behind a hazy substance like a luminous veil. The words that issued from it were an otherworldly, childlike quaver—the voice of a little girl.

"Mommy? Is that you, Mommy?"

"Oh thank God! Bernice!" Margaret Buckley's cry was rapturous. "Cyrus, it's our darling Bernice!"

Her husband made no response.

"I love you, Mommy. Do you love me?"

"Oh yes! Bernice, dearest, I prayed and prayed you'd come. Are you happy in the Afterworld? Tell Mommy."

"Yes, I'm very happy. But I must go back now."

"No, not so soon! Bernice, wait—"

"Will you come again, Mommy? Promise me you'll come again. Then the Auras will let me come too."

"I'll come, darling, I promise!"

The radiant image vanished.

Mrs. Buckley began to weep softly.

Quincannon was fed up with this hokum. Good and angry, too. It was despicable enough for fake mediums to dupe the gullible, but when they resorted to the exploitation of a middle-aged woman's yearning for her long-dead child the game became intolerable. The sooner he and Sabina put finish to it, the better for all concerned. If there was even one more materialization . . .

There wasn't. He heard scratchings, the unmistakable sound of the slate pencil writing on a slate. This was followed by yet another protracted silence, broken only by the faintest of scraping and clicking sounds that Quincannon couldn't identify.

Vargas said abruptly, "The spirits have grown restless. All except Angkar are returning now to the land beyond the Border. Angkar will leave too, but first he will free me from my bonds, just as one day we will all be freed from our mortal ties—"

The last word was chopped off in a meaty smacking noise and an explosive grunt of pain. Another smack, a gurgling moan.

Sabina called out in alarm, "John! Something's happened to Vargas!" Other voices rose in frightened confusion. Quincannon pushed up from the table, fumbling in his pocket for a lucifer. His thumbnail scratched it alight.

In the smoky flare he saw the others scrambling to their feet around the table, all except Professor Vargas. The medium, still roped to his chair, was slumped forward with his chin on his chest, unmoving. Quincannon kicked his own chair out of the way, carried the lucifer across to the nearest wall sconce. The gas was off; he turned it on and applied the flame. Flickery light burst forth, chasing shadows back into the room's corners.

Outside in the hallway, hands began to beat on the door panel. Annabelle's voice rose shrilly: "Let me in! I heard a cry . . . let me in!"

"Dear Lord, he's been stabbed!"

The exclamation came from Cyrus Buckley. There were other cries overridden by a shriek from Mrs. Buckley; Quincannon turned in time to see her swoon in her husband's arms. He ran to where Sabina stood staring down at the medium's slumped body.

Stabbed, for a fact. The weapon, a dagger whose ornate hilt bore a series of hieroglyphics, jutted from the back of his neck. Another wound, the first one struck for it still oozed blood, showed through a rent in Vargas's robe lower down, between the shoulder blades.

Ashen-faced, Dr. Cobb bent to feel for a pulse in the professor's neck. He shook his head and said, "Expired," a few moments later.

"It isn't possible," his wife whispered. "How *could* he have been stabbed?"

Buckley had lowered his wife onto one of the chairs and was fanning her flushed face with his hand. He said shakily, "How—and by whom?"

Quincannon caught Sabina's eye. She wagged her head to tell him she didn't know, or couldn't be sure, what had happened in those last few seconds of darkness.

The psychic assistant, Annabelle, was still beating on the door, clamoring for admittance. Quincannon went to the sideboard. The brass key lay where Vargas had set it down before the seance began; he used it to unlock the door. Annabelle rushed in from the dark hallway, her eyes wide and fearful. She gave a little moan when she saw Vargas and ran to his side, knelt to peer into his dead face.

When she straightened again her own face was as white as milk. She said tremulously, "One of you did this?"

"No," Dr. Cobb told her. "It couldn't have been one of us. No one broke the circle until after the professor was stabbed."

"Then . . . it was the spirits."

"He did perceive antagonistic waves tonight. But why would a malevolent spirit—?"

"He made all the Auras angry. I warned him but he didn't listen."

Sabina said, "How did he make the Auras angry, Annabelle?"

The woman shuddered and shook her head. Then her eyes shifted into a long stare across the room. "The slates," she said.

"What about the slates?"

"Did the spirits leave a message? Have you looked?"

Quincannon swung around to the sideboard; the others, except for Margaret Buckley, crowded close behind him. The tied slates were in the center of the stack where Vargas had placed them. He lifted those two out, undid the knot in his handkerchief, parted them for his eyes and the eyes of the others.

Murmurs and a mildly blasphemous exclamation from Buckley.

In a ghostlike hand beneath the "John Quinn" signatures on each, one message upside down and backwards as if it were a mirror image of the other, was written: *I Angkar destroyed the evil one.*

"Angkar!" Dr. Cobb said. "Why would the professor's guide and guardian turn on him that way?"

"The spirits are not mocked," Annabelle said. "They know evil when it is done in their name and guardian becomes avenger."

"Madame, what are you saying?"

"I warned him," she said again. "He would not listen and now he has paid the price. His torment will continue on the Other Side, until his essence has been cleansed of wickedness."

Quincannon said, "Enough talk and speculation," in authoritarian tones that swivelled all heads in his direction. "There'll be time for that later. Now there's work to be done."

"Quite right," Cobb agreed. "The police—"

"Not the police, doctor. Not yet."

"Here, Quinn, who are you to take charge?"

"The name isn't Quinn, it's Quincannon. John Quincannon. Of Carpenter and Quincannon, Professional Detective Services."

Cobb gaped at him. "A detective? You?"

"Two detectives." He gestured to Sabina. "My partner, Mrs. Carpenter."

"A *woman?*" Grace Cobb said. She sounded as shocked as if Sabina had been revealed as a soiled dove.

Sabina, testily: "And why not, pray tell?"

Dr. Cobb: "Who hired you. Who brought you here under false pretenses?"

Quincannon and Sabina both looked at Buckley. To his credit, the financier wasted no time in admitting he was their client.

"You, Cyrus?" Margaret Buckley had revived and was regarding them dazedly. "I don't understand. Why would you engage detectives?"

Before her husband could reply, Quincannon said, "Mr. Buckley will explain in the parlor. Be so good, all of you, as to go there and wait."

"For what?" Cobb demanded.

"For Mrs. Carpenter and me to do what no other detective, police officer, or private citizen can do half so well." False modesty was not one of Quincannon's character flaws, despite Sabina's occasional attempts to convince him otherwise. "Solve a baffling crime."

No one protested, although Dr. Cobb wore an expression of disapproval and Annabelle said, "What good are earthly detectives when it is the spirits who have taken vengeance?" as they left the room. Within a minute Quincannon and Sabina were alone with the dead man.

He turned the key in the lock to insure their privacy. He said then, "Well, my dear, a pretty puzzle, eh?"

Instead of answering, Sabina fetched him a stinging slap that rattled his eyelids. "That," she said, "is for the rude remark about sharing your bed."

For once, he was speechless. He might have argued that she had pre-cipitated the remark with her own sly comments, but this was neither the time nor the place. Besides, he could not recall ever having won an argument with Sabina over anything of consequence. There had been numerous draws, yes, but never a clearcut victory. At times he felt downright impotent in her presence. Impotent in the figurative sense of the word, of course.

"Now then," she said briskly, "shall we see if we can make good on your boast?"

They proceeded, first to extinguish the incense burner and to open a window so that cold night air could refresh the room, and then with an examination of the walls, fireplace, and floor. All were solid; there were no secret openings, crawlspaces, hidey holes, or trapdoors. Quincannon then went to inspect the corpse, while Sabina examined the jar-encased bell on the table.

The first thing he noticed was that although the rope still bound Professor Vargas to his chair, it was somewhat loose across forearms and sternum. When he lifted the limp left hand he found that it had been freed of the bonds. Vargas's right foot had also been freed. Confirmation of his suspicions in both cases. He had also more or less expected his next discovery, the two items concealed inside the sleeve of the medium's robe.

He was studying the items when Sabina said, "Just as I thought. The jar was fastened to the table with gum adhesive."

"Can you pry it loose?"

"I already have. The clapper on the bell—"

"—is either missing or frozen. Eh?"

"Frozen. Vargas used another bell to produce his spirit rings, obviously."

"This one." Quincannon held up the tiny hand-bell with its gauze-muffled clapper. "Made and struck so as to produce a hollow ring, as if it were coming from the bell inside the jar. The directionless quality of sounds in total darkness, and the power of suggestion, completed the deception."

"What else have you got there?"

He showed her the second item from Vargas's sleeve.

"A reaching rod," she said. "Mmm, yes."

Quincannon said, "His left hand was holding yours on the table. Could you tell when he freed it?"

"No, and I was waiting for just that. I think he may have done it when he coughed. You recall?"

"I do."

"He was really quite cunning," Sabina said. "A charlatan among charlatans, to paraphrase Mr. Buckley."

Medium rare, Quincannon thought again, and now medium dead. Plucked and done to a turn, for a fact, though not at all in the way anticipated. "Have you a suggestion as to who stabbed him?"

"None yet, except that it wasn't Angkar or any other supernatural agency. Annabelle may believe in spirits who wield daggers, but I don't."

"Nor I."

"One of the others at the table. A person clever enough to break the circle in the same way Vargas did and then to stand up, commit the deed, and return to his chair—all in utter darkness."

"Doesn't seem possible, does it."

"No more impossible than any of the other humbug we witnessed tonight. We've encountered such enigmas before, John."

"Too often for my liking. Well, we already have some of the answers to the evening's queer show. Find the rest and we'll solve the riddle of Vargas's death as well."

One of the missing answers came from an examination of the professor's mystic rings. The one on his left hand that he had referred to as an Egyptian Signet and Seal Talisman Ring had a hidden fingernail catch; when it was flipped, the entire top hinged upward to reveal a small sturdy hook within. Quincannon had no doubt that were he to get down on all fours and peer under the table where the medium sat, he would find a tiny metal eye screwed to the wood.

The miraculous self-playing guitar, which of course was nothing of the kind, drew him next. He already knew how its dancing levitation had been managed; a close scrutiny of the instrument revealed the rest of the gaffe.

"John, look at this."

Sabina was at the sideboard, fingering a small bottle. When he'd set the guitar down and joined her he saw that she had removed the bottle's glass stopper. "This was among the others on the tray," she told him, and held it up for him to sniff its contents.

"Ah," he said. "Almond oil."

"Mixed with white phosphorous, surely."

He nodded. "The contents of the other bottles?"

"Liquor and incense oils. Nothing more than window dressing."

Quincannon stood looking at the sideboard. At length he knelt and ran his hands over its smooth front, its fancily inlayed center top. There seemed to be neither doors nor a way to lift open the top, as if the sideboard might be a sealed wooden box. This proved not to be the case, however. It took him several minutes to locate the secret spring catch, cleverly concealed as it was among the dark-squared inlays. As soon as he pressed it, the catch released noiselessly and the entire top slid up and back on oiled hinges.

The interior was a narrow, hollow space—a box, in fact, that seemed more like a child's toy chest than a sideboard. A clutch of items were pushed into one corner. Quincannon lifted them out one by one.

A yard or two of white silk.

Another yard of fine white netting, so fine that it could he wadded into a ball no larger than a walnut.

A two-foot square piece of black cloth.

A small container of safety matches.

A theatrical mask.

And a pair of rubber gloves almost but not quite identical, both of which had been stuffed with cotton and dipped in melted paraffin.

He returned each item to the sideboard, finally closed the lid. He said with satisfaction, "That leaves only the writing on the slates. And we know now how that was done, don't we, my dear?"

"And how Professor Vargas was murdered."

"And by whom."

They smiled at each other. Smiles that gleamed wolfishly in the trembling gaslight.

♦ ♦ ♦

Neither the Buckleys nor the Cobbs took kindly to being ushered back into the seance room, even though Quincannon had moved both Vargas's body and chair away from the table and draped them with a cloth Sabina had found in another room. There was some grumbling when he asked them to assume their former positions around the table, but they all complied. A seventh chair had been added at Vargas's place; he invited Annabelle to sit there. She, too, complied, maintaining a stoic silence.

Buckley asked, "Will this take long, Quincannon? My wife has borne the worst of this ordeal. She isn't well."

"Not long, Mr. Buckley, I assure you."

"Is it absolutely necessary for us to be in here?"

"It is." Quincannon looked around at the others. "We have nothing to fear from the dead, past or present. The spirits were not responsible for what took place here tonight. Not any of it."

Grace Cobb: "Are you saying one of us stabbed Professor Vargas?"

"I am.

Annabelle: "No. It was Angkar. You mustn't deny the spirits. The penalties—"

"A pox on the penalties," Quincannon said. "Professor Vargas was murdered by a living, flesh-and-blood individual."

Dr. Cobb: "Who? If you're so all-fired certain it was one of us, name him."

"Perhaps it was you, doctor."

"See here—! What motive could I possibly have?"

"Any one of several. Such as a discovery prior to tonight that Vargas was a fake—"

"A fake!"

"—and you were so enraged by his duplicity that you determined to put a stop to it once and for all."

"Preposterous."

Quincannon was enjoying himself now. Dramatic situations appealed to his nature; he was, as Sabina had more than once pointed out, a bit of a ham. He turned his gaze on Grace Cobb. "Or you, Mrs. Cobb. Perhaps you're the guilty party."

She regarded him haughtily. "If that is an accusation—"

"Not at all. Merely a suggestion of possibility, of hidden motives of your own." Such as an interest in the medium that had gone beyond the spiritual and ended in a spurned lover's—or even a blackmail victim's—murderous rage.

"Or it could be you, Mr. Buckley, and your hiring of Carpenter and Quincannon but a smokescreen to hide your lethal intentions for this evening."

The financier's eyes glittered with anger. Sabina said warningly, "That'll do, John."

"It had better do," Buckley said, "if you entertain any hope of receiving the balance of your fee. You know full well neither I nor my wife ended that scoundrel's life."

Dr. Cobb: "I don't see how it could have been any of us. We were all seated here—all except Annabelle, and she was on the other side of the locked door. And none of us broke the circle."

"Are you certain of that, doctor?" Quincannon asked.

"Of course I'm certain."

"But you're wrong. Vargas himself broke it."

"That's impossible."

"Not at all. Neither impossible nor difficult to manage."

"*Why* would he do such a thing? For a medium to break the mystic circle is to risk the wrath of the spirits, endanger his own life. He told us so himself."

"He had already incurred the wrath of the Auras," Annabelle said fervidly. "It was Angkar, I tell you. Angkar who plunged the dagger into his body—"

Quincannon ignored her. He said to no one in particular, "You don't seem to have grasped my words to you a minute ago. Professor Vargas was a fake. The Unified College of the Attuned Impulses is a fake. He was no more sensitive to the spirit world than you or I or President Cleveland."

"That . . . that can't be true!" Margaret Buckley's face was strained, her eyes feverish. "Everything we saw and heard tonight . . . the visitations . . . my daughter . . ."

"Sham and illusion, the lot of it," Sabina said gently. "I'm sorry, Mrs. Buckley."

"But . . . but how?"

"We'll explain," Quincannon told her, "all of Vargas's tricks during the seance. To begin with, the way in which he freed his left hand while seeming to maintain an unbroken clasp of hands.

"The essence of that trick lies in the fact that the hand consists of both a wrist and fingers and the wrist is able to bend in different directions. The fingers of Vargas's left hand, you remember, were holding Mrs. Carpenter's wrist, while Mrs. Cobb's fingers were gripping his right wrist. By maneuvering his hands closer and closer together as he talked, in a series of small spasmodic movements, he also brought the ladies' hands closer together. When they were near enough for his own thumbs to touch, he freed his left hand in one quick movement and immediately reestablished control with his right—the same hand's fingers holding Mrs. Carpenter while its wrist was being gripped by Mrs. Cobb."

Buckley: "But how could he manage that when we were all concentrating on tight control?"

"He coughed once, rather loudly, if you recall. The sound was a calculated aural distraction. In that instant—and an instant was all it took—he completed the maneuver. He also relied on the fact that a person's senses become unreliable after a protracted period of sitting in total darkness. What you think you see, hear, feel at any given moment may in fact be partly or completely erroneous."

There was a brief silence while the others digested this. Dr. Cobb said then, "Even with one hand free, how could he have rung the spirit bell? I bound him myself, Quincannon, and I am morally certain the loops and knots were tight."

"You may be certain in your own mind, doctor, but the facts are otherwise. It is a near impossibility for anyone, even a professional detective, to securely tie a man to a chair with a single length of rope. And you were flurried, self-conscious, anxious to acquit yourself well of the business, and you are a gentleman besides. You would hardly bind a man such as Professor Vargas, whom you admired and respected, with enough constriction of the rope to cut into his flesh. A fraction of an inch of slack is all a man who has been tied many times before, who is skilled in muscular control, requires in order to free one hand."

Cobb was unable to refute the logic of this. He lapsed into a somewhat daunted silence as Quincannon went on to explain and demonstrate the bell-ringing trick.

"Next we have the table tipping and levitation. Vargas accomplished this phenomenon with but one hand and one foot, the right lower extremity having been freed with the aid of the upper left." Quincannon had removed the Egyptian talisman ring from the medium's finger; he held it up, released the fingernail catch to reveal the hook within. "He attached this hook to a small eye screwed beneath the table, after which he gave a sharp upward jerk. The table legs on his end were lifted off the carpet just far enough for him to slip the toe of his shoe under one of them, thus creating a 'human clamp' which gave him full control of the table. By lifting with his ring and elevating his toe while the heel remained on the carpet, he was able to make the table tilt, rock, gyrate at will."

Sabina added, "And when he was ready for the table to appear to levitate, he simply unhooked his ring and thrust upward with his foot, withdrawing it immediately afterward. The illusion of the table seeming to float under our hands for a second or two before it fell was enhanced by both the circumstances and the darkness."

Buckley, with some bitterness: "Seems so blasted obvious when explained."

"Such flummery always is, Mr. Buckley. It's the trappings and manipulation that make it mystifying. The so-called spirit lights are another example." Sabina placed the stoppered glass bottle on the table and described where she'd found it and what it contained. "Mix white phosphorous with any fatty oil, and the result is a bottle filled with hidden light. As long as the bottle remains stoppered the phosphorous gives off no glow, but as soon as the cork is removed and air is permitted to reach the phosphorous, a faint unearthly shine results. Wave the bottle in the air and the light seems to dart about. Replace the stopper and the light fades away as the air inside is used up."

"The little winking lights were more of the same, I suppose?"

"Not quite," Quincannon said. "Match-heads were their source. Hold a match-head between the moistened forefinger and thumb of each hand, wiggle the forefinger enough to expose and then once more quickly conceal the match-head, and you have flitting fireflies."

Grace Cobb asked, "The guitar that seemed to dance and play itself—how was that done?"

Quincannon fetched the guitar, brought it back to the table. Beside it he set the reaching rod from Vargas's sleeve. The rod was only a few inches in length when closed, but when he opened out each of its sections after the fashion of a telescope, it extended the full length of the table and beyond—more than six feet overall. "Vargas extended this rod in his left hand," he said, "inserted it in the hole in the neck of the instrument, raised and slowly turned the guitar this way and that to create the illusion of air-dancing. As for the music . . ."

He reached into the hole under the strings, gave a quick twist. The weird strumming they had heard during the seance began to emanate from within.

Mrs. Cobb: "A music box!"

"A one-tune music box, to be precise, affixed to the wood inside with gum adhesive."

Buckley: "The hand that touched Mrs. Cobb's cheek? The manifestations? The spirit writing on the slate?"

"All part and parcel of the same flummery," Quincannon told him. Again he went to the sideboard, where he pressed the hidden release to raise its top. From inside he took out the two stuffed and wax-coated rubber gloves, held them up for the others to view.

"These are the ghostly fingers that touched Mrs. Cobb and my neck as well. The smoothness of the paraffin gives them the feel of human flesh. One 'hand' has been treated with luminous paint; it was kept covered under this"—he showed them the black cloth—"until the time came to reveal it as a glowing disembodied entity."

He lifted out the silk drapery and theatrical mask. "The mask has been treated in the same way. The combination of these two items were used to create the manifestation alleged to be Philip Cobb."

He raised the fine white netting. "Likewise made phosphorescent and draped over the head to create the manifestation purported to be the Buckleys' daughter."

"But . . . I heard Bernice speak," Margaret Buckley said weakly. "It was her voice, I'm sure it was . . ."

Her husband took her hand in both of his. "No, Margaret, it wasn't. You only imagined it to be."

"An imitation of a child's voice," Quincannon said, "just as the other voice was an imitation of a man's deep articulation."

He picked up the two slates which bore the "spirit message" under his false signatures. " 'I Angkar destroyed the evil one.' Vargas's murderer wrote those words, in sequence on one slate and upside down and backwards on the other to heighten the illusion of spirit writing. Before the murder was done, in anticipation of it."

"Who?" Buckley demanded. "Name the person, Quincannon."

"Professor Vargas's accomplice, of course."

"Accomplice?"

"Certainly. No one individual, no matter how skilled in supernatural fakery, could have arranged and carried out all the tricks we were subjected to even if he hadn't been roped to his chair. Someone else had to direct the reaching rod to the guitar and then turn the spring on the music box. Someone else had to jangle the tambourine, make the wailing noises, carry the phosphorous bottle to different parts of the room and up onto the love seat there so as to make the light seem to float near the ceiling. Someone else had to manipulate the waxed gloves, don the mask and drapery and netting, imitate the spirit voices."

"Annabelle? Are you saying it was Annabelle?"

"None other."

They all stared at the pale, silent woman at the head of the table. Her expression remained frozen, but her gaze burned with a zealot's fire.

Dr. Cobb said, "But she wasn't in the room with us . . ."

"Ah, but she was, doctor. At first I believed her to have been in another part of the house—not because of the locked door but because of the way in which the lights dimmed and extinguished to begin the seance. It seemed she must have turned the gas off at a prearranged time. Not so. Some type of automatic timing mechanism was used for that purpose. Annabelle, you see, was already present here before the rest of us entered and Vargas locked the door."

"Before, you say?"

"She disappeared from the parlor, you'll recall, as soon as she announced that all was in readiness. While Vargas detained us with his call for 'donations,' Annabelle slipped into this room and hid herself."

"Where? There are no hiding places . . . unless you expect us to believe she crawled up inside the fireplace chimney."

"Not there, no. Nor are there any secret closets or passages or any other such hocus-pocus. She was hidden—"

"—in the same place as her spirit props," Sabina interrupted, "within the sideboard." Her testy glance at Quincannon said he'd hogged center-stage long enough; she wasn't above a bit of a flare for the dramatic herself, he thought fondly. "The interior is hollow, and she is both tiny and enough of a contortionist to fold her body into such a short, narrow space. The catch that releases the hinged top can be operated from within as well. Once the room was in total darkness and Vargas began invoking the spirits, she climbed out to commence her preparations. Under her robe, I'll warrant, is an all-black, close-fitting garment. Black gloves and a mask of some sort to cover her white face completed the costume. And her familiarity with the room allowed her to move about in silence."

"All well and good," Buckley said, "but the woman was *outside* the locked door, pounding on it, less than a minute after Vargas was stabbed. Explain that."

"Simple misdirection, Mr. Buckley. Before the stabbing she replaced all props in the sideboard and closed the top, then unlocked the door; the key made a faint scraping and the bolt clicked, sounds which John and I both heard.

Then she crossed the room, plunged her dagger into Vargas, recrossed the room immediately after the second thrust, let herself out into the darkened hallway, and relocked the door from that side. Not with Vargas's key, which remained on the sideboard, but with a duplicate key of her own."

No one spoke for a cluster of seconds. In hushed tones, then, Grace Cobb asked, "Why did you do it, Annabelle?"

The psychic assistant's mouth twisted. Her voice, when it came, was fiery with passion. "He was an evil unbeliever. He mocked the spirits with his schemes, laughed and derided them and those of us who truly believe. I did his bidding because I loved him, I obeyed him until the spirits came in the night and told me I must obey no longer. They said I must destroy him. Angkar guided my hand tonight. Angkar showed me the path to the truth and light of the Afterworld . . ."

Her words trailed off; she sat staring fixedly. Looking at no one there with her blazing eyes, Quincannon thought, but at whatever she believed waited for her beyond the pale.

♦ ♦ ♦

It was after midnight before the bumbling constabulary (Quincannon considered all city policemen to be bumbling) finished with their questions, took Annabelle away, and permitted the others to depart. On the mist-wet walk in front, while they waited for hansoms, Cyrus Buckley drew Quincannon aside.

"You and Mrs. Carpenter are competent detectives, sir, I'll grant you that even though I don't wholly approve of your methods. You'll have my check for the balance of our arrangement tomorrow morning."

Quincannon bowed and accepted the financier's hand. "If you should find yourself in need of our services again . . ."

"I trust I won't." Buckley paused to unwrap a long-nine cigar. "One question before we part. As I told you in your offices, the first seance Mrs. Buckley and I attended here was concluded by Vargas's claim that Angkar had untied him. We heard the rope flung through the air, and when the gas was turned up we saw it lying unknotted on the floor. He couldn't have untied all those knots himself, with only one free hand."

"Hardly. Annabelle assisted in that trick too."

"I don't quite see how it was worked. Can you make a guess?"

"I can. The unknotted rope, which he himself hurled across the room, was not the same one with which he was tied. Annabelle slipped up behind him and cut the knotted rope into pieces with her dagger, then hid the pieces in the sideboard. The second rope was concealed there with the props and given to Vargas after she'd severed the first."

"His planned finale for tonight's seance too, I fancy."

"No doubt. Instead, Annabelle improvised a far more shocking finish."

"Made him pay dearly for mocking the spirits, eh?"

"If you like, Mr. Buckley. If you like."

Quincannon had time to smoke a bowlful of shag tobacco before a hansom arrived for him and Sabina. Settled in the darkened coach on the way to Russian Hill, he said, "All's well that ends well. But I must say I'm glad this case is closed. Psychic phenomena, theocratic unity . . . bah. The lot of it is—"

"—horsefeathers," Sabina said. "Yes, I know. But are you quite sure there's no truth in it?"

"Spiritualism? None whatsoever."

"Not spiritualism. The existence of a spirit afterlife."

"Don't tell me you give a whit of credence to such folly?"

"I have an open mind."

"So do I, my dear, on most matters."

"But not the paranormal."

"Not a bit of it."

For a time they sat in companionable stillness broken only by the jangle of the horses' bit chains, the clatter of the iron wheels on rough cobblestones. Then there was a faint stirring in the heavy darkness, and to Quincannon's utter amazement, a pair of soft, sweet lips brushed his, clung passionately for an instant, then withdrew.

He sat stunned for several beats. At which point his lusty natural instincts took over; he twisted on the seat, reached out to Sabina with eager hands and mouth. Both found yielding flesh. He kissed her soundly.

In the next second he found himself embracing a struggling, squirming spitfire. She pulled free, and the crack of her hand on his cheek was twice as hard as the slap in Vargas's spirit room. "What makes you think you can take such liberties, John Quincannon!" she demanded indignantly.

"But . . . I was only returning your affection . . ."

"*My* affection?"

"You kissed me first. Why, if you didn't care to have it reciprocated?"

"What are you gabbling about? I didn't kiss you."

"Of course you did. A few moments ago."

"Faugh! I did no such thing and you know it." Her dress rustled as she slid farther away from him. "Now I'll thank you to keep your distance and behave yourself."

He sat and behaved, not happily. Had he imagined the kiss? No, he wasn't that moonstruck. She had kissed him, for a fact; he could still feel her lips against his. Some sort of woman's game to devil him. He imagined her smiling secretly in the dark—but then the hack passed close to a streetlamp, and he saw that she was leaning against the far door with her arms folded, unsmiling and wearing an injured look.

The only other explanation for the kiss . . . but that was sheer lunacy, not worth a moment's consideration. It must have been Sabina. Of course it was Sabina. And yet . . .

The hansom clattered on into the cold, damp night.

THE HIGHBINDERS

I n his twenty years as a detective Quincannon had visited a great many strange and sinister places, but this May night was his first time in an opium den. And not just one—four of them, so far. Four too many.

Blind Annie's Cellar, this one was called. Another of the reputed three hundred such resorts that infested the dark heart of San Francisco's Chinatown. Located in Ross Alley, it was a foulsmelling cave full of scurrying cats and yellowish-blue smoke that hung in ribbons and layers. The smoke seemed to move lumpily, limp at the ends; its thick-sweet odor, not unlike that of burning orange peel, turned Quincannon's seldom-tender stomach for the fourth straight time.

"The gentleman want to smoke?"

The question came in a scratchy singsong from a rag-encased crone seated on a mat just inside the door. On her lap was a tray laden with nickels—the price of admittance. Quincannon said, "No, I'm looking for someone," and added a coin to the litter in the tray. The old woman nodded and grinned, revealing toothless gums. It was a statement, he thought sourly, she had heard a hundred times before. Blind Annie's, like the other three he'd entered, was a democratic resort that catered to Caucasian "dude fiends"—well-dressed ladies and diamond-studded gentlemen—as well as to Chinese coolies with twenty-cent *yenshee* habits. Concerned friends and relatives would come looking whenever one of these casual, and in many cases not so casual, hop-smokers failed to return at an appointed time.

Quincannon moved deeper into the lamp-streaked gloom. Tiers of bunks lined both walls, each outfitted with nut-oil lamp, needle, pipe, bowl, and supply of *ah pin vin*. All of the bunks in the nearest tier were occupied. Most smokers lay still, carried to sticky slumber by the black stuff in their pipes. Only one was Caucasian, a man who lay propped on one elbow, smiling fatuously as he held a lichee-nut shell of opium over the flame of his lamp. It made a spluttering, hissing noise as it cooked. Quincannon stepped close enough to determine that the man wasn't James Scarlett, then turned toward the far side of the den.

And there, finally, he found his quarry.

The young attorney lay motionless on one of the lower bunks at the rear, his lips shaping words as if he were chanting some song to himself. Quincannon shook him, slapped his face. No response. Scarlett was a serious addict; he regularly "swallowed a cloud and puffed out fog," as the Chinese said, and escaped for hours, sometimes days, deep inside his pipe dreams.

"You're a blasted fool, all right," Quincannon told the deaf ears. "This is the last section of the city you should've ventured into on this night. It's a wonder you're not dead already." He took a grip on the attorney's rumpled frock coat, hauled him around and off the bunk. There was no protest as he hoisted the slender body over his shoulder.

He was halfway to the door with his burden when his foot struck one of the darting cats. It yowled and clawed at his leg, pitching him off balance. He reeled cursing against one of the bunks, dislodged a lamp from its edge; the glass chimney shattered on impact, splashing oil and wick onto the filthy floor matting. The flame that sprouted was thin, shaky; the lack of oxygen in the room kept it from flaring high and spreading. Quincannon stamped out the meager fire and then strained over at the waist, righted the lamp with his free hand. When he stood straight again he heard someone giggle, someone else begin to sing in a low tone. None of the pipers whose eyes were still open paid him the slightest attention. Neither did the smiling crone by the door.

He shifted Scarlett's inert weight on his shoulder. "Opium fiends, tong rivalry, body snatching," he muttered as he staggered past the hag. "Bah, what a case!"

Outside he paused to breathe deeply several times. The cold night air cleared his lungs of the *ah pin vin* smoke and restored his equilibrium. It also roused Scarlett somewhat from his stupor. He stirred, mumbled incoherent words, but his body remained flaccid in Quincannon's grasp.

Nearby, a streetlamp cast a feeble puddle of light; farther down Ross Alley, toward Jackson Street where the hired buggy and driver waited, a few strings of paper lanterns and the glowing brazier of a lone sidewalk foodseller opened small holes in the darkness. It was late enough, nearing midnight, so that few pedestrians were abroad. Not many law-abiding Chinese ventured out at this hour. Nor had in the past fifteen years, since the rise of the murderous tongs in the early 'eighties. The Quarter's nights belonged to the hop-smokers and fantan gamblers, the slave-girl prostitutes ludicrously called "flower willows," and the *boo how doy*, the tongs' paid hatchet men.

Quincannon carried his burden toward Jackson, his footsteps echoing on the rough cobbles. James Scarlett mumbled again, close enough to Quincannon's ear and with enough lucidity for the words—and the low, fearful tone in which he uttered them—to be distinguishable.

"Fowler Alley," he said.

"What's that, my lad?"

A moan. Then something that might have been "Blue shadow."

"Not out here tonight," Quincannon grumbled. "They're all black as the devil's fundament."

Ahead he saw the buggy's driver hunched fretfully on the seat, one hand holding the horse's reins and the other tucked inside his coat, doubtless resting on the handle of a revolver. Quincannon had had to pay him handsomely for this night's work—too handsomely to suit his thrifty Scot's nature, even though he would see to it that Mrs. James Scarlett paid the expense. If it had not been for the fact that highbinders almost never preyed on Caucasians, even a pile of greenbacks wouldn't have been enough to bring the driver into Chinatown at midnight.

Twenty feet from the corner, Quincannon passed the lone foodseller huddled over his brazier. He glanced at the man, noted the black coolie blouse with its drooping sleeves, the long queue, the head bent and shadow-hidden beneath a black slouch hat surmounted by a topknot. He shifted his gaze to the buggy again, took two more steps—

Coolie foodsellers don't wear slouch hats . . . one of the badges of the highbinder . . .

The sudden thought caused him to break stride and turn awkwardly under Scarlett's weight, his hand groping beneath his coat for the holstered Navy Colt. The Chinese was already on his feet. From inside one sleeve he had drawn a long-barreled revolver; he aimed and fired before Quincannon could free his weapon.

The bullet struck the limp form of James Scarlett, made it jerk and slide free. The gunman fired twice more, loud reports in the close confines of the alley, but Quincannon was already falling sideways, his feet torn from under him by the attorney's toppling weight. Both slugs missed in the darkness, one singing in ricochet off the cobbles.

Quincannon struggled out from under the tangle of Scarlett's arms and legs. As he lurched to one knee he heard the retreating thud of the highbinder's footfalls. Heard, too, the rattle and slap of harness leather and bit chains, the staccato beat of horse's hooves as the buggy driver whipped out of harm's way. The gunman was a dim figure racing diagonally across Jackson. By the time Quincannon gained his feet, the man had vanished into the black maw of Ragpickers' Alley.

Fury drove Quincannon into giving chase even though he knew it was futile. Other narrow passages opened off Ragpickers'—Bull Run, Butchers' Alley with its clotted smells of poultry and fish. It was a maze made for the *boo how doy*; if he tried to navigate it in the dark, he was liable to become lost—or worse, leave himself wide open for ambush. The wisdom of this finally cooled his blood, slowed him to a halt ten rods into the lightless alleyway. He stood listening, breathing through his mouth. He could still hear the assassin's footfalls, but they were directionless now, fading. Seconds later, they were gone.

Quickly he returned to Jackson Street. The thoroughfare was empty, the driver and his rig long away. Ross Alley appeared deserted, too, but he could feel eyes peering at him from behind curtains and glass. The highbinder's brazier still burned; in its orange glow James Scarlett was a motionless bulk on the cobbles where he'd fallen. Quincannon went to one knee, probed with fingers that grew wet with blood. One bullet had entered the middle of the attorney's back, shattering the spine and no doubt killing him instantly.

If the Kwong Dock tong was responsible for this, Quincannon thought grimly, war between them and the Hip Sing could erupt at any time. The theft of Bing Ah Kee's corpse was bad enough, but the murder of a Hip Sing shyster —and a white man at that—was worse because of the strong threat of retaliation by police raiders and mobs of Barbary Coast and Tar-Flat toughs. All of Chinatown, in short, was soon to be a powderkeg with a lighted fuse.

♦ ♦ ♦

The Hall of Justice, an imposing gray stone pile at Kearney and Washington streets, was within stampeding distance of the Chinese Quarter. Quincannon had never felt comfortable inside the building. For one thing, he'd had a run-in or two with the city's constabulary, who did not care to have their thunder stolen by a private investigator who was better at their jobs than they were. For another thing, police corruption had grown rampant in recent times. Just last year there had been a departmental shakeup in which several officers and Police Clerk William E. Hall were discharged. Chief Crowley claimed all the bad apples had been removed and the barrel was now clean, but Quincannon remained skeptical.

He hid his edginess from the other three men present in the Chief's office by carefully loading and lighting his favorite briar. One of the men he knew well enough, even grudgingly respected; this was Lieutenant William Price, head of the Chinatown "flying squad" that had been formed in an effort to control tong crime. He had mixed feelings about Crowley, and liked Sergeant Adam Gentry, Price's assistant, not at all. Gentry was contentious and made no bones about his distaste for flycops.

Short and wiry, a rooster of a man in his gold-buttoned uniform, Gentry watched with a flinty gaze as Quincannon shook out the sulphur match. "Little Pete's behind this, sure as hell. No one else in Chinatown would have the audacity to order the shooting of a white man."

"So it would seem," Quincannon allowed.

"Seem? That bloody devil controls every tong in the Quarter except the Hip Sing."

This was an exaggeration. Fong Ching, alias F.C. Peters, alias Little Pete, was a powerful man, no question—a curious mix of East and West, honest and crooked. He ran several successful businesses, participated in both Chinatown and city politics, and was cultured enough to write Chinese stage operas, yet he ruled much of Chinatown crime with such cleverness that he had never been prosecuted. But his power was limited to a few sin-and-vice tongs. Most tongs were law-abiding, self-governing, and benevolent.

Quincannon said, "The Hip Sing is Pete's strongest rival, I'll grant you that."

"Yes, and he's not above starting a bloodbath in Chinatown to gain control of it. He's a menace to white and yellow alike."

"Not so bad as that," Price said. "He already controls the blackmail, extortion, and slave-girl rackets, and the Hip Sing is no threat to him there. Gambling is their game, and under Bing Ah Kee there was never any serious trouble between the two. That won't change much under the new president, Mock Don Yuen, though it could if that sneaky son of his, Mock Quan, ever takes over."

"Pete's power-mad," Gentry argued. "He wants the whole of Chinatown in his pocket."

"But he's not crazy. He might order the snatching of Bing's remains— though even the Hip Sing aren't convinced he's behind that business or there'd have been war declared already—but I can't see him risking the public execution of a white man, not for any reason. He knows it'd bring us down on him and his highbinders with a vengeance. He's too smart by half to allow that to happen."

"I say he's not. There's not another man in that rathole of vice who'd dare to do it."

Quincannon said, "Hidden forces at work, mayhap?"

"Not bloody likely."

"No, it's possible," Price said. He ran a forefinger across his thick mustache. He was a big man, imposing in both bulk and countenance; he had a deserved reputation in Chinatown as the "American Terror," the result of raiding parties he'd led into the Quarter's dens of sin. "I've had a feeling that there's more than meets the eye and ear in Chinatown these days. Yet we've learned nothing to corroborate it."

"Well, I don't care which way the wind is blowing over there," the Chief said. "I don't like this damned shooting tonight." Crowley was an overweight sixty, florid and pompous. Politics was his game; his policeman's instincts were suspect, a lacking which sometimes led him to rash judgment and action. "The *boo how doy* have always left Caucasians strictly alone. Scarlett's murder sets a deadly precedent and I'm not going to stand by and do nothing about it."

Gentry had lighted a cigar; he waved it for emphasis as he said, "Bully! Finish off Little Pete and his gang before he has more innocent citizens murdered, that's what I say."

"James Scarlett wasn't innocent," Price reminded him. "He sold his soul to the Hip Sing for opium, defended their hatchet men in court. And he had guilty knowledge of the theft of Bing's corpse, possibly even a hand in the deed, according to what Quincannon has told us."

"According to what Scarlett's wife told my partner and me," Quincannon corrected, "though she said nothing of an actual involvement in the body snatching. Only that he had knowledge of the crime and was in mortal fear of his life. Whatever he knew, he kept it to himself. He never spoke of Little Pete or the Kwong Dock to Mrs. Scarlett."

"They're guilty as sin, just the same," Gentry said. "By God, the only way to ensure public safety is to send the flying squad out to the tong headquarters and Pete's hangouts. Axes, hammers, and pistols will write their epitaphs in a hurry."

"Not yet," Price said. "Not without proof."

"Well, then, why don't we take the squad and find some? Evidence that Pete's behind the killing. Evidence to point to the cold storage where old Bing's bones are stashed."

"Pete's too clever to leave evidence for us to find."

"He is, but maybe his highbinders aren't."

"The sergeant has a good point," Chief Crowley said. "Will, take half a dozen men and go over those places with a fine tooth comb. And don't take any guff from Pete and his highbinders while you're about it."

"Just as you say, Chief." Price turned to his assistant. "Round up an interpreter and assemble the men we'll need."

"Right away." Gentry hurried from the office.

Quincannon asked through a cloud of pipe smoke, "What do you know of Fowler Alley, Lieutenant?"

"Fowler Alley? Why do you ask that?"

"Scarlett mumbled the name after I carried him out of Blind Annie's. I wonder if it might have significance."

"I can't imagine how. Little Pete hangs out at his shoe factory in Bartlett Alley and Bartlett is where the Kwong Dock Company is located, too. As far as I know, there are no tongs headquartered in Fowler Alley. And no illegal activity."

"Are any of the businesses there run by Pete?"

"Not to my knowledge. I'll look into it."

Quincannon nodded, thinking: Not before I do, I'll wager. He got to his feet. "I'll be going now, if you've no objection."

Chief Crowley waved a hand. "We'll notify you if you're needed again."

"Will you bring Mrs. Scarlett word of her husband's death?"

"I'll dispatch a man." The Chief added wryly, "I imagine she'd rather not hear it from you, under the circumstances."

Quincannon said, "I expect not," between his teeth and took his leave.

♦ ♦ ♦

The law offices of James Scarlett were on the southern fringe of Chinatown, less than half a mile from the Hall of Justice. Quincannon had visited the dingy, two-story building earlier in the day, after leaving Andrea Scarlett with Sabina. The place had been dark and locked up tight then; the same was true when he arrived there a few minutes past midnight.

He paid the hansom driver at the corner, walked back through heavy shadows to the entranceway. Brooding the while, as he had in the cab, about the incident in Ross Alley.

How had the gunman known enough to lie in ambush as he had? If he'd been following Scarlett, why not simply enter the opium resort and shoot him there? Witnesses were never a worry to highbinders. The other explanation was that it was Quincannon who had been followed, though it seemed impossible that anyone in Chinatown could know that Carpenter and Quincannon, Professional Detective Services had been hired by Mrs. Scarlett to find and protect her husband.

Then there was the fact that the assassin had fired three shots, the last two of which had come perilously close to sending Quincannon to join *his* ancestors. Poor and hurried shooting caused by darkness? Or had he also been a target? Something about the gunman fretted him, too, something he could not quite put his finger on.

The whole business smacked of hidden motives, for a fact. And hidden dangers. He did not like to be made a pawn in any piece of intrigue. He liked it almost as little as being shot at, intentionally or otherwise, and failing at a job he had been retained to do. He meant to get to the bottom of it, with or without official sanction.

Few door latches had ever withstood his ministrations, and the one on James Scarlett's building was no exception. Another attorney occupied the downstairs rooms; Quincannon climbed a creaky staircase to the second floor. The pebbled glass door imprinted with the words *J.H. Scarlett, Attorney-at-Law* was not locked. This puzzled him slightly, though not for long.

Inside, he struck a sulphur match, found the gas outlet—the building was too old and shabby to have been wired for electricity—and lit the flame. Its pale glow showed him a dusty anteroom containing two desks whose bare surfaces indicated that it had been some while since they had been occupied by either law clerk or secretary. He proceeded through a doorway into Scarlett's private sanctum.

His first impression was that the lawyer had been a remarkably untidy individual. A few seconds later he revised this opinion; the office had been searched in a hurried but rather thorough fashion. Papers littered the top of a large oak desk, the floor around it and the floor under a bank of wooden file cases. Two of the file drawers were partly open. A wastebasket behind the desk had been overturned and its contents gone through. A shelf of lawbooks showed signs of having been examined as well.

The fine hand of a highbinder? Possibly, though the methods used here were a good deal less destructive than those usually employed by the *boo how doy*.

The smell of must and mildew wrinkled his nostrils as he crossed to the desk, giving him to wonder just how much time Scarlett had spent in these premises. The office wanted a good airing, if not a match to purge it completely. Scowling, he sifted through the papers on and below the desk. They told him nothing except that almost all of Scarlett's recent clients had been Chinese; none of the names was familiar and none of the addresses was on Fowler Alley. The desk drawers yielded even less of interest, and the slim accumulation of briefs, letters, and invoices in the file drawers was likewise unproductive. None bore any direct reference to either the Hip Sing or Kwong Dock tongs, or to Fong Ching under his own name or any of his known aliases.

The only interesting thing about the late Mr. Scarlett's office, in fact, was the state in which Quincannon had found it. What had the previous intruder been searching for? And whatever it was, had he found it?

♦ ♦ ♦

Sabina was already at her desk when he arrived at the Market Street offices of Carpenter and Quincannon, Professional Detective Services at nine a.m. She looked bright and well-scrubbed, her glossy black hair piled high on her head and fastened with a jade barrette. As always, Quincannon's hard heart softened and his pulses quickened at sight of her. A fine figure of a woman, Mrs. Sabina Carpenter. For a few seconds, as he shed his derby but not his Chesterfield, the wicked side of his imagination speculated once again on what that fine figure would look like divested of its skirt and jacket, shirtwaist and lacy undergarments . . .

She narrowed her eyes at him as he crossed the room. "Before we get down to business," she said, "I'll thank you to put my clothes back on."

"Eh?" Sudden warmth crept out of Quincannon's collar. "My dear Sabina! You can't think that I—"

"I don't think it, I know it. I know you, John Quincannon, far better than you think I do."

He sighed. "Perhaps, though you often mistake my motives."

"I doubt that. Was your sleepless night a reward of that lascivious mind of yours?"

"How did you know—"

"Bloodshot eyes in saggy pouches. If I didn't know better, I'd think you had forsaken your temperance pledge."

"Observant wench. No, it was neither Demon Rum nor impure thoughts nor my misunderstood affections for you that kept me awake most of the blasted night."

"What, then?"

"The death of James Scarlett and the near death of your most obedient servant."

The words startled her, though only someone who knew Sabina as he did would have been aware of it; her round face betrayed only the barest shadow of her surprise. "What happened, John?"

He told her in detail, including the things that bothered him about the incident and the speculations shared with the three police officers. The smooth skin of her forehead and around her generous mouth bore lines of concern when he finished.

"Bad business," she said. "And bad for business, losing a man we were hired to protect to an assassin's bullet. Not that you're to be blamed, of course."

"Of course," Quincannon said sardonically. "But others will blame me, The only way to undo the damage is for me to find the scoundrel responsible before the police do."

"Us to find him, you mean."

"Us," he agreed.

"I suppose it's back to Chinatown for you."

"It's where the whole of the answer lies."

"Fowler Alley?"

"If Scarlett's mutterings were significant and not part of a hop dream."

"You said he sounded frightened when he spoke the name. Opium dreams are seldom nightmares, John. Men and women use the stuff to escape from nightmares, real or imaginary."

"True."

"Scarlett's other words—'blue shadow.' A connection of some sort to Fowler Alley?"

"Possibly. I'm not sure but what I misheard him and the phrase only sounded like 'blue shadow.' "

"Spoken in the same frightened tone?"

Quincannon cudgeled his memory. "I can't be certain."

"Well, our client may have some idea. While you're in Chinatown, I'll pay a call on her."

"I was about to suggest that." He didn't add that this was a task he himself wished to avoid at all costs. Facing a female client whom he had failed would have embarrassed him mightily. The job required Sabina's fine, tactful hand. "Ask her if she knows of any incriminating documents her husband might have had in his possession. And where he kept his private papers. If it wasn't at his office, the mugg who searched it before me may not have found what he was after."

"I will. Who would the mugg be, do you suppose, if not one of Little Pete's highbinders?"

"I don't say that it wasn't a highbinder. Only that the job seemed to have a more professional touch than the hatchet man's usual ham-fisted tactics."

"Is there anything you can remember about the gunman?" Sabina asked. "It's possible he was known to Mrs. Scarlett as well as her husband."

"It was too dark and his hat pulled too low for a clear squint at his face. Average size, average height." Quincannon scratched irritably at his free-booter's whiskers. "Still, there was something odd about him . . ."

"Appearance? Movements? Did he say anything?"

"Not a word. Hell and damn! I can't seem to dredge the thing up."

"Let it be and it'll come to you eventually."

"Eventually may be too late." Quincannon clamped his derby on his head, squarely, the way he always wore it when he was on an important mission. "Enough talk. It's action I crave and action I'll have."

"Not too much of it, I hope. Shall we meet back here at one o'clock?"

"If I'm not here by then," Quincannon said, "it'll be because I'm some-where with my hands around a highbinder's throat."

♦ ♦ ♦

Fowler Alley was a typical Chinatown passage: narrow, crooked, packed with men and women mostly dressed in the black clothing of the lower-caste Chinese. Paper lanterns strung along rickety balconies and the glowing braziers of foodsellers added the only color and light to a tunnellike expanse made even more gloomy by an overcast sky.

Quincannon, one of the few Caucasians among the throng, wandered along looking at storefronts and the upper floors of sagging firetraps roofed in tar-paper and gravel. Many of the second and third floors were private apartments, hidden from view behind dusty, curtained windows. Some of the business establishments were identifiable from their displayed wares: restaurants, herb shops, a clothiers, a vegetable market. Others, tucked away behind closed doors, darkened windows, and signs in inexplicable Chinese characters, remained a mystery.

Nothing in the alley aroused his suspicions or pricked his curiosity. There were no tong headquarters here, no opium resorts or fantan parlors or houses of ill repute; and nothing even remotely suggestive of blue shadows.

Quincannon retraced his steps through the passage, stopping the one other white man he saw and several Chinese. Did anyone know James Scarlett? The Caucasian was a dry goods drummer on his second and what he obviously hoped would be his last visit to the Quarter; he had never heard of Scarlett, he said. All the Chinese either didn't speak English or pretended they didn't.

Fowler Alley lay open on both ends, debouching into other passages, but at least for the present, Quincannon thought sourly as he left it, it was a dead-end.

◆ ◆ ◆

The Hip Sing tong was headquartered on Waverly Place, once called Pike Street, one of Chinatown's more notorious thoroughfares. Here, temples and fraternal buildings stood cheek by jowl with opium and gambling dens and the cribs of the flower willows. Last night, when Quincannon had started his hunt for James Scarlett, the passage had been mostly empty; by daylight it teemed with carts, wagons, buggies, half-starved dogs and cats, and human pedestrians. The noise level was high and constant, a shrill tide dominated by the lilting dialects of Canton, Shanghai, and the provinces of Old China.

Two doors down from the three-story tong building was the Four Families Temple, a building of equal height but a much more ornate facade, its balconies carved and painted and decorated with pagoda cornices. On impulse Quincannon turned in through the entrance doors and proceeded to what was known as the Hall of Sorrows, where funeral services were conducted and the bodies of the high-born were laid out in their caskets for viewing. Candlelight flickered; the pungent odor of incense assailed him. The long room, deserted at the moment, was ceiled with a massive scrolled wood carving covered in gold leaf, from which hung dozens of lanterns in pink and green, red and gold. At the far end were a pair of altars with a red prayer bench fronting one. Smaller altars on either side wore embroidered cloths on which fruit, flowers, candles, and joss urns had been arranged.

It was from here that the remains of Bing Ah Kee, venerable president of the Hip Sing Company, had disappeared two nights ago. The old man had died of natural causes and his corpse, after having been honored with a lavish funeral parade, had been returned to the temple for one last night; the next morning it was scheduled to be placed in storage to await passage to Bing's ancestral home in Canton for burial. The thieves had removed the body from its coffin and made off with it sometime during the early morning hours—a particularly bold deed considering the close proximity of the Hip Sing building. Yet they had managed it unseen and unheard, leaving no clue as to their identity or purpose.

Body snatching was uncommon but not unheard of in Chinatown. When such ghoulishness did occur, tong rivalry was almost always the motivating factor—a fact which supported Sergeant Gentry's contention that the disappearance of Bing Ah Kee's husk was the work of Little Pete and the Kwong Dock. Yet stealing an enemy leader's bones without openly claiming responsibility was a damned odd way of warmongering. The usual ploy was a series of assassinations of key figures in the rival tong by local or imported hatchet men.

Why, then, if Little Pete wanted all-out warfare with the Hip Sing, would he order the murder of a white attorney to shut his mouth, but not also order the deaths of Hip Sing highbinders and elders?

The odor of fish was strong in Quincannon's nostrils as he left the temple. And the stench did not come from the fish market on the opposite side of the street.

The ground floor of the Hip Sing Company was a fraternal gathering place, open to the street; the two upper floors, where tong business was conducted, were closed off and would be well guarded. Quincannon entered freely, passed down a corridor into a large common room. Several black-garbed men, most of them elderly, were playing mah-jongg at a table at one end. Other men sat on cushions and benches, sipping tea, smoking, reading newspapers. A few cast wary glances at the *fan kwei* intruder, but most ignored him.

A middle-aged fellow, his skull completely bald except for a long, braided queue, approached him, bowed, and asking in halting English, "There is something the gentleman seeks?"

Quincannon said, "An audience with Mock Don Yuen," and handed over one of his business cards.

"Please to wait here, honorable sir." The Chinese bowed again, took the card away through a doorway covered by a worn silk tapestry.

Quincannon waited. No one paid him the slightest attention now. He was loading his pipe when the bald man returned and said, "You will follow me, please."

They passed through the tapestried doorway, up a stairway so narrow Quincannon had to turn his body slightly as he ascended. Another man waited at the top, this one young, thickset, with a curved scar under one eye and both hands hidden inside the voluminous sleeves of his blouse. Highbinder on guard duty: those sleeves would conceal revolver or knife or short, sharp hatchet, or possibly all three.

As the bald one retreated down the stairs, highbinder and "foreign devil" eyed one another impassively. Quincannon had no intention of relinquishing his Navy Colt: if any effort were made to search him, he would draw the weapon and take his chances. But the guard made no such attempt. In swift, gliding movements he turned and went sideways along a hallway, his gaze on Quincannon the whole while. At an open doorway at the far end, he stopped and stood as if at attention. When Quincannon entered the room beyond, the highbinder filled the doorway behind him as effectively as any panel of wood.

The chamber might have been an office in any building in San Francisco. There was a long, high desk, a safe, stools, a round table set with a tea service. The only oriental touches were a red silk wall tapestry embroidered with threads of gold, a statue of Buddha, and an incense bowl that emitted a rich, spicy scent. Lamplight highlighted the face of the man standing behind the desk—a man of no more than thirty, slender, clean-shaven, his hair worn long but unqueued, western style, his body encased in a robe of red brocaded silk that didn't quite conceal the shirt and string tie underneath. On one corner of the desk lay a black slouch hat with a red topknot.

Quincannon said, "You're not Mock Don Yuen."

"No. I am Mock Quan, his son."

"I asked for an audience with your father."

"My father is not here, Mr. Quincannon." Mock Quan's English was unaccented and precise. "I have been expecting you."

"Have you now."

"Your reputation is such that I knew you would come to ask questions about the unfortunate occurrence last night."

"Questions which you'll answer truthfully, of course."

"Truth is supreme in the house of Hip Sing."

"And what is the truth of James Scarlett's death?"

"It was arranged by the Kwong Dock and their cowardly leader, Fong Ching. You must know this."

Quincannon shrugged. "For what purpose?"

"Fong is vicious and unscrupulous and his hunger for power has never been sated. He hates and fears the Hip Sing, for we are stronger than any of the tongs under his yoke. He wishes to destroy the Hip Sing so he may reign as king of Chinatown."

"He's the king now, isn't he?"

"No!" Mock Quan's anger came like the sudden flare of a match. Almost as quickly it was extinguished, but not before Quincannon had a glimpse beneath the erudite mask. "He is a fat jackal in lion's skin, the son of a turtle."

That last revealed the depth of Mock Quan's loathing for Little Pete; it was the bitterest of Chinese insults. Quincannon said, "Jackals feed on the dead. The dead such as Bing Ah Kee?"

"Oh yes, it is beyond question Fong Ching is responsible for that outrage as well."

"What do you suppose was done with the body?"

Mock Quan made a slicing gesture with one slim hand. "Should the vessel of the honorable Bing Ah Kee have been destroyed, may Fong Ching suffer the death of a thousand cuts ten thousand times through eternity."

"If the Hip Sing is so sure he's responsible, why has nothing been done to retaliate?"

"Without proof of Fong Ching's treachery, the decision of the counsel of elders was that the wisest course was to withhold a declaration of war."

"Even after what happened to James Scarlett? His murder could be termed an act of open aggression."

"Mr. Scarlett was neither Chinese nor a member of the Hip Sing Company, merely an employee." Mock Quan took a pre-rolled cigarette from a box on his desk, fitted it into a carved ivory holder. "The counsel met again this morning. It was decided then to permit the American Terror, Lieutenant Price, and his raiders to punish Fong Ching and the Kwong Dock, thus to avoid the shedding of Hip Sing blood. This will be soon done."

"What makes you so sure?"

"The police now have evidence of Fong Ching's guilt."

"Evidence?" Quincannon scowled. "What evidence?"

"The Kwong Dock highbinder who shot Mr. Scarlett was himself shot and killed early this morning, during a raid on Fong Ching's shoe factory. A letter was found on the *kwei chan* bearing the letterhead and signature of the esteemed attorney."

"What kind of letter?"

"I do not know," Mock Quan said. "I know only that the American Terror is preparing to lead other raids which will crush the life from the turtle's offspring."

Quincannon was silent for a time, while he digested this new information. If anything, it deepened the piscine odor of things. At length he asked, "Whose idea was it to leave the job to the police? Yours or your father's?"

The question discomfited Mock Quan. His eyes narrowed; he exhaled smoke in a thin jet. "I am not privileged to sit on the counsel of elders."

"No, but your father is. And I'll wager you have his confidence as well as his ear, and that your powers of persuasion are considerable."

"Such matters are of no concern to you."

"They're of great concern to me. I was nearly shot, too, in Ross Alley. And I'm not as convinced as the police that Little Pete is behind the death of James Scarlett or the disappearance of Bing Ah Kee's remains."

Mock Quan made an odd hissing sound with his lips, a Chinese expression of anger and contempt. There was less oil and more steel in his voice when he spoke again. "You would do well to bow to the superior intelligence of the police, Mr. Quincannon. Lest your blood stain a Chinatown alley after all."

"I don't like warnings, Mock Quan."

"A humble Chinese warn a distinguished Occidental detective? They were merely words of caution and prudence."

Quincannon's smile was nothing more than a lip-stretch. He said, "I have no intention of leaving a single drop of my blood in Chinatown."

"Then you would be wise not to venture here again after the cloak of night has fallen." Mock Quan's smile was as specious as Quincannon's. So was the invitation which followed: "Will you join me in a cup of excellent rose-petal tea before you leave?"

"Another time, perhaps."

"Perhaps. *Ho hang la*—I hope you have a safe walk."

"Health and long life to you, too."

As he made his way out of the building, Quincannon felt a definite lift in spirits. The briny aroma had grown so strong that now he had a very good idea of its source, its species, and its cause.

Your hat, Mock Quan, he thought with grim humor. In your blasted hat!

♦ ♦ ♦

Sabina said, "Mrs. Scarlett has taken to her bed with grief and the comfort of a bottle of creme de menthe. It made questioning her difficult, to say the least."

"Were you able to find out anything?"

"Little enough. Her husband, as far as she is aware, had no incriminating documents in his possession, nor does she know where he might have put such a document for safekeeping. And she has no recollection of his ever mentioning Fowler Alley in her presence."

"I was afraid that would be the case."

"Judging from your expression, your visit to Fowler Alley proved enlightening."

"Not Fowler Alley; that piece of the puzzle is still elusive. My call at the Hip Sing Company,"

She raised an eyebrow. "You went there? I don't see a puncture wound anywhere. No bullets fired or hatchets or knives thrown your way?"

"Bah. I've bearded fiercer lions in their dens than Mock Quan."

"Who is Mock Quan?"

"The son of Mock Don Yuen, new leader of the tong. A sly gent with delusions of grandeur and a hunger for power as great as Little Pete's. Unless I miss my guess, he is the murderer of James Scarlett and the near murderer of your devoted partner."

Sabina's other eyebrow arched even higher. "What led you to that conclusion?"

"His hat," Quincannon said.

"His— Are you quite serious, John?"

"Never more so. The gunman outside Blind Annie's Cellar wore a black slouch hat with a red what-do-you-call-it on top—"

"A *mow-yung*," Sabina said.

He frowned. "How do you know that?"

"And why shouldn't a woman know something you don't? A *mow-yung* is a symbol of high caste in Chinese society."

"That much I do know," Quincannon growled. "Coolie foodsellers don't wear 'em and neither do the *boo how doy*. That's what has been bothering me about the assassin from the first. He wasn't a highbinder but an upper-class Chinese masquerading as one."

"How do you know it was Mock Quan?"

"I don't know it for sure. A hunch, a strong one. Mock Quan is ambitious, foolhardy, corrupt, and ruthless. He covets Little Pete's empire in Chinatown. He as much as said so."

"Why would he risk killing Scarlett himself?"

"If my hunch is correct, he's working at cross-purposes to those of his father and the Hip Sing elders. It's his plan to let Lieutenant Price and the flying squad finish off his enemies and then to take over Little Pete's position as crime boss—with or without the blessings of his father and the tong. He has allies in the Hip Sing, certainly, but none he trusted enough to do the job on Scarlett. He's the sort to have no qualms about committing cold-blooded murder."

"For the dual purpose of stirring up the police and silencing Scarlett? Mock Quan is behind the body snatching, too, if you're right."

"I'd bet five gold eagles on it," Quincannon agreed. "And another five he's at least partly responsible for the letter of Scarlett's found on the Kwong Dock highbinder who was killed by the police this morning."

"That's fresh news," Sabina said. "Tell me."

He told her.

"I wonder how Mock Quan could have managed such flummery as that?"

"I can think of one way,"

"Yes," she said slowly, "so can I. But proving it may be difficult. The case against Mock Quan, too."

"I know it. But there has to be a way to expose him before the kettle boils over. His plan is mad, but madder ones have succeeded and will again." He began to pace the office. "If we only knew the significance of Fowler Alley . . . Did you manage to have a look around the Scarlett lodgings?"

Sabina nodded. "Scarlett kept a desk there, but it contained nothing revealing. I did learn one small item of interest from Mrs. Scarlett before she fell asleep. It answers one question, while posing another."

"Yes?"

"She was followed when she came to see us yesterday. She intended to mention the fact but she was too upset about her husband."

"Followed? Not by a Chinese?"

"No, a Caucasian. A stranger to her."

"What did he look like?"

"She wasn't able to get a clear look at him. A man in a blue suit was all the description she could provide."

Quincannon muttered, "Blue shadow, eh?"

"Evidently. Another Caucasian on the Hip Sing payroll, one of Mock Quan's allies. And the explanation of how Mock Quan was able to follow you on your rounds of the opium resorts."

"Mmm." Quincannon continued to pace for a time. Then, abruptly, he stopped and said, "Perhaps not such a *small* item of interest after all, my dear."

"Have you thought of something?"

"Been bitten by another hunch is more like it." He reached for his coat and derby.

"Where are you off to?"

"Scarlett's law offices. My search last night was hasty and it's possible I overlooked something of importance. Or rather, spent my time looking for the wrong thing."

♦ ♦ ♦

No one else had passed through the portal marked *J.H. Scarlett, Attorney-at-Law* since Quincannon's nocturnal visit. Or if anyone had, it'd been without any further disturbance of the premises.

With a close curb on his impatience, he set about once more sifting through the lawyer's papers. He examined each document carefully, some more than once. The hunch that had bitten him had plenty of teeth: One name kept reappearing in similar context, and the more he saw it, the more furiously his nimble brain clicked and whirred. When he stood at last from the desk, his smile and the profane oath he uttered through it had a wolfish satisfaction.

He was certain, now, that he knew most of what there was to know. The only piece of the game he didn't have, in fact, was the one that had eluded him since last night—Fowler Alley.

♦ ♦ ♦

A sharp, chill wind blew along the alley's close confines. Litter swirled; pig-tailed men and work-stooped women hurried on their errands, not half so many as there had been earlier. Quincannon sensed an urgency in their movements, an almost palpable tension in the air. Word had spread of the flying squad's planned raids and the law-abiding were eager to be off the streets before dark.

Quincannon walked slowly, hands buried in the pockets of his Chesterfield, his shoulders hunched and his head swiveling left and right. The buildings in the first block, with their grimy windows and indecipherable calligraphy, told him no more than they had earlier. He entered the second block, frustration mounting in him again.

He was halfway along when he noticed a high-sided black wagon drawn up in front of some sort of business establishment. A small clutter of citizens stood watching something being loaded into the rear of the wagon. Quincannon moved closer. He was taller than most Chinese; he could see over the tops of the watchers' heads as he neared. One clear look at the object being loaded and he fetched up in a sudden standstill.

Casket.

Hearse.

Undertaking parlor!

He turned swiftly, ran back on that side of the alley until he came to an opening between the buildings. A tunnellike walkway brought him into a deeply rutted dirt passage that paralleled Fowler's Alley. He counted buildings to the rear of the one that housed the undertaker's. The door there was neither barred nor latched; he pushed it open with his left hand, drawing his Navy Colt with his right, and entered the gloomy corridor within.

The sickish odor of formaldehyde dilated his nostrils, set him to breathing through his mouth as he eased along the hall. From the front of the building the singsong of Chinese dialect came to him, but back here there was no sound.

The lanternlit chamber into which he emerged was empty except for rows of coffins, most of them plain, a few of the lacquered teakwood favored by the high-born and the wealthy. A tapestried doorway opened to the right. Quincannon went there, pushed the covering aside.

Here was the embalming room, the source of the formaldehyde odor. He crossed it, past a metal table, an herb cabinet, another cabinet in which needles, razors, and other tools of the mortician's trade gleamed, to where a row of three slender storage vaults were set into the wall. The first vault he opened was empty. The second contained the body of a very old Mandarin whose skin was so wrinkled he might have been mummified. Quincannon opened the third.

The body in this vault was also an old man's, but one who had lived a much more pampered life. It was dressed in an intricately embroidered robe of gold silk; the cheeks had been powdered, the thin drooping mustaches trimmed; a prayerbook was still clutched between the gnarled hands.

"Bing Ah Kee," Quincannon said under his breath, "or I'm not the master detective I believe I am."

He closed the vault, retraced his steps to the doorway, pushed the tapestry aside. And came face to face with a youngish individual wearing a stained leather apron over his blouse and pantaloons. The man let out a startled bleat and an oath or epithet that threatened to escalate into a full-fledged cry of alarm. As he turned to flee, voice just starting to rise, Quincannon tapped him with the barrel of his Navy at the spot where queue met scalp. Flight and cry both ended instantly.

Quincannon stepped over the fallen Chinese, hurried across the coffin room and into the rear corridor. Fortunately for him, he had the presence of mind to ease the outside door open and his head out for a look around, instead of rushing through. It saved him from having some tender and perhaps vital portion of his anatomy punctured by a bullet.

As it was, the gunman lying in wait in a nearby doorway fired too hastily; the slug thwacked into the wall several inches from Quincannon's head, which he quickly jerked back inside. There were no more shots. He stood tensely, listening. Was that the slap of footfalls? He edged the door open again and poked his head out at a lower point than the first time.

Footfalls, indeed. The assassin was on the run. Quincannon straightened and stepped outside, but before he could trigger a shot the black-outfitted figure vanished into the walkway to Fowler's Alley.

Mock Quan, of course, in his highbinder's guise. The fact that he'd made this attempt at homicide in broad daylight was an indication of just how desperate Quincannon's discovery had made him. So was the craven way he'd taken flight after his first shot missed its mark.

That was the difference between despots such as Little Pete and would-be despots such as Mock Quan, Quincannon mused. Both were rapacious and reckless, but the true tyrant was too arrogant to give himself up to panic. The would-be tyrant was far easier to bring down because his arrogance was no more than a thin membrane over a shell of cowardice.

♦ ♦ ♦

When Quincannon arrived at the Hall of Justice he found Price, Gentry, and a dozen other men of the flying squad already preparing for the night's assault on Chinatown. The basement assembly room was strewn with coils of rope, firemen's axes, sledgehammers, artillery, and bulletproof vests similar to the coats of chain mail worn by the *boo how doy*.

He drew the lieutenant aside and did some fast talking, the gist of which was that he had information which would render the raids unnecessary. Fifteen minutes later he was once again seated in the Chief's office, holding court before the same three officers as on his previous visit. As he spoke, he noted that the expressions worn by the trio were more or less the same, too: Crowley's stern and disapproving, Price's intently thoughtful, Gentry's hostile. None of them commented until he finished and leaned back in his chair. Then each spoke in rapid succession.

Crowley: "That's quite a tale, Quincannon."

Gentry: "Hogwash, I say."

Price: "Fact or fiction, we'll find out soon enough. I want my own look inside that undertaking parlor."

"What good will that do?" Gentry argued. "Even if Mock Quan is behind all that's happened, old Bing's bones will be long gone by the time we get there."

"I think not, Sergeant," Quincannon said. "Mock Quan likely has nowhere to move the body on short notice. And he won't destroy it for the same reason he didn't before—fear of the wrath of the gods and all of Chinatown. Even if he were able to remove the body, there are bound to be ties between him and the mortician. Put pressure on that party and his terror of tong reprisal will bring out the truth. I'll warrant the whole house of cards can be collapsed around Mock Quan in a few hours, and that he knows it as well as I do. I wouldn't be surprised to hear that he has already left the city—on the run ever since his bullet missed my head."

"Nor would I, if you're right," Price said. "And I'm beginning to believe you are."

The Chief leaned forward. "You really think Mock Quan is capable of plotting such a scheme, Will?"

"I wouldn't have until now. He's sneaky and ruthless, yes, but not half so clever as Little Pete. Still . . ."

"The plan wasn't his alone," Quincannon said. "He had help in its devising."

"Help? Help from whom?"

"A blue shadow."

". . . What the devil are you talking about?"

"James Scarlett said two things before he was killed. One was 'Fowler Alley'; the other was 'blue shadow.' And the truth is, he was as afraid of a blue shadow as he was of Mock Quan. His guilty knowledge wasn't only of the body snatching, but of the identity of Mock Quan's partner—the man who followed Scarlett's wife to my offices yesterday and who arranged for Mock Quan to follow me in Chinatown last night."

"*What* partner?" Chief Crowley demanded. "What does blue shadow mean?"

"It means a shadowy person in blue," Quincannon said. "Not a plain blue suit, as the partner wore yesterday, but a blue uniform—a policeman's uniform." He paused dramatically. "One of the policemen in this room is Mock Quan's accomplice."

All three officers came to their feet as one. Gentry aimed a quivering forefinger as if it were the barrel of his sidearm. "Preposterous nonsense! How dare you accuse one of us—"

"You, Sergeant. I am accusing you."

The smoky air fairly crackled. Price and Crowley were both staring at Gentry; the sergeant's eyes threw sparks at Quincannon. The cords in the short man's neck bulged. His color was a shade less purple than an eggplant's.

"It's a dirty lie!" he shouted.

"Cold, hard fact."

Price said with contained fury, "Can you prove this allegation, Quincannon?"

"I can, to your satisfaction. After I left here last night, I went to James Scarlett's law offices. They had already been searched sometime earlier, likely soon after Mrs. Scarlett visited my offices. At first I believed the job was done by one of the highbinders, hunting any incriminating evidence Scarlett may have had in his possession. But that wasn't the case. The search hadn't the stamp of the tong man; it was much more professionally conducted, as a policeman goes about such a frisk. Gentry's work, gentlemen."

"For the same reason?"

"More probably to look for evidence of his conspiracy with Mock Quan. If there was any such evidence, Gentry made off with it. He also made off with a letter written on Scarlett's stationery and signed by the attorney—the same letter you found on the Kwong Dock highbinder who was killed last night. Killed by Gentry, wasn't he? And the letter found by Gentry afterward?"

"Yes, by God. Right on both counts."

"He tried to put a knife in me!" Gentry cried. "You saw him, Lieutenant—"

"I saw nothing of the kind. I took your word for it."

"A clever attempt to tighten the frame against Little Pete," Quincannon said. "As was Gentry's constant urging of you and Chief Crowley to crush Pete and the Kwong Dock."

"Lies! Don't listen to him—"

The other two officers ignored him. Price said, "Go on, Quincannon."

"When Gentry searched Scarlett's offices he carried off any direct evidence he may have found, as I said. But he failed to notice indirect evidence just as damning. Scarlett's legal records indicate the sergeant was in the pay of the Hip Sing, just as Scarlett himself was, long *before* Gentry and Mock Quan cooked up their takeover scheme. He was mixed up in nearly all of the cases in which Scarlett successfully defended a Hip Sing member. In some, his testimony—false or distorted—resulted in acquittal. In others, it's plain that he suppressed evidence or suborned perjury or both."

Gentry started toward Quincannon with murder in his eye. "If there are any such lies in Scarlett's records, you put them there, you damned flycop! You're the one trying to pull a frame—"

Price stepped in front of him. "Stand where you are, Sergeant," he said in a voice that brooked no disobedience.

Quincannon went on, "Another piece of proof: Last night, if you recall, Gentry suggested taking the flying squad to find evidence of Little Pete's guilt in Scarlett's death—the bogus evidence he later planted himself. He also said, 'Evidence to point to the cold storage where old Bing's bones are stashed.' Yet for all any of us knew at that point, the body might have been burned, or buried, or weighted and cast into the Bay, or had any of a dozen other things done with it or to it. Why would he use the specific term 'cold storage' unless he knew that was what had been done with the remains?"

Gentry called him a name and tried once again to mount a charge. The Lieutenant shoved him back, none too gently.

"And if all that isn't sufficient validation of his duplicity," Quincannon concluded, "there is Mrs. Scarlett. She had a good look at the man who followed her yesterday and can easily identify him." A bald lie, this, but an effective capper nonetheless. "Gentry had no official reason to be following the woman, did he, Lieutenant?"

"No," Price said darkly, "he didn't."

The Chief stalked around his desk and fixed Gentry with a gimlet eye. "A damned highbinder no better than Little Pete or Mock Quan—is that what you are, Gentry?"

"No! No, I swear—"

"Because if so I'll see your mangy hide strung from the highest flagpole in the city."

Gentry shook his head, his eyes rolling, sweat shining on his forehead and cheeks. He was still wagging his head as Quincannon judiciously slipped out and went to find a quiet corner where he could smoke his pipe and enjoy his vindication.

♦ ♦ ♦

"Gentry's shell was no harder to crack than a Dungeness crab's," he told Sabina a while later. "It took Crowley and Price less than fifteen minutes to break him wide open."

"No doubt with the aid of some gentle persuasion."

"Have you ever known the blue shadows to use another kind?"

She laughed. "What was his motive? Power and greed, the same as Mock Quan's?"

"Those, and severe gambling losses. Which was why he sold himself to the Hip Sing in the first place. It seems the sergeant has a fondness for roulette and fantan, and little skill at any game of chance."

"Well, I must say you've plenty of skill at your particular game."

"I have, haven't I?"

"Exceeded only by your modesty," Sabina said. "Still, it's thanks to you that the crisis in Chinatown has been averted."

"For the time being. Until another, smarter Mock Quan emerges or something or someone else lights the fuse. Mark my words—one of these days, the whole Quarter will go up in flames."

"You may be right. In any event, this is one case it will be a relief, if not a pleasure to mark closed. We'll waive Mrs. Scarlett's fee, of course. I'll post a letter to her tomorrow— Why are you looking at me that way?"

Quincannon was aghast. He said, "Waive her fee?"

"It's the least we can do for the poor woman."

"Sabina, have you forgotten that I was shot at twice and almost killed? As well as made to trek through low Chinatown alleys, prowl opium dens, and invade an undertaking parlor in search of a snatched corpse?"

"I haven't forgotten."

"Well then? All of that, not to mention a near tarnish on our fine reputation as detectives, for not so much as a copper cent?"

"I'm afraid so, my erstwhile Scot. It's the proper thing to do and you know it."

"Bah. I know nothing of the kind."

Her expression softened. After a silence during which she seemed to be doing a bit of weighing and balancing, she said, "I suppose you should have one small reward, at least."

"Yes? And what would that be?"

"An evening out with me, if you like. Dinner at the Palace, then a performance of Gilbert and Sullivan's new opera at the Tivoli Theatre. I've been wanting to see *Patience* since it opened."

Quincannon's gloom evaporated as swiftly as an ice cube in a furnace. Smiling jauntily, he said, "And after the performance?"

"You may escort me to my flat."

"And after that?"

Sabina sighed. "You never give up, do you, John Quincannon?"

"Never. For my intentions are honorable, my passions sweet and pure. No, never, as long as a breath remains in my body."

The word Sabina uttered in response to that was heartfelt and decidedly unladylike.

CARPENTER AND QUINCANNON

Carpenter and Quincannon: Professional Detective Services by Bill Pronzini is printed on 55-pound Glatfelter Supple Opaque recycled acid-free paper, primarily from 12-point Caslon Old Face, a computer-version of a typeface designed in 1725 by William Caslon; typefaces used for telegrams, signs, and some handwritten notes are Courier New, Antique Olive, and John Handy. The cover painting is by Carol Heyer, and the design by Deborah Miller. The first edition is comprised of approximately one thousand, two hundred copies in trade softcover, and two hundred fifty copies sewn in cloth, signed and numbered by the author. Each of the clothbound copies contains an original typescript page from the author's files of one of the stories in this book. *Carpenter and Quincannon: Professional Detective Services* was printed and bound by Thomson-Shore, Inc., Dexter, Michigan, and published in October 1998 by Crippen & Landru Publishers, Norfolk, Virginia.

CRIPPEN & LANDRU, PUBLISHERS
P. O. Box 9315
Norfolk, VA 23505

Crippen & Landru publishes first editions of important works by detective and mystery writers, specializing in short-story collections. Most books are published both in trade softcover and in signed, limited clothbound with either a typescript page from the author's files or an additional story in a separate pamphlet. The following books have been published:

Speak of the Devil by John Dickson Carr. Eight-part impossible crime mystery broadcast on BBC radio. Introduction by Tony Medawar; cover design by Deborah Miller.   Out of Print

The McCone Files by Marcia Muller. Fifteen Sharon McCone short stories by the creator of the modern female private eye, including two written especially for the collection. Winner of the Anthony Award for Best Short Story collection. Introduction by the author; cover painting by Carol Heyer.

Signed, limited edition, Out of Print
Softcover, third printing, $15.00

The Darings of the Red Rose by Margery Allingham. Eight crook stories about a female Robin Hood, written in 1930 by the creator of the classic sleuth, Albert Campion. Introduction by B. A. Pike; cover design by Deborah Miller.

Softcover, Out of Print

Diagnosis: Impossible, The Problems of Dr. Sam Hawthorne by Edward D. Hoch. Twelve stories about the country doctor who solves "miracle problems," written by the greatest current expert on the challenge-to-the-reader story. Introduction by the author; chronology by Marvin Lachman; cover painting by Carol Heyer.

Signed (a few copies remain of out-of-series overrun), $30.00
Softcover, Out of Stock

Spadework: A Collection of "Nameless Detective" Stories by Bill Pronzini. Fifteen stories, including two written for the collection, by a Grandmaster of the Private Eye tale. Introduction by Marcia Muller; afterword by the author; cover painting by Carol Heyer.

Signed, limited edition, $40.00
Softcover, $16.00

Who Killed Father Christmas? And Other Unseasonable Demises by Patricia Moyes. Twenty-one stories ranging from holiday homicides to village villainies to Caribbean crimes. Introduction by the author; cover design by Deborah Miller.

Signed, limited edition, $40.00
Softcover, $16.00

My Mother, The Detective: The Complete "Mom" Short Stories, by James Yaffe. Eight stories about the Bronx armchair maven who solves crimes between the chicken soup and the *schnecken*. Introduction by the author; cover painting by Carol Heyer.

Signed, limited edition, Out of Print
Softcover, $15.00

In Kensington Gardens Once . . . by H. R. F. Keating. Ten crime and mystery stories taking place in London's famous park, including two written for this collection, by the recipient of the Cartier Diamond Dagger for Lifetime Achievement. Illustrations and cover by Gwen Mandley.

Signed, limited edition, $35.00
Softcover, $12.00

Shoveling Smoke: Selected Mystery Stories by Margaret Maron. Twenty-two stories by the Edgar award winning author, including all the short cases of Sigrid Harald and Deborah Knott, including a new Knott story. Introduction and prefaces to each story by the author; cover painting by Victoria Russell.

Signed, limited edition, Out of Print
Softcover, second printing, $16.00

The Man Who Hated Banks and Other Mysteries by Michael Gilbert. Eighteen stories by the recipient of the Mystery Writers of America's Grandmaster Award, including mysteries featuring Inspectors Petrella and Hazlerigg, rogue cop Bill Mercer, and solicitor Henry Bohun. Introduction by the author; cover painting by Deborah Miller.

Signed, limited edition, Out of Print
Softcover, second printing, $16.00

The Ripper of Storyville and Other Ben Snow Tales by Edward D. Hoch. The first fourteen historical detective stories about Ben Snow, the wandering gunslinger who is often confused with Billy the Kid. Introduction by the author; Ben Snow chronology by Marvin Lachman; cover painting by Barbara Mitchell.

Signed, limited edition, Out of Print
Softcover, $16.00

Do Not Exceed the Stated Dose by Peter Lovesey. Fifteen crime and mystery stories, including two featuring Peter Diamond and two featuring Bertie, Prince of Wales. Preface by the author; cover painting by Carol Heyer.

Signed, limited edition, Out of Print
Softcover, $16.00

Renowned Be Thy Grave; Or, The Murderous Miss Mooney by P. M. Carlson. Ten stories about Bridget Mooney, the Victorian actress who becomes involved in important historical events. Introduction by the author; cover design by Deborah Miller.

Signed, limited edition, $40.00
Softcover, $16.00

Carpenter and Quincannon, Professional Detective Services by Bill Pronzini. Nine detective stories, including one written for this volume, set in San Francisco during the 1890's. Introduction by the author; cover painting by Carol Heyer.

Signed, limited edition, $40.00
Softcover, $16.00

Not Safe After Dark and Other Stories by Peter Robinson. Thirteen stories, including one written for this volume, about Inspector Banks and others. Introduction and prefaces to each story by the author; cover painting by Victoria Russell.

Signed, limited edition, $40.00
Softcover, $16.00

The following short-story collections are forthcoming:

The Concise Cuddy: The First Collection of John Francis Cuddy Stories by Jeremiah Healy.
One Night Stands by Lawrence Block.
All Creatures Mysterious: The Dr. David Westbrook Stories by Doug Allyn.
Silent Prayers by Ed Gorman.
Fortune's Fortunes: Dan Fortune's Casebook by Michael Collins.
The Tragedy of Errors and Others: The Lost Stories of Ellery Queen.
McCone and Friends by Marcia Muller.
Challenge the Widow Maker and Others by Clark Howard.
The Velvet Touch by Edward D. Hoch.
The Spotted Cat and Other Mysteries: The Casebook of Inspector Cockrill by Christianna Brand.
Tales Out of School by Carolyn Wheat.
The Adventure of the Murdered Moths and Other Radio Mysteries by Ellery Queen.

Crippen & Landru offers discounts to individuals and institutions who place Standing Order Subscriptions for its forthcoming publications. Please write for details.

June 3

May